# Never Been Ready



USA TODAY BESTSELLING AUTHOR

# J.L. BERG

# ALSO BY J.L. BERG

## THE READY SERIES

*When You're Ready*

*Never Been Ready*

*Ready to Wed*

*Ready for You*

*Ready or Not*

*The Ready Series Box Set*

*When You're Ready - 10th Anniversary Edition*

## THE WALLS SERIES

*Within These Walls*

*Beyond These Walls*

*Behind Closed Doors*

*The Cavenaugh Brothers - A Box Set*

## THE LOST & FOUND SERIES

*Forgetting August*

*Remembering Everly*

## BY THE BAY SERIES

*The Choices I've Made*

*The Scars I Bare*

*The Lies I've Told*

*The Mistakes I've Made*

*The Secrets We Keep*

*By The Bay Series: A Box Set (Books 1-4)*

## STANDALONES

*Fraud*

*The Tattered Gloves*

*The Affair*

Like all novels in this series, **Never Been Ready** can be read as a standalone. However, for frame of reference, this story takes place three months after the last chapter of **When You're Ready**. The events that take place in the epilogue of that story have not yet occurred.

# Prologue

LEAH

I remember the shattering glass most of all. The sound still echoes through my head to this day. It was deafening to my child-sized eardrums, and I awoke quickly, covering my ears to try to mute the piercing sound.

The shrill voices came next. Heated, angry words were shouted outside my frilly pink bedroom that my mother and I had decorated from things we'd found at Goodwill. I was used to the shouting. My parents lived to fight. I spent a good part of my early childhood hidden behind the walls of that room. I'd play with my Barbies and dream of a normal family. Barbie would bake apple pie and sing Etta James in the kitchen, and Ken would take her out dancing. He would never raise his voice...or his hand. When I awoke that night though, it felt different...scarier. Even at seven, I knew something major was about to happen, and my world would never be the same.

Angry stomping passed my door, followed by hysterical cries and pleading words. Someone rushed down the hall, stopping briefly by my door, and then I heard the front door slam. Jumping out of my bed, I peeked my head out the door in the direction of our small living room. It was empty, and dark. The glass coffee table was in shards, and pieces were scattered all over the shaggy brown carpet. The dark shadows of the room seemed to be closing in on me from all angles. With the curiosity of a young child getting the best of me, I pressed on and walked farther into the room. No one was to be seen anywhere, and my exploration proved fruitless. Not knowing what else to do or where else to go, I picked a spot in the corner, curled myself into a ball, and started to count the glittery pieces of glass.

"What the hell are you doing out of bed?" my father asked when he found me some time later. My count had reached the hundreds by then, and my feet were ice cold from the lack of heat in the house. I looked up at the man I both loved and feared. Both of his hands were wrapped in bloody bandages and his clothes looked askew and out of place. I remember wondering if he had a hard time getting dressed with those bandages on his hands and that's why he looked so funny. I reminded myself to help Daddy button his shirt the next day. Children have such innocent minds.

"I couldn't sleep," I answered quietly, "Where's Mommy?"

"She's gone. For good."

# Chapter One



"How are you feeling, sweetie?" I asked the soon-to-be-mother as I walked into the birthing room carrying her chart and a cup of ice chips.

"I'm okay," she groaned before grimacing in pain as another contraction rolled through her tiny body.

Natural childbirth —I would never understand it. It was like going to the dentist and saying, "Novocain? No thanks. Just go in there Doc and rip that sucker right out!" Epidural was the way to go and it made my job so much easier.

I was a labor and delivery nurse and my current mother-to-be was named Hillary. With her granola eating boyfriend, Teegan, she had come in tonight with mild contractions after her water had broken. They were like any soon-to-be-parents —excited, nervous and scared. They were also very adamant in what they did and did not want. They had a three-page birthing plan. Three fucking pages that were single spaced no less. Hillary had promptly handed it to me in between her Lamaze breathing, and she'd instructed me to read and follow it to the letter.

Hippie chick was bossy. Five hours later, she was also bitch-ass tired and hadn't progressed at all. Stuck at six centimeters dilated, she was in a hell of a lot of pain and completely miserable.

Handing her the ice chips, I asked, "Can I get you anything?"

She shook her head and tried to give a polite smile, but I could see it waver. She was losing her strength fast. Hard lines from exertion showed in her forehead, sweat trickled down her brow and her eyes were heavy from exhaustion.

"Okay, I'll come back in a few and check on you." I gave a reassuring smile to Teegan before exiting the room.

Walking down the hall, I headed for the nurses station and spotted one of the other nurses on shift.

"Hey Trish. How's your night going?"

"Just finished delivering a baby boy. It was her third, so I think she could have done my job for me."

"I love the repeat offenders. They're so much easier."

"Yeah, but the newbies are fun too. Hey, I heard you went out with Susan's brother, Neil. How'd that go?" she asked, her eyes flickering with unshed laughter.

Neil and I had gone out the other night, and unfortunately it was three hours of my life I'd never get back. He was a financial advisor and he really loved his job. It had been all he talked about, and by the end of the evening — after repeated attempts at keeping myself from stabbing my own eyes out with a fork —I faked a stomachache and fled. It had been my first date in months —six months to be exact.

"Yes. Why do you say it like that? I asked, eyeing her suspiciously. "What do you know?"

"I'm surprised you made it out alive. Did he talk you to death? I thought I was going to bleed out from my ears from the endless chatter I had to endure on our date," she confessed.

"Oh my God! You went out with him, too? And you didn't feel the need to warn me? Shit, you could have told me he was a walking, talking, ad campaign for abstinence, " I scolded, causing her to burst into laughter.

She muffled the sound with her hand as a doctor walked by, and gave us a look that clearly held judgment, but I ignored it and pressed on.

"Seriously Trish! I thought you were my friend!"

"I'm sorry, Leah. I am. I didn't know. I found out afterwards, when Susan was talking about it in the cafeteria. She was so proud. She thought she'd finally found her new sister-in-law. Man, she is going to be disappointed."

"I have news for her. She's never, ever going to marry that man off. The only chance she has is finding a nice young girl who happens to be deaf."

We continued giggling and talking as I checked charts and entered a few things into the computer. When Susan asked if she could set me up with her hot brother, I leaped at the chance. My love life had taken a serious nose dive lately, and I was sick of sitting on the couch being utterly boring. I had no one to blame but myself. Well, that wasn't true. There was one other person I could blame for my complete lack of interest in the male species —Declan James.

Declan was childhood pals with my best friend's husband, Logan Matthews. Declan and I had met one night at a bar when Clare and Logan were dating. Declan had been an up-and-coming star in Hollywood, and well...he was gorgeous —like, sizzling hot, forgot-every-other-man-in-the-world-but-him-hot. Tall and rugged, with dark chocolate brown hair, he had hazel eyes that seemed to take on a life of their own, depending on his mood. Despite his obvious attempts to hide his appearance, I'd known who he was the minute he'd walked into that bar. Even with his dark sunglasses and baseball cap pulled tight against his head, I'd known.

I would recognize that weathered jawline and chiseled body anywhere. I'd spent enough hours looking at him on the internet, and even more time lying in bed, thinking of all the naughty things I could do to him if given the chance.

And suddenly there he had been, staring at me from across the bar. My wet dream had come to life. His eyes had locked with mine, making me feel hot and flustered. I didn't do flustered. Up until that point, I hadn't even been sure I'd understood the complete definition of the word.

I'd always been confident around men. They were fun and nice to be around, but some time ago, I'd come to the realization that they just weren't worth the trouble. I spent many good years of my adult life with one man who I thought was *the* man. When things got rough, he bailed. I was sick of investing my emotions and feelings into the part of our species who seemed unable to reciprocate. Men never followed through with their promise and they never loved me enough to stay. So, I'd sworn them off —until my eyes found Declan James, standing in a crowded bar, and I suddenly found myself unable to breathe.

By the time Logan and Declan had made it to our table that night, I had been nearly panting. My nether regions were on high alert, and wanted to play. I had to bite the inside of my cheek to keep from whimpering. By the time the two of us had been left alone, I had barely said two words to him. It hadn't been because I was star struck. The problem was I was so goddamn horny that my brain wouldn't function.

I kept telling myself, He's just another man...a really hot, yummy, lickable man. Stop drooling and say something.

But nothing had come out.

Eventually he'd spoken, and I had managed to get a few things out. What had I said? I had no fucking clue. I could have told him about puppies or the weather for all I knew. It was a wonder the man had wanted anything to do with me at all after that. But he had. We'd left together, and stopped at a local cemetery I'd apparently mentioned during our chat. He'd wanted to check it out before leaving town as a possible location for his upcoming film. It was a Civil War movie and Richmond, our home town, had been picked as one of the filming locations.

I'd watched him walk through the cemetery, looking at old graves and bending down to get different angles and views. His body had moved and flexed as he'd shifted positions, and I had to bite my lip to keep from groaning.

I'd known him for all of two seconds, but I knew he was in his element in that cemetery.

After about fifteen minutes, I'd took him all in as he'd made his way back to where I had been standing, towards the entrance. His jeans had sat low on his hips and his black T-shirt accentuated the ridges of his abs. His eyes, no longer focused on the cemetery, had been dead set on me. He was male perfection.

"Looks good," he had announced, taking one final glance around. "I'll have the crew come out tomorrow during the day to take some photos that we can take back with us. But I think it's definitely a place we could use."

"This is your passion," I'd said softly.

He'd seemed a little taken aback by my sudden ability to form a coherent sentence, but he'd nodded, smiling.

"Yes. Acting is fun, but this is what I really want to do. Being behind the camera and creating something from start to finish is an amazing feeling."

It had been the first honest moment we had shared that evening. I finally hadn't felt flustered and it was the first time I noticed he wasn't paranoid about being recognized. He'd looked younger and more at ease. I'd smiled and relaxed a bit. I was still horny as hell, but calmer.

We'd eventually made it back to my townhouse where he'd showed me that all the ways he'd earned that bad-boy, lady-killer reputation he was known for. He'd ruined me for all other men that night.

For six months, I'd moped around, thinking about that night, unable to move on. I hadn't slept with another man, and every time I had gone to open my drawer full of stand-ins, the thought of using a vibrator had seemed less than thrilling when I knew what I was missing. The only times I'd managed to release some of the built-up steam had been when I thought of him. When I would touch myself, while remembering his hands touching me, and his lips tasting me, I could find bliss again. It was never as sweet, but it was as close as I'd ever get to him again. He was a player and I wasn't about to be his side dish. We had been doomed from the start.

I huffed out a sigh and said my good-byes to Trish before making my way back to the birthing room that held my New Age couple. Standing outside the room was Teegan. Bent forward, his hands were on his thighs, and his head was lowered. He looked ill. I knew this look well. It was the look of an expectant father about to lose his shit.

"Hey Teegan. How's it going?" I asked cautiously.

"It's...God, it's too fucking hard. She's in so much pain. I don't know what to do. I can't do this. I'm not ready." His breathing became labored as his head sank further between his knees.

"Teegan, look at me."

Nothing —he didn't budge.

"Teegan. It's time to man the fuck up. Look at me."

His eyes shot up to mine. That had gotten his attention. It usually did. I'd done this speech more than once.

"Hillary needs you right now. You need to get your shit together, go back in that room and take care of her. She doesn't have anyone else in there, except for you and me. As much as I want to help her, it's you she needs and loves. So, if you need to, give yourself a few more moments if you need them to breathe it out, but in a couple of minutes, you are going to walk back into that room and you will be the calm supportive man I know you can be. Got it?"

He looked at me. He was completely bewildered for a few seconds, but then he nodded and his lost vacant eyes changed. He became determined and full of driven purpose. I knew then that he was back where he needed to be.

We entered the room again together, and he immediately went to Hillary's side. He gave her a tender kiss on the forehead before he whispered something in her ear that made her smile.

It was a rough few more hours, but eventually baby Kai entered the world. After cutting the umbilical cord, Teegan watched as I cleaned off his newborn son and then placed the baby into his arms.

I loved this part of my job. Humans were perfect in this moment. A new life was born, completely void of selfishness or sin. It was humanity at its best. When I saw a mother and father hold their child for the first time, I could see so many possibilities. A blank slate that could do and be anything, and I loved being the one to help usher him or her into the world.

"Thank you Leah," Teegan said, giving me a knowing smile.

"No problem pops. You did good."

"Do you have any children?" Hillary asked lovingly as she watched the two men in her life meet for the first time.

She smiled as Teegan carefully leaned down, nuzzling the three of them close together as a happy new family.

"No. No kids for me."

"Well there's still time. You will be a wonderful mother," Teegan said encouragingly.

I just smiled. There would be no children in my future. Children deserved to grow up in a loving home, with two parents who adored each other. I didn't have that. Besides, I had been raised in a house that was anything but loving. *What would I know about properly raising a child?*

<hr>

The night air was chilly against my skin as I pulled my coat closer to my body. The thin scrubs that covered my legs were doing little to block the wind gusting through the parking lot of the hospital. Just as I reached my car, my purse started vibrating and playing the Superman theme song. I was a ringtone whore. I must have spent half my paycheck downloading songs and ringtones in iTunes store. I had a different ringtone for every person in my Contact List. I hand-selected the tone based on the person, making sure each song fit their personality. This particular ringtone, the one from the original movie, with its sweeping melodic ballad, was for Logan. He always reminded me of a superhero because he was so giving and selfless, so I made him one —on my phone at least.

"Hey Superman. What's up?"

"Hey Leah. You still at work?"

"Well, technically, yes." I said, starting to do a little dance in the middle of the deserted parking lot in an effort to keep my toes from falling off.

"I'm in the parking lot. Why? Are you okay?"

Suddenly I was concerned. Logan had been diagnosed with Hodgkin's disease several months earlier, and although the prognosis looked good, after several rounds of chemotherapy and radiation, I still worried.

"Yeah, I'm fine. I'm actually here at work too."

Logan was a doctor and we worked at the same hospital. He worked in the emergency room though, so we very rarely saw each other.

"I wanted to ask a favor. We just had a pretty bad car accident come through. Trucker fell asleep at the wheel and veered off into oncoming traffic. Clipped a car, sending it head-on into a tree. We did everything we could for the driver, but she didn't make it. The trucker is fine, of course."

"What do you need me for Logan? You know I'm not trained in trauma, and it sounds like it's too late anyway."

"No, I know that." He paused as he let out a deep breath. "Leah, there's a kid."

I felt all the air leave my lungs at once. *Oh God, that poor child.*

"How old, Logan?"

"Seven."

"I'll be right there."

I walked back into the hospital, and headed towards the ER. Thoughts swarmed my mind as I tried to figure out what to do or say to a child who had just lost his mother. I was the same age when I'd lost mine. Granted, it wasn't the same situation. His hadn't chosen to leave him. But it was still a loss. I knew what it could do to a child. The loss could eat away, slowly taking that childhood innocence until there's nothing but bitterness and long-ing. If it hadn't been for my best friend Clare and her family, I would have been swallowed by it.

I rounded the corner and found Logan reviewing a file at the nurse's station. He looked tired and worn. We'd tried to talk him into taking time off, but he'd refused. He'd said he would go fucking nuts if he was left with nothing to do. We had managed to get him to reduce his hours and work part-time during his treatments, but on nights like this, when the job got rough, I could see it wearing on him.

"Hey, how are you doing?" I asked.

He looked up at me and at that moment, I knew what losing a patient meant to him. He was destroyed.

"Oh God, Logan...I'm sorry," I said, pulling him into a tight hug.

I'd lost patients before. I knew the pain and guilt, worrying that I could have done more. I remembered the few I'd lost like it was yesterday. I remembered their names, the parents who grieved the lost lives and the years that had passed by without them.

"I don't know why this one is affecting me so much more. It's not like this is the first time I've lost someone on the table."

"You're a father now Logan." I said, pulling back from our embrace.

"Every mother you save is Clare. Every child you bandage up is Maddie. It's harder now to separate your-self from your patients because *you* feel so much more."

"You're right. I can't stop thinking about that child. He's parentless now. There is no father on record and the police can't find a next of kin. He told the officers at the scene they were on their way to visit a close family friend so I guess they're trying to make contact with them. Social services is on their way."

"Hey, it's okay. You did everything you could. Go home. Be with your wife and daughter and let them help you get through this. I've got this. I'll take care of him until Social Services come, all right?"

He nodded before pulling me into another hug.

We said our good-byes, and I made my way towards the room that held the child. His name was Connor. He sustained only mild injuries from the accident, since he'd been in the back of the car.

Right before I was about to push open the door open, I paused, feeling panic rise in my chest.

*What was I doing?*

I should find someone else to go in there —a mother maybe, someone who would know what to say or do. I didn't have any experience with children beyond my goddaughter, Maddie. What the hell did I know about caring for a hopeless child? Isn't that something I should have learned from my own parents? All I learned from my mother and father was how to abandon and hurt.

Looking around the empty hallway, I realized there was no one else. It was only me. I had to do something. I entered the room, and my heart fell. He was sitting in the center of the bed with knees pulled to the center of his chest and his head lowered. He was clutching something in his left hand, but I couldn't make out what it was. *A paper, or a photo maybe?* Tears trickled down his legs, and I heard him heave in a breath as he sobbed.

As I clicked the door shut, his eyes jerked up and found me. They were hazel and looked like paint splatters. Blue, green, and brown were mixed together to create one of the most beautiful sets of eyes I'd ever seen. They were so unique, yet familiar. I felt the overwhelming need to pull him into my arms and tell him everything would be okay even though I had no proof otherwise.

"Who are you?" he questioned.

"I'm Leah."

"Are you here to take me away?" he asked cautiously.

"No, I'm not taking you anywhere. I'm a nurse."

"They already put bandages on me."

"I know," I said.

"So, why are you here?" he asked softly. He quickly wiped away the tears from his eyes in a halfhearted effort to cover up the fact that he'd been crying.

"I'm here so you don't have to be alone. You can talk to me if you want, or you can ignore me, but I'm going to sit here with you until it's time to leave because I think you need a friend right now."

"You're not my friend," he retorted.

"No, but I'd like to be."

DECLAN

The flight attendant had just announced our final descent into Richmond. In twenty minutes, I would be stepping foot in Virginia for the first time in six months. After months of delays, we were finally ready to start filming the Civil War movie I was both the star and executive producer. If given the choice, I would hand the acting role to someone else. Let them deal with the constant attention and the never-ending chatter. But that was a condition the studio had put into my contract. If I wanted my name added to the list of producers in the credits, I had to take the lead role. It was an honorary title mostly, but it would hopefully get me to where I wanted to go.

Acting was never my intention. I had come to Hollywood to direct, but I'd had a hard time getting my foot in the door. So, I'd auditioned for a small role, and got it.

One thing had led to another and before I knew it, acting had become my full-time career.

When a little known film I'd done struck it big with several Oscar nominations last year, my name had been plastered over every gossip magazine and Internet site known to man. I had been dubbed the newest up-and-coming Hollywood hunk.

I fucking hated it.

I couldn't leave my apartment for weeks without some dick with a camera following me around asking me about anything from the weather to who I'd fucked last night. I had been offered every role imaginable. I'd turned them all down. I didn't want to be the next action hero or the newest heart-throb. I just wanted to be left alone to retire from acting so I could get behind the camera.

When the script for this movie had come across my desk, I'd seen an opportunity. It had a small budget, and was an independent film —exactly the type of thing I needed. I'd approached the director and asked if I could step in as an assistant director —only. They'd given me a flat-out no, which wasn't a total surprise since I hadn't directed a single thing since college. But they had offered the title of executive producer —if I agreed to star as well. It was an olive branch and my hope was that by getting my name recognized for something other than acting credit, it could be a step in the right direction.

I'd accepted, hating the fact that I had to add another acting gig to my schedule, but I was grateful for the opportunity. The director needed my name in the starring role to gain the necessary attention. With Declan James, the hot new thing in Hollywood, cast as the lead, they had been able to land a top-notch actress to costar. It was a compromise, but at least I had my foot in the door now. My only wish was that it hadn't taken so long to get going. Spending six months in Hollywood, sitting around while they finalized everything, had about killed me.

I'd felt like a caged animal waiting to get out of confinement. All my life, I'd been able to go wherever and do whatever I wanted. It was what I'd demanded and expected, and no one had ever stood in my way. Now that my face was everywhere, I couldn't have a private moment to save my life —which meant that every second of my life was watched and scrutinized. If I walked down the street with a woman, she was automatically my girl-friend. If we were seen together twice, we were obviously engaged. It was fucking ridiculous. I'd managed to hang low long enough that the attention from my last movie had died down a bit. Eventually the paparazzi had gotten bored and stopped stalking my house, but I would still get the occasional flash when going into Starbucks or a club. If my last name were Pitt or Pattinson, I didn't think I would have gotten off so easily. But the entire experience had left me paranoid and edgy.

After six months, I would finally be out. Returning to Richmond, I knew exactly where I was going and who I was going to see first —Leah Morgan.

The blonde bombshell had become a permanent fixture in my mind since that one amazing night we'd spent together so many months ago. She haunted me, filled my dreams and made me ache. I'd tried to rid myself of her by losing myself in other women but no matter how beautiful, or sexy, they didn't hold a fucking candle to Leah. It was her face I'd pictured every time I'd come, her body I'd felt every time I touched another and her moans I'd heard echoing through my ears.

She was like an addiction running rampant in my system, and I knew only one way to cure it.

The Captain came on the intercom and said something, probably telling the flight attendant to plant her ass in her seat. The plane angled downward toward the ground and the landing gear locked into place. I looked out the window and saw the darkened city, taking note of the lights dotting the landscape. Anticipation took over as I waited for the plane to touch down. I had been waiting for this moment for months now —ever since I'd decided Leah's invasion of my mind wasn't going to go away on its own. It was going to require drastic measures. I never slept with the same female twice. Repeat performances in one night were fine, encouraged even, but I never, ever returned for seconds. That made them think you had feelings, and I didn't.

*Couldn't. Wouldn't. Not ever again.*

I wasn't built that way anymore. Monogamy wasn't something I wanted with anyone. I was sure it worked out for some people. But for the majority? *No.* It was something people did out of obligation or guilt, even though they would rather be screwing their hot secretary or racquetball instructor.

So, I had rules —well, one rule really. Never sleep with the same woman twice. It was a brilliant fucking rule, and it had worked —until Leah. I didn't know what it was that had me so hooked. When I'd picked her out in that bar so many months ago, I had pegged her as just another gorgeous woman. Granted, I'd never seen any other woman who equaled her. With her long honey-wheat hair, striking blue eyes and curves that could kill a man, she was the whole fucking package. The fact that she was friends with Logan's girlfriend just made things easier. She would have been going home with me that night no matter the circumstances. When we'd all sat down together, she had begun fumbling all over her words, and I'd thought "bingo", knowing I had her. The only coherent thing I had gotten out of her all night was the mention of a cemetery when I'd asked her about the history of Richmond.

Trusting my instincts, we had stopped by the old cemetery that dated back several hundred years so I could get a good look for the camera crew to consider as a possible location. Now the location was actually going to be used, thanks to me. As I roamed, taking note of head-stones of generals and fallen soldiers, and the various different angles that could be shot, she had seen me. No, it had been more than that. She had seen through me. I'd never felt so exposed before. Usually women saw what they wanted to see with me, and I would let them. It was easier that way. Let them sleep with the playboy movie star for a night, and their expectations are set nearly as high. When I would disappear the next day, they expected it. Leah? She had seen the real me, and it was chilling.

I'd never craved a woman after she left my bed like I did with Leah. Days, weeks and now months after that night, I still remembered everything —her smell, the touch of her skin and the way she had trembled when she broke apart beneath me. It had to stop. I couldn't go on like this, obsessing about a woman I didn't want anything permanent with. I figured after one more night, maybe two, with her...and I'd be cured. I could move on with my life —without the beautiful blonde ghost following my every step. It was a good plan. It was goddamn brilliant. Soon, I'd be back to my normal self again, and I could put this crazy Leah business behind me.

I took a deep breath of air as the plane landed and made its way to the gate. We all filed out of the plane, and while I walked into the terminal, I swore I could hear laughter in my head. It was as if my conscience were saying, *you think you're going to get off that easy?*

*Yeah, buddy I do.*

I was so fucking wrong.


LEAH

Looking into the bathroom mirror, I finished securing my blonde hair into a messy bun on the top my head and then I removed my makeup. I took a quick glance at my reflection, seeing the spitting image of my mother staring back at me and I sighed before shutting off the light and walking into my bedroom. My father always said I'd grow up to look just like her. *Guess the bastard was right.* The few pictures I had tucked away that I'd managed to steal from home were like staring into my own reflection. It was one giant reminder of what was left behind.

After slipping into my favorite robe and fuzzy slippers, I made a beeline for my modern small kitchen decorated shades of my favorite color —teal. I opened the freezer and pulled out the pint of rocky road that was currently calling my name.

It had been a long, emotional night. Watching social services walk in and eventually escort Connor out of the hospital was heartbreaking. They'd promised me they would take good care of him, and they really had been gentle and loving with him. They were going to follow through with trying to contact the family friends Connor mentioned. He told them their name and said they were the only other family he had. He wasn't even from here. He was visiting from out of state. I couldn't imagine how scared he must have been.

He had eventually agreed to be my friend. We'd sat quietly in that exam room for probably thirty minutes as I listened to him try to hide his tears.

Then he'd asked, "Do you have a Mommy?"

I'd answered, "No."

I'd told him I had lost my mommy when I was seven also. He'd asked if she died in a car crash, too. I'd just shook my head. He'd looked up at me with those big mesmerizing eyes so full of hurt and he leaped into my arms. He'd cried and cried, and I'd just let him, knowing he needed it. I'd held him for an hour as he'd let every last drop of moisture leak from his body. I knew the feeling. I remembered doing the same thing at the very same age. *The only difference? I hadn't had anyone to hold me.* I was so grateful that I could be that person for him. I just hoped there was someone else willing to take up where I'd left off.

He had shown me the picture he'd held so tightly to his body. The EMT had recovered it from the car before it had been towed away. It was a photo of him and his mother that had been attached to the sun visor. She stood behind him at what appeared to be a state fair of some sort. Carnival rides and food stands dotted the canvas behind them, and Connor held a giant cotton candy in his tiny hands. He was covered in blue sugar and his mom just smiled, not seeming to care that he was a giant mess. She was beautiful, a lot like him, but she had lighter hair and different colored eyes. They looked happy and so full of love.

I'd bitten my lip to keep the tears from falling down my cheek. He'd told me about the fair and the day his mom had taken him. He'd talked about the fun things they did and the trip they were supposed to take to Virginia to see his Mom's friend. I didn't know much about children, but being there with him had felt right. Giving him that chance to cry and talk about his mother with me had been all l I could give him in that short amount of time. I just hoped it had helped.

When I'd gotten home from my twelve-hour shift and my emotional evening, the only thing I'd wanted was ice cream, pajamas and a sappy romance movie. I loved chick flicks. They were my dirty little secret. I didn't even think Clare knew of my obsession. Yes, I'd given up on men...but in films, they were perfect. They always came through in the end, kept their promises and loved with every fiber of their being.

I loved seeing that moment when the man would hover, right before he leaned in to kiss a woman, and I found myself screaming, "Kiss her!! Kiss her!!"

Then he would, and it was just so toe curling, heart

melting and good. I knew it was a movie magic lie, but the girl in me loved seeing it even if it weren't true. Although, I guessed a few men like this did exist. Logan loved Clare to the moon and back, but I think he was a special breed, and I didn't have the energy to comb through the male species looking for an anomaly anymore.

After walking from the kitchen to my living room, I snuggled down onto my comfy brown suede sofa, grabbed my favorite furry red fleece blanket and sighed in happiness. *Who needed to date?* This was perfect —Ice cream, fuzzy slippers and perfect men on film who didn't expect anything in return. Perfect.

Just as I hit Play on the Blu-ray player to watch *Dirty Dancing* for the four hundredth time, my doorbell rang. Confusion hit me as I looked at the clock. It was ten at night.

*Who was ringing my doorbell at such a late hour? And since when did ten at night become so late? Damn, I was boring.*

*Who the hell could that be?* I briefly hoped it was my hot new neighbor from three doors down needing to borrow a cup of sugar, but knowing my luck, it would probably be a punk-ass kid playing Ding-Dong ditch.

I threw off the blanket, and with the ice cream still in hand, I stormed to the door, slightly annoyed that I wasn't beginning my cha-cha lessons with Patrick Swayze at that moment.

I opened the front door, and froze.

*Holy fucking hell.*

Declan James. On my porch. Looking sexy as hell.

And I was...in a bathrobe and fuzzy slippers. *Shit!*

His hazel green eyes ran down my body, scanning my

attire, lingering on my legs peeking through the parting of my robe, before stopping at my hand.

"Do you always eat ice cream in a coffee mug?" He leisurely leaned against my door frame.

He was sporting a cocky smile that had my hormones going haywire.

"What? Yes, the handle keeps my hand from getting cold," I blurted out.

*Oh my God, why was he here? At my house. And holy hell, why did he have to smell so good?*

"What the hell are you doing here?" I finally asked.

His eyes found mine, and he smirked. He was clearly amused. God, six months hadn't made him any less sexy. His wavy brown hair was pushed back, making his piercing hazel eyes stand out against his handsome face. Unshaven, and wearing a leather jacket, he was the epitome of a bad boy.

Every part of me wanted to take him for a ride — again.

*Oh God, my greatest weakness had come for a visit.*

"My film got the green light, so I'm in town for the next three months or so. Thought I'd stop by and pay you a visit," he answered.

He brushed past me, entering the house like he'd just been invited in, which he hadn't.

My lust filled haze cleared a bit, and it was replaced with a bit of annoyance.

*Who the hell did this guy think he was?*

"So, you got into town, and you thought you'd pay me a visit? Why? To say hello? Needed a friendly chat Declan?" I asked, clearly peeved.

I'd had an emotional day.

He sat himself on my sofa, draping his arms over the back like he owned the fucking place as he grinned at me. He was too big for the room. My living room was literally being swallowed up by his presence.

"No, I think you know exactly why I'm here Leah," he said, he voice deepening.

His eyes darkened, sending shivers down my spine and straight to my core. All traces of playfulness disappeared. This was the Declan I remembered —the predator, the great seducer.

The man who had taken me again and again all night, sending me over the edge more times than I could count. His hands had touched every inch of my skin. His mouth had kissed every intimate part of my body. No man had ever filled me so completely and owned me as he had.

And here he was, like an offering from the gods.

"No," I whispered.

"No?" Are you seeing someone?" he asked, suddenly jumping off the couch and stalking toward me.

"No, I'm not seeing anyone."

His movements slowed, and he visibly relaxed. He continued his journey toward me, but it changed from an angry stalk to a casual swagger. I watched him, loving the confidence in his gait and the determination in his eyes, knowing it was all focused on me.

"Then I don't see a problem here, Leah," he whispered in my ear as he pressed his firm body against mine. "We were good together. Don't you remember?"

Brushing back the golden strands off my neck, he slowly pushed the bathrobe off my shoulder, taking my tank top strap with it. Undoing the belt of my robe with his other hand, he let it fall to the floor in a heap, leaving me in my tank top and tight pajama shorts. His eyes took an appreciative gaze over my exposed flesh, causing my nipples to harden instantly. He smiled, knowing the effect his touch was having on me.

Leaning forward, Declan grazed his lips over my bare shoulder, making me shudder from the touch.

"I can remind you, one more time. Don't you want that?"

I heard the words, and tried to process them in the foggy mush that was my brain. *One more time.* He'd just arrived. He wasn't here because he needed me, or wanted me as much as much as I wanted him. I was his fucking booty call, an easy lay for someone who had just gotten into town.

Anger flooded my system, and I pushed him away. I'd had a long day and this was just the icing on the cake. *A movie star coming by for a quick fuck. Perfect.*

"Get out."

He looked confused, but then his trademark smile came back. I could tell he was ready to throw out more bullshit that I wouldn't fall for again.

"No, seriously, get out. I'm not your booty call, Declan. I'm not going to spread my legs just because you showed up at my doorstep. Just because you're in town for three months doesn't mean I suddenly have an open-door policy. I am not your fucking groupie."

Momentarily stunned, he looked around the room until he saw a pen and a notepad resting on the coffee table. He stalked over to the small table, grabbed the pen and angrily scribbled something before ripping the sheet of paper off the notepad and handing it to me.

"This is where I'm staying in town and the name my room is booked under."

Rejection must be a new thing for Declan because he looked conflicted, pissed and seriously sexy. With his eyes wild and intense, he took a deep breath as he ran his hands through that unruly hair. Suddenly, he grabbed me around the waist, and took my mouth in a fierce kiss. Surprise, lust, anger, and confusion all invaded my system and I both pulled him closer and tried to push him away. His taste was exactly the same —completely addictive. Instincts had me diving in, needing him like my next breath, but the logical side of me that had been hurt too many times needed him to leave.

Before I could make a decision, he abruptly pushed away looking smug.

"Call me if you change your mind," he said before walking out the door, letting it close with a soft click behind him.

Making my way to the door, I let my head fall forward until it hit the hard wood with a thump, echoing my mood. "Fuck!" I cursed out in frustration.

"Heard that!" Declan yelled from the other side of the door, as his loud laughter faded away.

*Bastard.*

At least he didn't see my hand shake as I locked to the door. I could never let that man know how much he affected me. It would be my undoing.

"He just showed up at your doorstep?" Clare asked.

We nibbled on turkey sandwiches from the picnic basket she'd brought. Picnics in November were rare, considering the temperature in Virginia was usually in the fifties, but today was oddly warm, and we were taking advantage.

"Yep. Six months of nothing, and there he was, at my house in all of his sexy masculine glory."

"And he just expected you to fall down at his feet, thanking him for the opportunity to service him?" she asked.

"Pretty much."

"That arrogant bastard! Logan, did you know Declan was back in town?" Clare called out to her husband.

Logan was currently pushing their five-year-old daughter in the nearby swing. "No, baby," he said. "I haven't talked to him in months. We don't exactly run in the same circles anymore. Once he found out I was married, he figured he'd lost his wingman, so he hasn't called much."

Clare gave a quick snort. "Hmm, well, apparently, he's here for a while. I'm sure he'll stop by at some point. I mean, you would think a good friend would at least check in. Right, Leah?"

"Mmhmm," I answered. I was completely bored with this conversation now that I'd found something much better to focus on. I tried to be a good friend, I really did.

"Leah!" Clare scolded. "Can you please refrain from staring at my husband's ass?"

"Sweetie, you can ask all you want, but it's not going to change my answer. Besides, it's not like I have much else to look at," I answered halfheartedly. I completely dismissed my best friend's request as I continued to ogle.

Logan gave a quick grin and wink in our direction before returning his attention to his duties as the official swing pusher.

*Flirt.*

I tried pulling my eyes away from Logan, Clare's perfectly built husband. It was difficult. Even almost six months into cancer treatment, he was still a hot piece of ass. Long and lean, he was built like a swimmer. He'd lost a bit of weight when he started chemo, but he'd still kept his handsome features. He'd shaved his head, opting to take it all at once, and damn if the man didn't look sexier that way.

"Hey, Logan told me what you did for him the other night with the kid. Thank you. He was pretty wrecked when he got home," she said quietly while Logan's attention was diverted. She looked at me with a meaningful smile.

"Anytime, babe."

Successfully turning my attention away from Logan, my eyes traveled until they found something else entirely —my Maddie, my beautiful goddaughter. She was the best present a best friend could give. She was the spitting image of Clare and her late husband, Ethan. Sometimes, it hurt to look at Maddie, seeing Ethan's eyes shining through, but knowing he lived on brought me hope. She carried his wisdom and love, and being around her always made me want to be a better person. Clare was the best mother a child could have, having been raised by amazing parents herself, and it showed in everything Maddie did. She was perfection.

Logan laughed while Maddie kicked her feet back and forth excitedly as he pushed her higher and higher. He was healing. I could see it. Two months ago, he wouldn't have been able to do this, but here he was, slowly regaining his strength. His doctors hadn't given him a clean bill of health yet, but it was coming. He was coming back to us slowly, and the outlook was very optimistic.

Knowing Clare wouldn't have to suffer the loss of another husband was a relief I couldn't put into words. Losing her first husband, Ethan, had almost killed her. The only thing that had kept her going was Maddie. Knowing she had to care for that tiny innocent child had given her the will to carry on. That was, until she'd met Logan. Then, I had seen her come alive again. That glowing radiance she carried with her in her movements, her voice, and her smile —it had all come back when Logan entered her life.

And then, we'd found out that Logan had cancer. It was ironic how life could be so cruel. But here we were, six months later, and I was finally able to take a breath again. I felt like I'd been stepping on eggshells for months, waiting for our world to come crashing down again. But seeing Logan playing with Maddie in the park gave me hope.

"So, what are you going to do?" Clare asked.

She knew full well that my dismissal the other evening wasn't the last I'd see of Declan James. My body and mind wouldn't allow it. Saying no to him had taken almost every bit of will I had. I was drawn to him, and it was just a matter of time before I found myself at that hotel, knocking on his door.

I needed this time to form a plan —or at least to make him sweat it out a bit. I couldn't be his sloppy seconds or his late-night booty call. I didn't want a relationship, but I wouldn't be a doormat either. I felt like I was being pulled in two different directions. I wanted to run as quickly and as far away as possible, knowing he could end me if he tried, yet the more I told myself to stay away, the more I wanted to throw caution to the wind and get to that hotel as quickly as possible. After Daniel, my college sweetheart that turned out to be anything but and a childhood of mistrust —thanks to a father who really gave definition to the word *deadbeat* —I couldn't afford to give my trust to another man who didn't deserve it.

"I don't know, but I do know one thing. It will be on my fucking terms."

# Chapter Three

DECLAN

"Just get it fucking done!" I roared, causing the personal assistant on the other end of the line to whimper in fear.

He sputtered off an acknowledgment, and I ended the call, sighing in frustration. I paced the floor of the hotel room that would be home for the next three months. I was usually calm and fairly easygoing. At times, I was intense maybe, but I was never one to cause a PA to piss himself with my voice alone. Angry and pissed-off Declan was a new thing. The people on the set didn't know how to react, and personally, I didn't either.

I had managed to screw up every one of my lines at the read-through yesterday, gotten in an argument with my director, and even pissed off the caterer because there wasn't enough coffee. I was now known as the bitchy diva on the set. *Fucking great.*

I couldn't concentrate. I was restless, irritable, and so goddamn horny.

Leah had said no. She had fucking said no...to me. In my entire adult life, I'd never been turned down by a woman I had pursued. Call me cocky, but when I put my sights on something, I always got my prize. I'd stepped off the plane that night, ready to put Leah Morgan in my past. She was an aching need I couldn't squelch, and I wanted nothing more than to sink into those silky thighs once more, so I could walk away a cured man. But then, she'd opened that door, wearing a bathrobe and slippers, with a mug in her hand, looking absolutely dumbstruck. It was...well, adorable. *Fuck! I hated that word.*

Seeing her flustered and off her game had given me great pleasure. It reminded me of the quiet woman I'd met that night in the bar. I'd thought, *This will be easy, simple. I'll be cured by morning, ready to start fresh and begin my life again —free of Leah Morgan.*

I had taken advantage of her shock, playing into her bewildered reaction to my surprising presence. I'd stalked her, reminding her of how good we had been together that night, and her body had instantly blossomed under my touch. I'd had her in my grasp. Everything had been perfect.

And then, she'd said no. Her eyes had heated in anger, and she had taken a firm stance that had clearly backed up her words. It had taken a total one-eighty from the woman I'd just seduced not a minute before. I was learning there were many sides to Leah Morgan.

I'd never felt so angry, frustrated, and more turned-on in my entire life. No? What the hell? I couldn't leave, but I couldn't stay. I'd practically thrown my hotel information at her before walking out the door. As the door had clicked into place, I'd heard her curse in frustration, and I'd known that this wasn't over.

She was playing me or simply delaying the inevitable, and it would only be a matter of time before she came knocking on my door, begging me for more. I just had to wait it out. She'd be crawling back to my hotel, begging me to take her, in a day, two tops. I couldn't contain the all-out grin I had spread all over my face that night as I'd driven back to my hotel.

But now, it had been a week —a motherfucking week. I didn't play games, and I wasn't a patient man. This cat-and-mouse game was making me restless, but I still couldn't back down. No matter how many women passed me in the hotel lobby, giving me a shy smile and wave, I couldn't give in. Even a blatant invite from my costar to visit her trailer had gotten nothing in return. I couldn't do it. I had unfinished business, and it demanded closure.

But now, it had been a week, and I felt like a fool. *Did she think this was funny? Was I a fucking joke to her? Did I misread the signals? Maybe she wasn't coming at all.*

Declan James wasn't some pussy who waited around for a woman. Women waited around for me, and it was time I got back in the game. This addiction or infatuation I had would cure itself over time. *Screw this. I was done waiting.*

After giving myself a pep talk that even I didn't believe, I made about fifty laps around my room trying to get my head in the game. Then, I threw on my leather jacket and stalked over to the front door, setting my sights for the hotel bar. It was an upscale hotel, and single women were always mingling around, hoping to score a lonely rich man on a business trip. Feeling much less excited than I should be, considering I was headed downstairs to pick up an easy lay, I opened the door and nearly ran headfirst into a stunned Leah, who had her fist raised in the air like she was about to knock.

"Holy shit! You just about killed me!" she yelled.

I steadied us both in the doorway. "What are you doing here?" I asked.

The look on her face abruptly changed from stunned to pissed, and I realized my question sounded more than a little rude.

"Sorry. I meant to say, how did you get up here, alone?"

I had left instructions with the front desk not to let anyone up without calling me first. I was booked under an alias. It sounds crazy, but there were all kinds of new requirements in the shitty life I'd acquired.

Leah grinned widely as we walked into the room.

"Men," she answered. "I can pretty much talk them into doing anything. And it just so happened that men were working the front desk, and they were very accommodating when I told them I wanted to surprise my boyfriend with an impromptu striptease, but I didn't want to ruin the surprise with a call."

"That's bullshit. That seriously didn't work," I countered.

"Oh, but it did. All I had to do was say the word *striptease*, and I had them eating out of my hand."

Much like I had done at her house, she settled herself

on the sofa, making herself comfortable without asking permission. She had her spunk back tonight. Dressed in a low-cut black sweater, a short pink skirt, and heels, she looked fierce and very tempting. The flustered girl I'd walked in on last week was gone, and Leah, the firecracker I'd met in bed all those months ago, was back. Having met both sides of her now, I couldn't decide which I liked better.

"So, when exactly do I get my striptease?" I asked.

"Well, that's up to you, Hotshot."

"Hotshot?"

"Yep. Cocky attitude, arrogant disposition, and sexy as fuck —it's a good nickname."

"All right, so what are your terms, Leah?"

I fought back the urge to touch her. Stuffing my hands into my pockets, I paced the room in a vain attempt at keeping myself from just saying, *Fuck it*, and pinning her against the wall before she could lay down any terms or requirements. Because whatever she was about to say, I was going to agree. She didn't know it, but she had my balls in her perfect little hands, and I was at her fucking mercy. I both hated and wanted her at the same time. She made me feel out of control and weak with need. I couldn't stop the pursuit, and I couldn't walk away.

"I will not be an easy fuck whenever you get too lazy to find a new bimbo for the evening. I will not allow you in my bed, wondering where you've been and what kind of sloppy seconds I'm getting," she declared.

Then, she said the one thing I never wanted to hear.

"I want to be exclusive with you —for however long we decide to do this. I don't care about labels or dates.

You don't have to take me out to dinner, bring me flowers, or buy me anniversary presents. The only thing I ask is that, for the time we are together, you are mine."

"Yes," I answered immediately, surprising us both.

"Yes? That's it? No counteroffer? No freak-out or temper tantrum, Declan?"

"No, Leah, no temper tantrum. Just one request,"

I joined her on the sofa. My thigh brushed hers, and I heard her breath falter.

"And what's that, Hotshot?"

"Make it two," I amended. "First, the same rules apply to you. While we're together, for however long, you're mine, Leah," I purred against her ear.

Her eyes widened, and her breath became ragged, giving me a quick sense of satisfaction because I'd broken through her calm and collected exterior.

"And second?" she asked timidly.

"Don't fucking call me Hotshot."

She visibly relaxed and snorted out a laugh before saying, "So not happening, Hotshot."


LEAH

He stood and circled the room like a predator stalking prey. I was the gazelle, and he was the hungry lion. I could still remember the feel of his lips from last week when they'd moved against my neck, so soft and warm. It had been six months, but every detail had been memorialized in my memory —every touch, every moan, every earth-shattering second.

My hands trembled in anticipation, knowing those

memories would finally become reality again. When you knew what you were missing, it was almost worse than anticipating something you'd never had. I was like a drug addict standing in front of a dealer, eagerly anticipating her next hit.

"I believe I was promised a striptease," Declan said, breaking the heavy silence that had filled the room. He sat down in a plush beige chair, kicking his legs up on the nearby desk. He placed his hands behind his gorgeous head and leaned back, like he was waiting for the show to begin.

"I don't recall promising you one," I fired back.

I was a little breathless at my new view. Seeing Declan sprawled out in front of me did dirty things to my mind. I wanted nothing more than to knock those legs off that desk and sink into his lap, so I could relive all the fantasies I'd been living off of for so long. But I was stubborn as a mule, and I refused to give in so easily. This was a game we were playing, and I definitely wanted to play with him.

"Mmm...well, seems you told the desk clerks you were here to give your boyfriend a striptease. We wouldn't want to disappoint the poor boys, would we, Leah?" he asked with a crooked grin.

"You're not my boyfriend."

"No, but you did just agree to be mine, didn't you? I think we'll start with the top. Lose it." His voice deepened, becoming darker, sensual, and sexy as hell.

My muscles tightened in response, and I instantly flushed. I felt like a raging inferno had erupted inside my body, melting me from within. Complying with his command, I rose from the sofa and slowly lifted my sweater up and over my head, letting it fall to the floor in a billowing heap. His hazel eyes darkened, becoming greener, as he took me in.

"Now, the skirt, Leah," he said, dropping his feet from the desk to the floor in front of him.

He leaned back in the chair, trying to appear relaxed, but his former calm was gone, replaced with the hum of sexual energy now coursing through his system. He looked feral, barely contained, and I loved that my presence was bringing the animal out in him.

Achingly slow, I slid the skirt down my long legs, still tan from the summer, until it joined my sweater in the growing pile of clothes. I was now standing before him in nothing but black lace and heels. Feeling emboldened, I reached for the closure of my bra.

Declan interrupted, "No, my turn."

The predator was now on the move, rising up from his chair in one fluid motion. He took a few steps, closing the gap between us, until our bodies were nearly flush. I could feel the heat radiating off his perfect body. He smelled like leather, aftershave, and something purely male. It was divine.

His eyes swept down my body before moving upward and finally meeting my own. They were bright, alive, and full of fire. His hand snaked around my torso, brushing my sensitive skin with his fingertips, until he found the clasp of my bra. With one flick of his wrist, it came undone, and I watched it fall to the floor. His sharp intake brought my focus upward again. His eyes swept hungrily over my breasts as his hands found my waist, pulling me against his hard frame.

"Do you remember me, Leah?" he asked.

*Like I could forget. Like I hadn't spent the last one-hundred-and-eighty-days trying to forget him.*

I shuddered as his lips found my collarbone and gently kissed my skin.

"Do you remember what it feels like to have me buried deep inside you?"

*Oh God.* I couldn't help it. I let out a small moan in response, and then I felt his lips upturn in a small smile against my shoulder.

"Do you think of me every time you come? Cry out my name when you screamed your release?"

His hand moved up my torso and squeezed my breast as his thumb rubbed my nipple into a hard peak. I instantly felt my panties drench at his touch. My body's physical reaction to him was so intense that I could feel my knees quivering beneath me. I hated that a man could make me feel this way, so helpless and out of control, but I couldn't get enough. I knew the moment Declan had shown up at my door last week that I'd end up here. It was only a matter of time. An addict can hold out for only so long before she needs another fix, especially when her fix is six plus feet of raw alpha male.

"You haven't answered my questions, Leah," he whispered against my ear.

"Yes. God, yes," I moaned.

His hand traveled down my body before reaching the lacy edge of my panties. When his hand stilled, I nearly screamed in frustration. I needed his touch like I needed air. He owned me in that moment, and he fucking knew it.

Taking a step back, his voice rough like gravel, he pointed to my panties and said, "Slide those down your pretty little legs, won't you?"

Happily agreeing because it meant I would be that much closer to my goal of being fucked to death by Declan, I started to step out of my heels.

"Uh-uh, Leah. Keep the heels. Just the panties," he instructed, his eyes dark and full of desire.

Giving him a small smirk, I hooked my fingers into the sides of my panties, and ever so slowly, I slid them down my slim legs, making a show of the process. My eyes locked with his again, and I noticed his fists tighten at his sides as his jaw ticked. Apparently, I wasn't the only one so overly affected by the other. He looked like a ticking time bomb waiting to blow.

"Back against the door," he commanded, motioning toward the suite entrance with a nod of his head.

He followed me as I walked backward, taking a couple of steps, until my back hit the cold wooden door. He drew near, and I felt his fully clothed body become flush with mine. Seeing him still wearing every article of clothing while I stood bare was thrilling. It made me feel wanton and desirable, and as I looked into his eyes, I knew he felt the same.

His hand found my breast again, and my nipple pebbled at his familiar touch. Declan kissed my collarbone —a favorite place for him, it seemed —and then his tongue swept up my neck until his teeth gently tugged my ear.

"From now on, Leah, you will only scream my name when you come."

I whimpered. The man made me freaking whimper in want. I needed him to touch me —right now. If I were stuck on a desert island without food or water and I was given the choice of a picnic basket filled with sustenance or an hour with Declan James, I wasn't sure what I would choose. Right now, I'd say, *Screw the food. I'll take the hot-as-fuck actor, please!*

His hand traveled from my breast, down my stomach until it found my slick core. I silently begged, pleaded, and offered him my entire 401(k) plan if he would just end the torture and stroke me.

"Oh God, Declan, please," I moaned.

He lazily ran his fingers over the smooth juncture of my thighs, clearly enjoying the wax I had done just a few days earlier.

"Please, what, Leah?"

"Please make me come. Damn it, Declan!"

He chuckled softly, and then that large alpha male dropped to his knees before me, never breaking eye contact. He shucked off his leather jacket quickly, and I took a moment to admire the new view. He was wearing a simple white T-shirt underneath, and it clung to him, showing the hard lines and muscles of his toned body.

*Yum.*

"Spread your legs," he said gruffly.

No sooner had I done as he'd commanded, he was on me, burying his head between my legs in one swift motion.

"Oh fuck!" I screamed.

His tongue found my clit, sending waves of pleasure rushing through my body. Back and forth, his tongue moved over the tiny bundle of nerves at the center of my body until I thought I was going to explode. Just when I was getting close to coming from that alone, he plunged his tongue into my core, causing me to cry out in ecstasy. He mouth fucked me with wild abandon, seeming to get lost in the process. His hands pushed me further into the door, and then he lifted one leg at a time over his shoulder until I was suspended against it, seated on his shoulders. He never stopped working me with his tongue, and the new angle allowed him to penetrate deeper.

"God, I forgot how sweet you taste," he said against my flesh.

In those minutes, I thought I fell in love with Declan's tongue. It was a work of art and should receive medals or trophies. If there were an award for the best tongue action, Declan would win, hands down.

I weaved my fingers through his dark locks as his thumb found my clit. The two sensations together sent me over the edge, making me free fall into bliss. My body shook from the force of my orgasm, and I silently thanked Declan's massive shoulders for holding me upright. He let my legs return to the floor, and slowly, he rose, licking his lips with the same tongue he'd just used to fuck me senseless.

Without a word, he began to give me a striptease of his own as he lifted his white T-shirt in one graceful, fluid move. My memories of his body hadn't done him justice, and the few films he'd done were strictly shirt-on type movies. Those directors were seriously stupid. They could make a shit-ton of money just by having Declan parade around shirtless for a few minutes. Women would line up for days to see that movie.

His broad tanned shoulders gave way to a torso made for stroking, petting, and licking. Along with his six-pack abs, he had a perfect V that pointed to all things dirty — things my mind and body couldn't wait to do again. As if he heard my naughty thoughts out loud, Declan smirked while his hands headed for his belt buckle. My libido cheered him on, begging his hands to work faster. He grabbed a condom from his back pocket, and then his faded jeans dropped to the floor, leaving him standing before me in a pair of black boxer briefs that left nothing to the imagination. He was hard, massive, and so ready for me under the thin barrier of fabric. As his hand went to the waistband of his boxers, I pushed off the door, stopping him.

"No, let me," I said boldly, needing to put my hands on him immediately.

He stilled, gave me the condom, and allowed me to take over. The instant my fingers touched the hot skin of his abdomen, he hissed in pleasure. His eyes flared an intense green as my hands wrapped around his back and slipped into his boxers to grab his tight ass. After giving it a firm squeeze, I pulled the boxers down his legs, dropped myself to the floor, and leaned back onto the balls of my feet. Ripping the wrapper of the condom apart with my teeth, I slowly slid it down the long length of his shaft.

Seeing me in this position must have been the last straw for Declan. Before I even had a chance to admire the view from below, I was hauled up, slammed against the wall, and devoured by his mouth. Our tongues tangled and moved together, and his hand fisted in my hair like he was punishing me for some unspoken act. I felt the same because no man should be this consuming or make me feel this unglued. Men were fun but on my terms. Declan had a way of turning me inside out, twisting me in knots, and just when I thought I had recovered, he'd do it all over again.

As we feverishly kissed, he reached a hand down my body until he found my center, and then he slid his fingers into my wet core.

"God, you're so wet," he said against my mouth, "so ready."

He removed his finger, lifted me up higher on the door, and then brought me down onto his rock-hard shaft. I cried out at the sudden invasion, but he gave no mercy as he pulled out and slammed back in again. The door shook and vibrated as he fucked me, and I gladly took all of it, letting out my cries of pleasure, completely uncaring what people passing by might think.

"That's it, Leah. Let those boys downstairs hear how much I like to please my *girlfriend*. Let them know whose name you scream out when you come."

"Oh God, yes!" I cried as he continued to thrust and fill me completely.

"No, wrong name...although I have been called him a time or two. Try again, Leah," he taunted.

His fingers found my sweet spot, and he began to rub my clit as he pounded me against the wall with his powerful strokes. I could feel my muscles beginning to tighten and clench, and I knew I was close as my stomach began to flutter.

Just when I thought I would pass out, I screamed, "Declan!"

I came undone, fisting his cock like a vice, which sent him over the edge and he joined me with a deep guttural moan.

Out of breath and completely sated, I sagged against the support of his body as his hand braced us against the door. I didn't think I'd ever been this tired from sex before, and I'd had sex with Declan before, so that was saying something.

As I lay against Declan's hard shoulder, I felt him beginning to harden again inside me. I lifted my head and met his eyes in surprise. His smug smile said it all.

"What? Did you think you were done? Silly girl." He laughed.

That man was like the Energizer Bunny. He kept me going all night long, never stopping longer than to change the condom and grab a glass of water. He was an unstoppable force.

*God bless Declan James.*

# Chapter Four



"Against the wall?" Clare squeaked as we sat on her bed, folding laundry on a chilly Tuesday afternoon.

We'd met for yoga, had lunch at one of our favorite little spots in town, and now, we were spending some quality time with her socks and underwear. I was an awesome best friend.

"Yep, and then he bent me over the desk and took me in the shower. Hell, we even did it on the floor before we made it to the actual bed."

"Wow, didn't your, um...girlie bits hurt after all that?" she asked.

I burst out laughing. I loved Clare. She and I were the perfect combo. I said whatever the fuck came to mind without a care for the consequences while Clare turned the color of a tomato and said things like *girlie bits* because she was too afraid to say *pussy* out loud.

"Of course they did. Every time I walked around the next day at work, I ached. That would only remind me of the night before, which of course, reminded me of Declan, which made me horny."

"You're crazy! I swear, you two are a match made in heaven! Two nymphos. I should start typing up the wedding announcement now. Hmm...that could be interesting! Do you think using the word *nymphomaniac* in a wedding invitation is tacky?"

"No!" I shouted a bit too loudly. "No weddings, no engagements, no matches made in heaven, Clare! We are screwing each other. That is it. It's for a few months, and then we are done. Okay? Consider it a long-term fuck buddy. Nothing more."

I had been reminded of that fact this morning when I had woken up to an empty hotel room —no note, no phone number...nothing. A boyfriend would have left a note explaining where he had gone. A lover would have at least left a phone number. Walking around the hotel room, I'd realized that Declan and I were neither of those things. I couldn't even consider us lovers because that just sounded too intimate. It involved feelings, and I couldn't risk any of those. I had given too many to the last one, and he'd left me high and dry. I had learned my lesson.

So, I had done the few things I could in that moment. I'd ordered the most expensive room service possible, making sure it was charged to my boyfriend's room, and then I'd taken the longest, hottest bubble bath known to man. I'd wandered around in his white hotel robe, enjoyed my overpriced Belgian waffle and French-pressed coffee, and told myself that this was the best possible relationship I could ever have. In fact, while soaking in the jetted tub, I'd told myself that I was a genius, pure genius.

Not only did I get to enjoy one of the hottest males on the planet, but I also didn't have to worry about when or if he would leave me. I wouldn't have to pace the floors, wondering if he was screwing someone behind my back or whether he would remember our anniversary. I knew exactly what he expected of me and how long our arrangement would last.

*It was perfect, right?*

*Right.*

"Are you sure? I mean, you don't want anything more permanent?" Clare asked hesitantly.

"No!" I snapped. "I mean, I am fine with this. He isn't my forever man, so why not have some fun?" I said with an encouraging smile.

I hadn't told Clare that I didn't plan on having a forever man. Whenever she had brought it up, I would deflect, saying I just hadn't found him yet. She wouldn't understand. She had one, and she would never compre-hend how a woman could go through life without someone as wonderful as Logan. Personally, if I had a Logan, I wouldn't either. But the super-awesome guy store was currently out of stock, and I heard the waiting list was endless.

"Okay...well, if you are sure, then I'm happy for you. I mean, I'm happy that you're happy," she fumbled. "You know the thing with Daniel isn't always going to happen, right? I mean, decent men are still out there. You can't compare them all to him."

Daniel was my ex —ex-boyfriend, ex-lover...ex-forever man. He was supposed to be my happily ever after, but he had left me when I decided being a friend while my best friend's husband was dying took precedence over Daniel. He'd felt it was a competition, and like the spoiled little boy that he was, he'd left me. Clare had blamed herself for it for a long time. It wasn't her fault the guy was a grade-A asshole.

"I know, Clare. I'm just not currently looking for anyone. We're just having a bit of fun."

She nodded her head, but I could tell she didn't quite agree. I knew she wasn't judging. She wanted me to be happy, as happy as she was, and I loved her for that. But I didn't think love was in the cards for me.

"Hey, you don't always have to help me with laundry, you know?" she said, changing the subject and chucking a pair of socks at my head.

"Um, yes, I do." I laughed, ducking to dodge the sock attack. "When I get injured doing something incredibly stupid —because we all know it will happen someday —I expect you will return all of these awesome favors with interest. So, you see, it's not a selfless act. I am really a selfish bitch trying to protect my own ass."

She gave me a look that said *whatever* as she continued to match tiny pink socks and throw them into the basket. She knew I would gladly fold a hundred loads of laundry with her if it meant less stress for her and Logan right now. After two months of chemo and a couple rounds of radiation, their lives had been hectic. Never-ending doctor and treatment appointments had taken time away from Maddie and household chores. I'd helped out in any way I could —from sitting at home with Maddie while they ran to the hospital to running quick errands for them so that they could enjoy a bit of free time together.

I remembered every second Clare had suffered during Ethan's sickness. Having to go through something similar, even if the chances were much better, was still a blow to the heart. Every time she had walked into the treatment room at the hospital, I knew she would see Ethan sitting in one of those chairs, remembering him growing weaker until his doctors had finally told him that it wasn't an option anymore. But she'd been so strong —so much stronger than I could ever be. She'd walked proudly by Logan's side to every appointment, braving every fear and memory head-on.

A knock on the door broke the brief bit of silence, and I glanced up to see Logan standing in the doorway, looking in on us.

"Hello, ladies. What are we doing up here?"

"Folding your tighty whities," I replied smugly.

"Hmm...well, I know that's a lie 'cause I go commando," he shot back, equally smug.

"Nice. That's a mental picture I'm keeping for my spank bank!"

"Leah!" Clare scolded.

Logan laughed as he came in, and then he sat next to his bride. He bent his head and kissed her softly before whispering something in her ear that caused her to blush.

"So, what are you two crazy kids up to today?" I asked, not exactly sure I wanted to know after seeing the blush that was currently taking over Clare's ivory skin.

With red hair and fair skin, it wasn't easy for her to hide any embarrassment. It was something I loved to exploit at all times. She was my best friend. Embarrassing her was my job. Apparently, Logan excelled at the subject as well.

"We are unfortunately headed for the hospital," Clare said.

"You are? You didn't ask me to babysit, did you? I can, if you need me to."

"Actually," Logan answered, "Garrett is watching Maddie today."

"Garrett? Seriously?"

Clare just grinned and nodded.

"How the hell did you talk him into that? And are you sure he's old enough?"

"Leah! I know he's my baby brother, but he's twenty-three! He's home this week, working in the regional office in town, and he wanted to help out. So, I told him his niece would love to hang out with him. He jumped at the chance. You know how much he loves her."

I did. It was just really weird to see Garrett —the kid who couldn't look at me between the ages of fourteen and eighteen without getting an instant boner —was all grown-up. It made me feel old, and I did not want to feel old at twenty-eight.

"Come on," Clare beckoned, rising from the bed, "let's head downstairs. He should be here any minute, and I know he'd love to see you."

It had been ages since I'd seen Garrett Finnegan. Growing up, he'd been the brother I never had. Being an only child to an alcoholic single father had meant that our house wasn't usually filled with the warm and fuzzy feelings most children had.

Clare's family had been my sanctuary from the hell that I'd had to return to every night. When I walked into her house, I felt safe and secure. Being there, I had a mother who hadn't left me, a father who had loved me, and a kid brother who I could taunt. It had been normal, boring, and something I'd so desperately wanted. Clare's mother had known this, and she'd let me stay over as often as I'd needed. I thought, at some point, she had even tried to take me away from my awful home life, but the courts hadn't agreed. *Figures.*

"Absolutely. I would love to see Goober. It's been ages," I said.

The three of us made our way downstairs. We found Maddie watching *Dora* and playing with Legos on the couch in the family room. I smiled and gave a silent laugh, seeing her watch the TV show that Clare despised. I knew it drove her batshit crazy, but she endured it because it was Maddie's absolute favorite. No matter how many other shows Clare introduced Maddie to, she always came back to that one. I think Clare had hoped she would grow out of it, but even now, several months into kindergarten, she still loved that stupid show.

I meandered into the remodeled kitchen and grabbed a bottle of water out of the fridge. I loved this house. Seeing Clare move out of the house she and Ethan had lived in was difficult, but I was glad to see her starting over with Logan. This was his home before they'd met, and it was perfect for them. It was historic but completely remodeled to live in comfortably. It was as if Logan had purchased it, waiting for Clare and Maddie to come and make it a home.

"Hello? Anyone home?" a deep male voice called out as the front door was pushed open.

"Uncle Garrett!" Maddie screamed with glee, running down the hall to greet Garrett.

He was now trying to juggle a very enthusiastic five-year-old and a box of pizza. I joined him halfway and took the pizza out of his hand, so he could hold on to Maddie with both hands.

"Thought you could use some help there, Goober," I said with a wry smile.

"God, seriously, Leah? Still? I'm an adult. Aren't we past the Goober phase?"

"Uh, no. You will always be Goober, dude. It doesn't matter how old or how hot you get, you will forever be the dorky, lanky six-year-old, who followed me around an entire summer, asking if I would marry you."

We settled back into the kitchen, and I set the pizza box down as he released Maddie. She lost interest in our discussion and ran off to the family room to continue her *Dora* marathon. Clare and Logan were sitting at the kitchen table, making googly eyes at each other.

"I was six! And you've got to admit that it was pretty damn cute. Besides, I'm way over my infatuation with you. Wait —you think I'm hot?"

Catching my earlier comment, he glanced at me with amusement. I loved Garrett for so many reasons, but one of the biggest reasons was he and I could trash-talk and banter like this for hours. He totally got me and my blunt sense of humor.

"Have you looked in a mirror lately, Goober? That baby face melted away and left you with nothing but sex-on-a-stick hotness. Now, this is coming from a purely objective opinion because anything beyond that makes me want to hurl. Hot or not, you're still like a brother to me."

It was true. Garrett had always been blessed in the looks department, but after he turned eighteen, he'd really blossomed. He'd filled out more, his slimmer body becoming harder and more defined. His jet black hair and piercing green eyes that mirrored his sister's made him quite the package.

"Right on, Leah. I feel the same way. You're crazy hot, but I'd never in a million years tap that. Gross." He laughed.

"Tell that to your dick. You used to have to sit around with a pillow on your lap whenever I was around. Don't think I didn't notice."

"I was a horny teenager. What do you expect? I popped wood over tampon commercials," he admitted.

Clare covered her ears and groaned.

"Yuck. All right, well, now that we've reestablished how fucking hot we are, how are you doing? Job okay? Seeing anyone? Getting enough protein?" I asked.

"Oh, don't even try to ask him about his love life. You won't get anywhere," Clare chimed in.

Garrett rolled his eyes. "It's because I don't have one. I don't have any time. When I'm not traveling, I'm working eighty-hour weeks. When I do get a day off, I have a side job, babysitting," he said with a grin. "It's a very lucrative career."

"Okay, Goober, just don't work too hard. You know there is a life beyond a paycheck. Try to actually spend it on something enjoyable."

He nodded and smiled, but his smile didn't quite reach his eyes, and I knew he wasn't listening. He was working himself to death, and I wondered why. There were many reasons people lost themselves in their work —to forget or to swap one addiction for another. What was his reason? At twenty-three, what could he possibly be trying to forget?


DECLAN

"Cut!" the director bellowed from his stance behind the cameraman. "What the hell was that, Declan? Your blocking is all over the place, and you look like you're headed out to pick up a fucking carton of milk! This is supposed to be your goddamn wife and children you are leaving behind. Show me some fucking emotion!" he barked.

*Damn it.* I needed to get my head in the game. The problem was that I was pretty sure I'd left my head among other things in that hotel room with Leah.

I couldn't believe we'd slept together. I knew we'd slept together. That part of the evening had been stuck on repeat like a broken record in my fucking head. Just like the first night, I remembered every single second. What I couldn't get past was when we'd reached the point of exhaustion, we'd both collapsed on the king-sized bed, entangled in each other, and fallen asleep. I'd awoken this morning, and the first thing that had hit me was her flowery vanilla scent. I'd opened my eyes to find her naked form wrapped in my arms, and her soft honey-colored hair fanned out over my chest. Her breathing had been slow and even, still far away and deep in sleep. I hadn't known what to do. I'd never spent the night with anyone I'd fucked around with...since Heather. I would either make excuses and get the hell out afterward or send the woman packing. Sleeping in the same bed was intimate, and I'd forgotten how much so until I'd had Leah's warm, naked body wrapped in mine.

I'd gently uncurled my body from hers and headed for the shower, knowing my morning call time was quickly approaching. I'd told myself I was being a nice guy, allowing her to sleep in and not disturbing her with my work schedule, but it had been all a lie. I had been running. Waking up with her tempting body flush against mine had brought something out in me —the same feeling I'd had when she asked me last night to be hers only. It had been that innate feeling of want. I had held on to the slim chance that after we had come together again, I would be over her, like I'd originally planned, but with some cruel twist of fate, I only wanted her more. It seemed every time I had her, it fueled my desire that much further.

I took my position again for the opening of the scene I had just botched as I cleared my head and tried to focus. It wasn't working. Leah's writhing body against that door as I'd licked her clean filled my memory, and when I opened my eyes, I saw my costar, Natasha, standing before me, waiting for me to deliver my line.

*Damn it, Declan. Concentrate.*

Natasha's fake tears trickled down her cheek as she portrayed a broken wife saying good-bye to her husband as he went off to war. It was supposed to be a heartbreaking scene, one that would make the women in the theater weep.

"Sorry, guys, give me a minute," I said.

The set crew groaned. Everyone gave me a look that clearly said, *Get your shit together*, before they shuffled off to get coffee.

I paced for a second or two, trying to focus on the scene and job ahead of me. I looked up to see Natasha closing the distance between us, swaying her hips in her nineteenth-century gown.

She gave me a sympathetic look and placed her hand on my own. "Everything okay, Dec?"

I hated when people called me Dec. I also hated when phony people tried to act like they cared. It wasn't even two days ago when Natasha —or Tasha Sinclair as she was known most of the time —had barreled into my trailer, offering me a blow job because she had been bored. She was the daughter of a movie producer, and she was spoiled beyond most people's imaginations. After playing around with her father's money for a few years, she had decided she wanted to get into the family business and act. When Daddy wouldn't hire her on as a leading lady, she'd realized she was going to have to work at it like the rest of us peons. She'd been working her way up ever since. The funny thing was, she was actually pretty damn good. Apparently, hanging around all those celebrities her entire life had taught her a thing or two.

I wished it would have given her more of a personality. I swore helium was coming out of her fucking ears.

"I'm fine, Tasha," I said flatly.

"I could make you better, you know. We have a lunch break coming up. I'll come to your trailer," she said as her fingers brushed my chest.

I glanced up at her then, seeing her perfectly sculpted lips and her deep brown eyes that made the caramel highlights in her hair seem to glow. Her body was sculpted after years of training and probably numerous surgeries. She was flawless in every way, and I just wasn't interested.

"I'm good, thanks."

I didn't even give her the chance to respond. I just extracted her bony fingers from my body and walked away. Normally, I'd be up for a quickie on a break, but this woman didn't want just a bit of fun. She wanted the status of being with me. She wanted to lure me in and then sink her fangs in, thinking she could make us the next celebrity couple. I knew women like her. In Hollywood, I ran away from a hundred just like her. They didn't give two fucks about me. They only cared about my name and how many magazine spreads I could get them.

And then, there was Leah. She was the other reason I'd stayed away from Natasha. It had been years since I'd given a woman my word, and I intended to keep it. I never made women promises that I couldn't keep. It was why I was so careful with how I treated them. When I'd agreed to Leah's terms last night, it wasn't something I had gone into lightly even though the words had tumbled out of my mouth instantly. Whatever crazy, fucked-up excuse we had for this relationship, I was going to keep my promise to her until we parted ways.

I just hoped she did the same because as I'd watched her shatter in my arms over and over again while screaming my name, I'd known one thing.

I'd kill any man who touched her.

# Chapter Five

LEAH

"Oh fuck...I'm gonna...oh God!" I screamed right before the orgasm racked through my body, sending pleasure to every nerve ending I possessed.

Declan hovered over me in bed, his gaze hot and intense. His mouth came down onto mine in a scorching kiss that mimicked what the rest of his body was doing as he thrust in and out of my pulsating core. His movements became urgent, and his pace quickened as his body grew closer to the edge of release.

My fingers bit into the skin of his back, and he muttered a curse while he pushed my legs forward, so he could drive in deeper. I could feel the beginning of a second orgasm, and I knew Declan was holding out. He was waiting, like a smug bastard, for me to come again. He always did this, holding back for the second one to come, like he was some sort of sexy god who could conjure an orgasm with the flick of his wrist.

*Not that I was complaining.*

*Nope, not one fucking bit.*

But the man could show a bit of humility. He worked my body like he owned it, making it move and explode to his will. And shit, maybe he did...but he could smile a little less about it.

The second orgasm tore through my body, and I convulsed beneath him, screaming his name, as he finally let go with a masculine cry and came with me. He collapsed onto the bed, taking a second to make sure he wouldn't land on top of me, but he still pulled me towards him, curling his arm around me with a firm grasp. Our combined labored breaths filled the small space of my bedroom.

Turning to my side, I watched as he tucked his other hand beneath his head and stared at the ceiling fan while it made lazy circles above us. He was so handsome, a perfect example of male beauty. He was simple yet rugged. He wasn't one of those pretty boys plastered all over the teen magazines. He was the exact personification of a bad boy—the kind daughters were always told to stay away from. And I'd just enjoyed every single inch of him —twice.

As my eyes roamed over his body, I focused on the tattoo centered over his heart. My fingers grazed over it, causing his attention to flitter back to me.

"What does it mean?" I asked as I traced the Celtic knot.

It was a circular design of twisting knots that wove their way over the middle of his chest, directly over his heart. The center of the tattoo was open, empty as if it were waiting for something.

He gave me a look that conveyed confusion and a bit of amusement. It'd been a few weeks since our little arrangement started, and this was probably the first personal question I'd asked. *So, sue me.* I was curious.

"Well, you know what it is, don't you?"

"Yeah, it's a Celtic knot. But I always thought a Celtic knot traditionally stood for love. So, did you have this tattoo done in honor of someone?" I asked, hoping like hell he wasn't going to tell me a story about some long lost love. I knew what we were doing here wasn't a relationship, but I wasn't keen on lying in bed, naked, while the guy I'd just fucked bared his soul about his broken heart.

*Shit, why did I even ask?*

"Yes. Me."

"What?" I asked, completely astonished as I slapped him on the chest. "You're so full of shit!"

"No." He laughed. "I'm serious. I got it to remind myself that when it comes down to it, out of everyone on this Earth, we will always choose ourselves."

"That's not true," I whispered.

"No?" he questioned. "We are a very selfish species. We might say we do things for one reason or another, but when push comes to shove, we do what we do for one specific reason —to put ourselves ahead. When a relationship falls apart and one person says it's for the best,, they're really just looking out for their own best interest.

I began to protest, but he just continued on.

"When you offer someone your space in line at the coffee shop, it's not out of the goodness of your heart. It's because you were hoping that person would notice you, or you wanted to be closer to the person behind them. Nothing we ever do is selfless. We love ourselves first."

"You sound like you speak from experience," I said softly.

"Don't we all? I come from a very selfish family. My dad snuck around on my mother and left her with nothing when he died. When I finally got out of there, I convinced myself that I'd never make the same mistake and fall in love, but I did. We all do. I met Heather the first week of my freshman year, and I was hooked. I thought we'd spend the rest of our lives together, but when I wanted to pursue my dreams and move to Hollywood, she told me she wasn't willing to make it work. She didn't want to come with me, and she wasn't willing to wait. Seven years together were gone like that...because she didn't want to take a chance on us. She chose herself instead," he said, keeping his focus on the fan as it continued its endless cycle of motion.

"Have you spoken to her since?" I asked, still running my fingers over his skin where the ink ran underneath.

"Not a single word," he answered with a bit of finality.

I knew the conversation was done then. I glanced out the window and saw the sun had set in the sky while we had been busy under the sheets.

It was a good thing I didn't have to work. We had wasted the entire day.

*Shit!* I did have to babysit though. I frantically whipped my head around, searching for the alarm clock on my nightstand. I didn't know why it took me so long to find it. It wasn't like it had taken a four-hour walk while I had been busy orgasming my brains out. Finally locating the clock, I sighed, seeing I had an hour before I had to be at Clare and Logan's.

"You okay?" Declan asked, rising up to lean on his elbows. He was clearly amused at having witnessed my twenty-second panic attack.

"Yeah, I guess I just lost track of time, and I realized I have to be somewhere tonight."

"Oh."

"I, uh...have to babysit for Clare and Logan. Logan has been having so many doctor appointments lately. They haven't really had any alone time outside of the hospital, so I volunteered to watch Maddie while they spent a few hours out. You do know that Logan has cancer, right?" I asked.

His brows furrowed together, and he nodded silently.

Declan and Logan had been friends since childhood, almost as long as Clare and I had known each other. I knew their relationship hadn't always been great, but I had thought it would have occurred to Declan to call Logan or check in on him since getting into town. But according to Clare, the two friends hadn't spoken in months. Logan had called him to break the news, and that was the last time Declan had spoken to him. I knew Logan was trying to be a man about the whole thing, but after being rejected by his father, he hadn't needed a shitty friend on top of everything.

"You want to go with me?" I asked.

His head jerked up in surprise. Hell, I was even a little surprised. He just looked so sad, lying there, stewing in his own thoughts.

"To babysit? Me? I don't think so," he said coolly.

"What? Are you scared of a little girl, Declan?"

"Fuck no. I'm not...well, yeah...maybe a little."

I couldn't help it. I giggled, causing him to smirk. Goddamn, he was sexy. Still leaning back on his elbows, he was completely naked and not ashamed in the least. He wasn't hiding a square inch of himself.

"Come on, it will be good for you. Live a little," I taunted.

"Live a little? How the hell is chasing around a six-year-old going to help me live a little? Besides, I'm pretty proficient with living the shit out of my life, thank you very much."

*Ah, yes, I forgot.* Logan had told me many stories of the mighty Declan James living it up all over the world as a glorified party animal and certified womanizer. I was fairly certain he was convinced that this was what life was about, what living was about. It was probably why he had that ridiculous tattoo on his body. If the man could look past his own finger, he would find being the life of the party wasn't fulfilling any cosmic purpose.

"That's it. You're coming. No more arguing. Get up and get dressed. We are going."

He gave me a hard stare before dragging his long body off the bed in an exaggerated pained movement. I rolled my eyes in the process.

"All right, but I'm going to take a shower first. I'm using your shit, so don't laugh when I come out smelling like a chick."

I squelched a laugh as I watched his tanned backside make its way into the adjoined bathroom. He didn't bother closing the door. I heard the faucet turn, and a moment later, the shower came on. The sound of water spraying against his body came next, and I suddenly was very jealous of water. This was a complete change for the few weeks of what I liked to call the Declan Days.

After our first night together, when we'd fallen asleep in the hotel room and I'd awoken to find myself alone in that same room, he hadn't stayed over at my place, and I'd never asked if I could stay at his hotel. We would meet, hook up, maybe talk a bit, joke around, and leave. This was the way it had been for two weeks. It was exactly how I'd expected a relationship with Declan James to be. We didn't hold hands, do late-night phone calls, or sit around, wondering what the other was thinking or doing when we were apart. We would text our schedules and find times to meet. It wasn't like we didn't talk. We did. We just didn't linger for hours afterward. We both had lives and demanding jobs, and I had a family. We would make the most of our time and then part ways.

He'd never asked to shower here. He always left, saying he had somewhere to be or an early call on the set. But over the last few days, things had slowly started to change. We were spending more time together. He would stay longer, and we'd even spent time chatting on the phone. Something between us was changing, like some new level of comfort, and I was trying desperately not to analyze it too closely.

The shower shut off, and I watched from my spot on the bed as he stepped out of the shower. The water droplets slid down his naked skin, and I had the sudden urge to lick every single one of them off his rock-hard body. We'd just spent hours devouring each other, and I was already eager for his touch again. I'd never felt this kind of desperate, raw passion for a man before. Even when I had been with Daniel, a man I'd thought I was going to marry, I hadn't felt this never-ending, consuming need to touch him, inhale his scent, and feel him buried deep inside me.

Just then, Declan caught me looking at him, which caused a slow grin to spread across his face. "So, are you going to stare at me all day? Or are we going to go do some babysitting?"

*So damn cocky.*

I threw him an equally smug grin as I crawled out of bed, creating a bit of a show as I went. His attention went directly to me as I bent down to pick up clothing, making sure my ass was in full view.

Turning around, I gave him a wink. "Be ready in twenty, Hotshot."


DECLAN

We pulled up to Logan and Clare's nineteenth-century home situated in a quaint neighborhood. It was tucked away in a small suburban neighborhood outside of Richmond. The trees were as old as homes, and the entire neighborhood had that perfect-postcard look everyone wished for. Children were running up and down the streets, some were on bicycles and skates, while people jogged by and waved as we exited my rental car.

It was nauseating. I felt like I was in a late-night Nickelodeon rerun. I couldn't believe this was Logan's life now. The man who, a year ago, had done body shots off a bikini model and then proceeded to take not only her but also her two best friends back to our hotel for an entire evening of debauchery. He was my legacy. I'd taken a quiet, reformed rich boy and turned him into a lesser version of me.

Well, I had until he'd met his first wife. He'd tamed down for a while, and we had drifted apart. But when those divorce papers had gone through, who had been the first person he'd contacted? His old buddy, Declan. I'd reminded him of how good being single was, and I'd thought he was cured until several months ago when I walked into a bar and came face-to-face with a certain blonde. That certain blonde knew my buddy, Logan...because she was his girlfriend's best friend.

*Girlfriend...and now wife...with a kid.*

*A kid that I am apparently babysitting.*

*Babysitting. Why the fuck did I agree to this?*

I walked behind Leah on the narrow walkway that led to the front door, noticing the way her ass seemed to be made for the jeans she was wearing. It was like she was poured into them. They molded to her curves perfectly. Her hips swayed as she walked, causing my dick to twitch. Her wheat-colored hair was loosely braided and draped elegantly to the side. It gave me visions of what it would be like to wrap that silky hair around my wrist and fuck her from behind. Just thinking of it was getting me in trouble. Lost in my thoughts, I barely noticed the door opening and the child barreling toward us.

"Leah!"

"Hey, Short Stack!" Leah said to the little girl who was

now wrapped in her arms. "Does Mommy know you're out here?"

"Um..." the girl responded.

"Come on, let's get you inside before we both get yelled at!" Leah said.

Leah shifted the child in her arms and hollered up at Clare that she had arrived as we all headed into the house. The girl was draped over Leah's shoulder, giving me a curious look as we walked passed family photos and portraits from Logan and Clare's wedding I never attended.

*Worst friend ever.*

We settled ourselves in the living room, and Leah set her precious cargo down.

The little girl immediately turned to me as I sat on the sofa with Leah. "My name is Maddie. Who are you?"

She smiled, and I couldn't help but return the gesture. She really was cute —for a kid. With strawberry-blonde curls and dark brown eyes, she was like a little angel, minus the talking.

"I'm Declan."

*"Are you my auntie's boyfriend?"*

*Wow, this kid is abrupt. Are all kids like this?*

"Uh...well..." I stammered.

"He's my friend, Maddie. Don't you have friends who are boys at preschool?"

Maddie thought about this momentarily. "Oh, yes! I have a friend named Tommy. He likes to make sandcastles with me, and he's fun to play with on the monkey bars!"

"Well, Declan is just like that!" Leah said, giving me a wry smile.

*Mmhmm, I would do a round with Leah on the monkey bars any day.*

"Oh! Okay! Hey, Declan, want to watch *Dora* with me?"

And just like that, we were buddies.

She took me over to the TV area where all the movies were stored, and we started to sort through them as she showed me her favorite ones. There was quite the collection. They also had a great selection of grown-up movies that I'd definitely have to check out later.

"Hey, Leah!" I heard someone shout from the top of the stairs. "Next time you see that good-for-nothing friend of my husband's, ask him if he suddenly forgot how to use a phone!"

I looked at Leah as she suddenly looked at me. Her hand flew to her mouth, trying to contain the laughter threatening to spill out.

"Oh my God, she's going to be so embarrassed when she gets down here," she whispered.

I hadn't really thought about this aspect of the evening —the fact that I hadn't seen or spoken to my friend in months. He'd been diagnosed with cancer, gotten married, and become a stepfather, and I hadn't called to check-in. He was in a different world now, and I didn't know how to relate. The cancer thing...I was honestly just scared shitless. It had been a dick move, but I just hadn't known what to say. People my age didn't get cancer. That was something we had to worry about when we got older, right? Apparently not. It had been a reality check that I wasn't prepared for, so I'd bailed on him, and now, I had to find the words to say I was sorry. And I had to find them fast because he was coming downstairs.

"Did you hear what I said, Leah?" Clare asked, entering the room.

She didn't see me sitting there, but Logan did. He looked surprised and then a bit of humor peeked through, knowing his wife was digging herself a bigger hole.

"I'm seriously sick of people treating him like —oh shit!" she said, finally noticing my presence.

Logan snorted, and Leah doubled over, laughing, while Clare began to turn a deep shade of red.

"Mommy said a bad word!" Maddie scolded, causing Leah to laugh harder.

"Hey, man," Logan greeted me, "long time, no see."

I arose from the couch, and we did the guy version of a hug with a quick pat on the back before I stepped away quickly. I stood there nervously, unsure what to say to my sick friend. I could see the difference. The loss of hair was obvious, but he'd also dropped some weight, and he just looked tired. He was still Logan though, I realized, so I went with what I knew best.

"So, cancer, huh? That blows."

A huge grin spread across his face along with a bit of relief.

"You're just jealous that I'm still hotter than you," he taunted.

And we instantly fell back into a comfortable place. The water was under the bridge. Men didn't need long, drawn-out conversations for these types of things. A few inappropriate jokes with a good laugh, and we were solid again. Easy.

"Not according to *People* magazine. Top one hundred, baby," I countered.

Leah started making gagging noises in the back-ground, and Clare immediately began laughing.

Logan grinned. "You've got your hands full with that one."

"So I've noticed."

A fter what seemed like hours of directions, instructions, and lessons, we were finally handed over the responsibility of watching the child for the evening. I found it hilarious that Leah was reminded half a dozen times to make sure Maddie brushed her teeth, ate dinner, and actually went to bed before midnight. Leah rolled her eyes and nodded, saying she'd done this gig a million times and would make sure Maddie was fed and watered.

As soon as they were out the door, Leah pulled Maddie up in her arms. "Thank goodness! I thought they'd never leave! Ready for some fun?"

Maddie nodded excitedly, and we started the evening with a game of hide-and-seek. It was Maddie's turn to be the counter, and Leah and I were in charge of hiding. Playing this game as an adult was much more difficult than as a child. We were too big to fit in any of the cool places, like the laundry basket or the cupboards.

As I listened to Maddie's voice downstairs, counting from one to sixty, I quickly moved through the house, looking for someplace to hide. Leah was nowhere to be seen, so she'd obviously found her sweet spot. Hearing

Maddie hit fifty-five, I dove into the nearest closet and shut the door.

"Ouch!"

"Leah?"

"Who the hell else would it be, Hotshot?" she whispered in annoyance. "You're in my hiding place!"

"Well, I guess it's our place now, isn't it?" I grinned, and knowing she couldn't do anything to stop me due to the enclosed space, I slowly ran my hand under her top, savoring the feel of her bare skin against mine.

"What are you doing? Maddie is right outside that door!"

"Is she? I can't hear her," I whispered in her ear right before claiming her lips with my own.

She moaned as I plunged my tongue into her mouth, caressing every luscious inch. Sliding my hands in her jeans pockets, I pulled her hard against my body, and she gasped.

*God, she's so fucking sexy.*

Her leg snaked around my hip, and she began rocking her pussy against my rock-hard erection. Just as my hand moved to the front of her jeans, fully intent on ripping them from her body and fucking her senseless, we heard Maddie giggling down the hall.

"Where are you? I'm coming to find you!" She laughed.

Still breathless and wrapped around each other like our lives depended on it, we burst into laughter, giving away our spot immediately. We managed to make ourselves look presentable before Maddie opened the door and proclaimed herself the winner.

"I can't take you anywhere, Hotshot," Leah said, shaking her head.

I gave her a wink. "I kind of like babysitting."

<hr>

Two hours, several pizzas, and a living room fort later, we had successfully put our young charge to sleep. Well, Leah had. My duties consisted mostly of standing around and supervising, considering I had no idea what went into the nightly rituals of a young girl. Hell, I didn't even know what a grown woman did before bed. Heather and I had never lived together, and I guessed I didn't care enough to pay attention when we had spent nights together.

I suddenly wondered what it would be like to watch Leah get ready for bed. She would probably be in that robe I'd seen her wear that first night when I came back to Richmond, and she'd stand in front of the mirror as she tenderly brushed her golden locks. I'd come up behind her and wrap my arms around her waist, watching her sigh in pleasure from my touch.

"Hey, you still here?" Leah asked, taking me out of my weird fantasy.

I was brought back into the present where we were settling onto the couch at Clare and Logan's. Leah had just pulled out a movie and was about to hit Play.

"Yep, I'm all here." I flashed my award-winning smile, hoping my little checkout from reality would go unnoticed.

*Where the hell did that come from?* Maybe I was letting

this friends-with-benefits thing go a little too far. I enjoyed spending time with Leah, and I actually considered her a friend now. The image I'd just had though went way beyond the level of friendship, and that was not okay. I needed to take it back a level —no more adventures like tonight. Things like this created feelings, and neither of us could risk that. *Nope, back to just good clean sex.* I was great at that. In fact, I excelled at it. It was everything else in a relationship that I sucked at.

We decided to watch a movie, *The Princess Bride*. Leah had chosen it when she found out I'd never seen it.

"How could you never have seen this movie, Declan? You're a self-declared movie expert! It's like the greatest movie ever created!" she had declared.

"The greatest? Really? What makes it so great?"

"It has everything —love, humor, mystery, honor, deceit, and a hot guy in a mask! What is there not to love?"

"All right, all right, put your damn movie on, woman!"

She'd laughed and we'd settled in to watch our movie. When the young kid from *The Wonder Years* appeared, I got really confused.

"Wait, is this a kid movie? Is there sex in this?"

She hit me on the arm and shushed me before telling me I was ruining it. I chuckled and found myself pulling her closer to me. We were lying together on the couch, watching the weirdest movie I'd ever seen. But she was right. It was good...in a strange eighties type of way.

When it finished, she looked up at me and asked, "So, what did you think, Hotshot?"

"Not half bad. I love watching older films even if they

are from the eighties and include Rodents of Unusual Size, and terrible accents. Older movies are so different from the films we create today."

"How so?" she asked, genuinely interested.

"Well, the filming alone is different. So many movies are filmed by digital cameras nowadays. It creates a different look on the screen. The picture is clearer...more vivid, but I think you lose that original quality that only film could produce. It's like every time we take a leap forward, we always lose something from the past in the process."

"You know, I've never heard you talk about acting the way you talk about creating a film. Why do you do it? Act, I mean," she asked.

I puffed out a breath of air and fiddled with a strand of her hair. "I hate acting. I honestly do. If I could act and not have all the bullshit that went along with it, I might be able to enjoy it. But you can't have one without the other in Hollywood, and I'm just not built that way. When I started getting noticed, I thought it was nice. Women paid more attention to me, and I got into bars without any problem, but then the cameras would show up every time I tried to exit a club or restaurant. Out here, away from it all, I can almost start to feel normal again. But in L.A., the paparazzi are relentless. Some people are able to handle the constant attention, but I'm not one of them. I can't live my life in a fucking fishbowl."

"So, what's your escape plan?"

"This movie. They agreed to let me executive produce it if I would also star in it. I figured if I could get my name in as a producer, it would help build my credibility, and eventually, someone might sign me in some role that doesn't require being in front of the camera."

"Well, I hope it works out for you, Hotshot. Everyone deserves happiness, especially if that means doing the one thing you were put on this earth to do."

I smiled, silently thanking her, before saying, "And what about you? What were you put on this earth to do?"

"I don't know yet. I'm still figuring that out."

# Chapter Six



The piles of dried leaves scattered all over the curb crunched under my tires as I pulled off the street. I looked out onto the disheveled yard. Mountains of acorns and twigs were scattered everywhere — reminders that winter was just around the corner. The grass was a mile high, and I knew my father probably hadn't stepped foot outside since the last time I'd visited. Or if he had, he had just been too drunk to notice his yard looked like a scene from *The Addams Family*.

I hated visiting my father. It was just one giant reminder of my childhood and how much it had utterly sucked. I was constantly being compared to a woman who he had both hated and loved with every fiber of his being. I was a never-ending reminder of the wife who had left him behind and the mother who hadn't wanted me. But it was Thanksgiving Day, and as much as I hated the man, he was my only family. Someone should check on him, and unfortunately, that someone was me. This was the part of my life I didn't share with most people. Not even Clare knew everything that went on in this house, and I intended to keep it that way.

Bundled up in a long wool sweater to combat the cooler temperatures, I hiked up the driveway and let myself in, not bothering to knock. He wouldn't hear me anyway. He was probably still passed out from the night before. The familiar stale stench of alcohol filled my nostrils, and I tried not to gag. *God, I hated that smell.*

When growing up, most children usually attributed certain memories with scents —the intoxicating aroma of their mother's homemade cookies, the way the house smelled after the freshly cut Christmas tree was brought in. For me, this pungent aroma of alcohol summed up my entire youth in one poignant statement. Booze was my father's best friend, lover, and soul mate. There was no other room for anything else in his life after my mother had left. He used it to fill the emptiness, regret, and anger that had consumed him.

I was just the byproduct that had come from it all, and I had been left to raise myself from the age of seven. If it weren't for Clare and her family, I didn't know how I would have survived. They had shown me what love was, and I had sought solace in their arms every second I could.

"Dad?" I called out into the silence.

No answer.

After dropping groceries and supplies off in the kitchen, I made my way through the dingy house, picking up trash along the way before depositing it into the overflowing trash can. As I went, I made a mental list of the things I needed to do before I left. Emptying the trash was the first on the list. I finally found my hero of a father slumped face-first on his twenty-year-old faded orange sofa. His clothes looked about two days old, and from the smell, he probably hadn't bathed in at least four days.

"Dad, wake up," I said a bit louder, reaching down to shake him.

He finally stirred, looking confused through his blood-shot eyes. He cocked his head toward me, taking a few moments for his sight and brain to sync before he figured out it was me.

"What the hell are you doing here?"

"Nice to see you, too, Dad."

"Come to rag on me some more, girl? That's all you do when you come around here," he muttered.

"I brought you groceries. Today is Thanksgiving Day. Did you know that?"

"Why the hell would I care about that? Do I look like I got anything to be thankful for?"

I ignored that question. Instead, I decided to go and unload the groceries. I first went through the fridge and pulled out all the expired items, which was mostly every-thing. I put in the lunch meat, cheese, and milk I'd bought, and then I placed the bread on top of the refrigerator. I took out the trash next and replaced all the liners with fresh ones, knowing they would all be full of bottles and empty take-out containers the next time I came. *Social security being spent wisely no doubt.*

Hearing shuffling, I turned to see my dad enter the

kitchen. He seated himself in one of the old wooden bar stools at the counter.

"You bring me any liquor, girl?"

"No, Dad. You know I don't buy you alcohol."

"You got any money then?"

"I'm not giving you any money, Dad," I said calmly, trying to keep my hands from shaking.

"Then, what the hell good are you?" he roared.

I flinched, knowing it was now time for me to leave. No good had ever come from this argument, and I'd learned my lesson before. I folded up the grocery bags and headed for the door. As I turned the handle, I took one last look at my father, seeing him hunched over the counter. His face was buried in his hands, and he looked about twenty years older than his actual age. I'd always wondered what life would have been like if he had just let her go. If he had been able to man up and be the father I so desperately needed him to be...but he hadn't. And this was the life we'd both ended up with.

"Happy Thanksgiving, Dad," I whispered before quickly walking out the door and taking my first full breath in minutes.

I cried the entire way home.

---

Hands covered in sticky dough and flour, I groaned when the sound of "SexyBack" by Justin Timberlake filled the tiny space of my kitchen. It was Declan's ringtone.

"Great," I muttered, looking down at my dough-covered hands. I tried to clean off at least one hand, so I could answer the phone without getting dough permanently stuck in the crevices.

"Hello?"

"What are you doing?" Declan's sultry voice asked.

"Making an apple pie."

"Mmm...from scratch? That's kind of kinky."

I laughed, loving the *American Pie* reference. "You and your manly parts stay the hell away from my pie, Hotshot!"

He chuckled, and we delved into a longer than necessary conversation about how the original movie was the best and none of the other ever compared. We were definitely products of our generation if we could have a ten-minute conversation about *American Pie*.

After our movie discussion was done, a silence took over, and I suddenly wondered why he was calling. Since our evening of babysitting, our arrangement had gone back to normal. We hadn't hung out or had any lengthy conversations. I got the hint that Declan was trying to keep space between us after last week, and as much as it had kind of stung, I understood. He was someone I was quickly starting to see as more than just a fuck buddy, and that could definitely complicate everything. He was easy to talk to and fun to be around. I felt at ease around him now, and I guessed he was probably feeling the same thing.

"So, what are you doing?"

"Nothing. I'm bored," he answered simply.

"You don't have any plans today?" *Doesn't everyone have plans on Thanksgiving?*

"Nope."

"You didn't go home?" I honestly didn't even know much about his parents to know if there was a home to go to, but I assumed he had family. Most people didn't come from the wreck of a home life like I did.

"No, my mom is up in New York. She's spending time with her sister."

"Do you want to come with me to Clare's parents' house?" I asked. I was completely blindsided by the words that had just come out of my mouth. *Wasn't I just thinking about how some distance would be good for us?* My head and mouth seriously needed to get together and agree on something. The disconnect was getting me into trouble more and more lately. He had just sounded so sad though.

"Are you sure that would be okay?" he asked.

*He actually wanted to go? That was a shocker. Well, no backing out now.*

"Clare's family takes all stragglers, even Hollywood movie stars. Be here in thirty minutes to pick me up."

"Okay."

"Oh, and, Hotshot?"

"Yes?" he growled at the mention of his pet name I insisted on using.

I laughed a little. He hated it, which was why I used it so often.

"Wear something nice."


DECLAN

I adjusted the tie around my neck for the hundredth time as we walked up to Clare's parents' house, and I pressed the buzzer. Not bothering to wait, Leah opened the door and ushered us in. The tie around my neck felt like a noose grabbing my body in a choke hold as it cut out all the oxygen one tiny breath at a time. I hated ties. They reminded me of my father, and that was a road I didn't like revisiting. He'd spent every damn day of his wasted existence wearing a tie, looking the part, playing the field. And all for what? So, he could screw us all over in the end.

*Bitter much? Me? Never.*

But here I was, wearing a fucking tie —on a holiday, no less. *Why? No fucking clue.* Actually, that wasn't true. I had a big clue, and it was tall and blonde and wearing a dress that made me want to throw her over my shoulder and run.

I'd looked over at her as we'd walked into the house. *Did she own anything that didn't make her ass look like it was being served up on a fucking platter?*

I'd woken up this morning, intent on spending the day with no one but a bottle of Jack and some room service. Instead, I'd spent the morning thinking about Leah — wondering what she was doing, who she was spending the day with. It was everything I had told myself to never do. Against my better judgment, I'd called her. I'd just needed to hear her voice.

I'd tried to distance myself from her over the last week. After our babysitting gig, I had known something had changed between us. Lines had blurred, and I'd felt myself growing closer to her. Although I still felt every ounce of fiery passion for her, I also felt something deeper brewing. I'd put the brakes on and only made our usual house calls, never lingering too long even though my gut had told me to stay.

These feelings weren't new. I'd felt them before, long before —although these were more intense. The thought of having feelings like that again scared the ever-living shit out of me, which is why I'd kept pushing her away. But as hard as I'd pushed, I'd pulled back —calling her when I had known I shouldn't...holding her too long when I had known I should let her go. This would all lead to my demise, yet I was unable to stop it.

So, here we were, together on Thanksgiving — attending a holiday gathering together —like a fucking couple. We hadn't even made it two steps into the house, and we were immediately greeted by about fifty people. At least, it felt that way. The house was packed like a sardine can. Laughter and happy voices filled the air as we made our way through the house. Leah said hello to a few and hugged several, introducing me as we went. We finally found Logan and Clare in the kitchen, helping an older couple —Clare's parents, I assumed —with food preparation. Clare was actually the only one helping. Logan was seated on a stool at the counter, chatting with three other men.

"Hey, Declan. Glad you could make it," Logan greeted, never once making a comment about the fact that I hadn't actually been invited.

I guessed Leah had been right about the open-door policy. No one seemed to mind the random new guy, and no one took a second glance at me, trying to figure out where they had seen me before. It was heaven.

"Good to see you, too, baldy. What are you drinking?" I asked, motioning to his drink.

"I have nonalcoholic beer here, O'Doul's. The real stuff does crazy things with my meds and makes me sicker than a dog, but I like to pretend. The good shit is in the fridge."

"Damn. No beer? Please tell me you can at least have sex," I joked.

"No worries on that front, man. They'd have to chain me to a fucking hospital bed to keep me from Clare. Even then, I might be inventive," he answered smugly.

I laughed, quickly grabbed a beer, and rejoined Logan.

He introduced me to the other guys in the group. "This is my brother-in-law, Garrett."

I shook hands with a younger version of the man cooking in the kitchen. Garrett was a few years younger than me, but he looked older than he should for his early twenties. His smile didn't quite make it to his eyes, and he looked permanently tired. But he seemed like a cool guy. He didn't look at Leah when she'd walked in, so he went on the okay list.

I also said, "Hey," to Colin.

He was Logan's best friend, who I had known for a long time. We gave each other a quick handshake, and he updated me on his new role as a father. He pointed across the room to his wife, Ella, who was holding his newborn son, Marshall.

I didn't know the other dude, Ian, a doctor who worked at the same hospital as Logan. After being introduced to Ian, I found his eyes following Leah as she moved around the kitchen while gathering dishes and plates for Clare's mom. I immediately didn't like him much.

"Oh, hey, Ian! I didn't know you were going to be here!" Leah said, catching the fucker as he watched her.

Apparently, they knew each other.

"Yeah, Logan took pity on the divorcé and invited me over. My first year single," he said, holding up his bare ring finger as proof.

*Well, isn't that swell?*

I made a mental note to give Logan an ass kicking for inviting the newly single doctor to the party. I'd wait until he was healthy though. Kicking the ass of a sick dude was just wrong.

"That's right. I'm sorry. I heard about you and Karen. How are you doing?" Leah asked sweetly.

He leaned in closer —*the loser* —and said, "Well, I'm doing a hell of a lot better now."

Leah gave a short laugh and slapped him on the arm before moving away to do something else in the kitchen. I had to restrain myself from planting my fist in the man's face. Possessiveness like I'd never felt before flooded my system, and I had to look away, fearful my death stare would actually cause bodily harm to the guy. After a while, dinner was set, and we all gathered around the various tables arranged in the house. There were so many people that card tables had been set up throughout several rooms to accommodate everyone. As luck would have it, Leah and I ended up sharing a table with our good friend, Dr. Ian. It turned out that Ian was an OB-GYN who worked with Leah, which is how they knew each other. Knowing he got to see the professional side of Leah, a part of her I'd never seen before, pissed me off. I didn't know why. Jealousy was a new thing for me.

"Leah, I heard you are volunteering in a nursing home now? Is there anything you don't do?" Ian asked.

He looked at me as if he were trying to gauge my reaction to this new piece of information. *Did I know Leah was doing this? No. Did it surprise me? No.* In the short time I'd known Leah, I had quickly figured out that she was one of the most selfless people I knew. She'd rush over to help her best friend at a moment's notice and check on her elderly neighbor during the day. She didn't do it for attention or praise. It was just who she was.

"So, what is it that you do, Declan?" Dr. Ian asked as we dug into the mounds of food scattered across the table.

Clare and Logan helped their daughter cut up her turkey while baskets of bread and side dishes were passed around. There was enough food to feed the entire U.S. Army.

Leah handed me the basket of rolls as I gave Ian a hard stare.

"I'm an actor and a producer," I answered.

"Around here?" he asked with a bit of amusement.

He was sizing me up since he had seen Leah and I come in together. He heard actor, and he figured I was a just a second-rate struggling loser. I gave him a smile right back as I took the time to butter my roll before answering.

*Hold on to your seat, Dr. Pussy. Shit is about to get real.*

"Oh no, Hollywood. I'm here on location, starring in a film that's shooting here. Surely, you've heard about it?" I asked casually while grabbing the bowl of mashed potatoes.

*He gaped at me, suddenly putting two and two together.*

*That's right, asshole.*

"You're Declan James!" he announced. "I saw you in *Invisible*. It was brilliant."

"Thank you," I said honestly. It was always nice to receive a compliment —even from an asshat trying to make moves on my date.

"So, Leah, dating a movie star, huh? That's...amazing!" he said with a bit of jealously. "I imagine you get to visit the set all the time. Have you met Tasha Sinclair yet?" he asked.

I looked at Leah as she opened her mouth and then closed it again, unsure what to say.

"We aren't...I mean, I haven't —" she stammered.

"I'm taking her tomorrow. She hasn't been yet because it's been a closed set until tomorrow. I can't wait to introduce her to everyone." I flashed a genuine smile at her before covering her hand with mine.

The look she gave me was priceless, and I thought I heard Clare choke on her water.

*Apparently, I was taking Leah to the set with me tomorrow.*

*That should be interesting.*

# Chapter Seven



It was early —like why-did-I-even-bother-going-to-sleep early. When the alarm had gone off this morning, I'd seriously doubted my sanity.

*Why am I going to a movie set at four in the morning? Right —because Declan asked me to.*

So, the day after Thanksgiving, at the butt crack of dawn, when everyone else was waking up to go stand in ridiculously long lines for stuff they really didn't need, I was sipping coffee in the freezing cold while a bunch of crew members curiously stared at me like I was from another planet. Declan had stepped away for hair and makeup, so I was all alone for the time being.

It was supposed to look like night for the scene they were shooting. When I'd asked why they just didn't film it at night, Declan had said the meteorologists were predicting fog that morning, and the director had switched around the schedule, so they could try and take advantage of the natural beauty, rather than adding it in after. It had sounded logical, but my sleepy brain was not agreeing with logic at that very moment. I was a nurse, so I was supposed to be used to odd hours, but I was pretty sure my body —the smart bitch —knew this was not work, and therefore, it didn't count. So, I was bitch-ass tired.

The weatherman had actually been right for a change. The fog hanging heavy in the air created a very ominous sight as we stood around the historic gravestones. This movie had brought Declan and I back full circle, and we were now at the cemetery we had walked through so many months ago. This was the place where I had seen Declan in his element, and I had known he was more than just some Hollywood poser.

Pulling my thick red peacoat closer to my body, I tried to keep myself from shivering. It was teeth-chattering cold this morning. Winter was slowly winning the battle against fall, and I felt like our autumn days were numbered. Soon, snow would come, and the trees would become bare. It made me a bit sad. I loved autumn in the South. It was breathtaking. Orange, red, and brown leaves would take over the landscape, almost overnight, and the air would finally become cool and crisp after months of suffocating heat.

As I snuggled into my scarf and coat, I felt warm hands encircle my waist.

Declan whispered in my ear, "Are you cold?"

It was such an intimate thing to do, and I felt off balance for a moment, not knowing where this sudden change had come from. All I could do was nod as he pulled my body closer to his. Looking around, I noticed a few of his costars watching us. He must have noticed, too, but he didn't pull away. He stayed there with me in his arms, like he was purposely staking his claim in front of the rest of the crew.

I turned in his arms, needing to see his face, in hopes that I could understand what was going on in his head. Looking in his eyes, I saw heat and desire, but I also saw something deeper. *Affection? Possession?* I wasn't sure, but it gave me chills. It created possibilities in my head that I didn't want to think about. I could not allow myself to hope with Declan. Hoping led to pain, and I knew one thing. I wanted Declan more than I wanted my next breath. Hope could be my ultimate downfall. I didn't think I would survive Declan like I had with Daniel.

"They're ready for me," he said.

I took notice of his makeup and costume for the first time. He looked...good. The Confederate soldier uniform made him look regal and handsome, and the makeup they had applied gave him an aged, worn appearance that fit the time period.

"You can sit over there. Someone from the crew will give you headphones, so you can listen, okay?"

I nodded, but before I could say anything else, he lowered his lips to mine in a slow, lingering kiss that showed anything but urgency. It left me branded. As he walked away, my hand drifted up to my mouth as if I were trying to make sure I was still real. I had been kissed by Declan James too many times to count. He seemed to have quite the obsession for my mouth —among other things. *But that kiss?* That kiss had left me awe-struck. It was earth-shattering in its simplicity, mind-numbing in its intimacy, and completely raw in its emotional depths.

*Did I miss something? What had changed?* Before I could take the necessary time to think through Declan's complete turnaround, I was ushered over to a set of chairs and handed large headphones.

Lights went on, and someone yelled, "Quiet on the set!" and "Action!"

*Holy shit, I was on a movie set!*

The reality of where I was solidified when I saw Declan dressed in his Civil War–era uniform, wandering through the graves. His eyes found mine briefly before he carried on through the foggy graveyard. Declan had told me they were filming the scene where his character came back after the war had ended, only to discover his wife and child had died. The scene they were currently filming had Declan's character, William, visiting their graves after he just heard the terrible news.

He stumbled, looking distraught and disheveled. He looked around from grave to grave with a small candle-light lamp, searching for their graves. Stopping, his eyes found what they were searching for. Falling to his knees in front of the graves, an angry cry tore through his body as he placed a hand on top of the granite slab, and then he began to sob.

I couldn't help it. Even though I knew he was acting, I felt tears trickle down my cheeks in response to the emotions he was expressing. He hadn't even delivered a line yet, and I was completely transfixed on him, mesmerized by his performance.

"I'm so sorry, Anne. I'm so sorry I wasn't here," he said.

He continued to cry and whisper to his wife until a woman entered the scene. Her real name was Sidney Monroe, and she was an amazing actress. She was around my age with chocolate brown skin and a curvy body that most women would kill for. She was cast as the head maid to the wealthy landowner played by Declan. She would also be his love interest after his wife died. That was what made the film so interesting —a wealthy man in the Civil War era falling in love with an emancipated slave in the South. It was beautiful, and I hoped to God Declan got the credit he deserved.

"Mr. Hamilton, sir..." Sidney said. "Mr. Hamilton," she said a bit louder.

Declan looked up, his eyes completely red and blood-shot from the tears he had shed.

"I'm so sorry. I tried, sir. I tried everything I could, but the sickness came so quickly..." She trailed off.

"Leave. Please. Just leave me," he said harshly.

The woman nodded and fled.

The director yelled, "Cut!"

And I was pulled out of my Declan-induced trance. I looked up in time to see Declan jogging toward the director, who was huddled in discussion with the cameraman. Declan glanced my way, giving me an expression that said he'd be with me as soon as possible. I just smiled and gave him a slight nod as he joined the small group. I watched as they looked through the film, pointing at different aspects and pausing to discuss. Both the director and lead cameraman listened to Declan as he provided his opinion and suggestions for the scenes they had moving forward. He was so passionate when he spoke and so in his element as he described his vision.

"Good job, Declan. Really, it was superb. Whatever you were thinking about and focusing on in that scene, harness it. It was the best work I've seen out of you yet," the director said.

The men ended their impromptu meeting, and Declan slowly made his way over to me, giving me time to look him up and down. Even dressed in a Civil War–era uniform, he looked sexy as hell. In fact, I was starting to think we needed to take that costume back to my place and do a little role-playing. I could do my best Scarlett O'Hara impression, and he could sweep me off my delicate Southern belle feet.

*Yeah, that could work.*

Declan's lips turned up into a sly smile as he closed the gap between us. He was obviously aware of the effect his presence had on me.

Pressing his body close to mine, he angled his mouth against my ear. "They've given us a bit of a break on account of my fabulous acting abilities. And the only thing I can think about right now is getting you into my trailer, out of these clothes, and burying myself deep inside you."

*Well, um...yeah.* I was pretty sure I could go for that.

I gave him a devilish grin, "Let's go."


DECLAN

I wanted to rip the throat out of every man on the entire set. No, first, I'd do something about their eyes, and then

I'd go for the throats. Then, at least, they wouldn't be able to stare at Leah while I was killing them.

*Fuckers.*

As soon as she had stepped foot on set, they had all looked her over and swarmed around her like vultures. She hadn't seemed to notice, but I sure as hell had. Their eyes, full of uninhibited lust, had lingered over her ass and fixated on her breasts —all the things that were mine, not theirs.

After the doctor yesterday and my overwhelming reaction to him, I'd gone back to my hotel and had a serious come-to-Jesus meeting with myself. *What the hell was I doing?* I had basically claimed her at that dinner table, and afterward, when I should have felt remorse or panic, I'd felt...good. As bad as I'd felt for the doctor and his shitty divorce, I hadn't wanted him looking at Leah or talking to her at all. She was mine, and I'd wanted to do anything and everything that night to make it perfectly clear. Those hadn't been the acts of a man who wanted a casual affair. They had been the thoughts and actions of a man who wanted more.

Figuring that out had made things a bit clearer for me. Coming to the set today and seeing the vultures descend had made it crystal clear. My sudden fierce possessiveness of Leah was more than a casual fling to me now. I wanted her, all of her. I didn't know how long this would last or how it would end up, but I was balls-in, and I hoped to God she was too.

I'd heard one of the crew members say, "Man, that is one hot piece of ass. How does Declan do it all the time?"

Then, I'd seen red. I didn't want Leah to be seen as

another skank I'd picked up from a bar or club, so I had done the only thing I could think of. I'd walked up to her and claimed her —not with a sloppy bar kiss, no. I'd given her the type of kiss that a man gave the woman he wanted to keep. And I did. She'd looked downright stunned and stupefied ever since. I kind of liked her this way. It was kind of humorous.

We made our way to my on-set trailer, passing by several of the men who had spent the better part of the early morning staring at Leah's butt. I wrapped my arm around her waist and slid my hand down her backside to cup her firm ass. It was my way of saying both, *Fuck off,* and, *Mine,* all at the same time. The men seemed to get the hint and scattered as we continued down the path.

Unlocking the door, I ushered Leah in first, making sure to secure the lock again after we'd entered. She took her time, taking the few steps into the tight space. There wasn't much room. Only a small table, a microwave, refrigerator, a tiny bed, and bathroom toward the back occupied the trailer. It wasn't meant to be lived in, but it did provide an escape during the day when I needed space or privacy.

"What are we doing, Declan?" she asked.

"I think you know, Leah."

I knew she wasn't speaking in the literal sense, but I didn't want to go there yet. I wasn't ready for the *us* discussion yet. I'd never wanted an *us* until now.

*What if she didn't feel the same way?*

Stalking toward her, I hooked my hand around her neck, drew her toward me, and captured her mouth with mine.

"You taste so damn good. Like peaches and cream, you're sweet and creamy and so fucking addictive," I said against her now swollen lips.

"I want you, Declan. Now," she moaned, nearly causing me to blow it right there.

*God, her voice.* It was the perfect combination of sexy porn star and the sweet girl next door.

Closing the small gap between us, I wrapped my arms around her waist and lifted her off the ground, pulling her body against mine. Her legs circled my torso, and I growled as her core pressed hard against my dick. Not wasting any time, my mouth devoured hers as we made our way to the bed in the back of the trailer. Even though our movements and kisses were frantic, I laid her gently on the bed, cradling her head like a priceless treasure.

Leaning back, I slid my hands under the hem of her sweater and lifted it over her head, exposing her red satin bra.

"Nice. Is this my early Christmas present?" I asked, grinning.

"I don't know. Have you been good?"

"No, I've been very, very bad. Let me show you."

Letting my hands ghost down her waist, I unsnapped her jeans and slid them down her lush, long legs. My gaze traveled upward, and I found a pair of matching satin panties, making my grin even wider.

"I don't think I've ever seen a more beautiful sight than you sprawled out on a bed, ready and eager for me." I removed my battered uniform coat and lifted my shirt up and over my head.

"You know, I was starting to think directors were

crazy for never giving you shirtless scenes. But now, I'm kind of relieved."

"Oh?" I asked, suddenly confused.

"I don't want to share you with all the females of the world," she whispered.

If I hadn't been so hard from the mere sight of her, I wouldn't have thought it would be possible to become more so. But hearing those possessive words made me hornier than a teenager in heat, and I attacked her. Fusing our lips together, I wrapped an arm underneath her body, pulling her up, so that her legs straddled me. I loved this position with her. My hands felt like they were everywhere at once, running up her back and then down to grab her ass, as she ground herself against me.

Realizing I'd mauled her with half my clothes still on, I lifted her, so she was straddled around my torso, high enough that I could slip off my shoes and pants without breaking our kiss. Now fully nude, I settled us back onto the bed. I removed Leah's bra and panties, so she was left completely bare, like an offering from the gods. I was so hard that it was nearly painful. All I wanted to do was plunge into her soft heat and never leave. But I needed to taste her first.

"Spread those beautiful legs for me, baby," I commanded.

A sly smile crossed her face as she leaned back on her elbows and slowly pulled her legs apart, like the parting of a curtain. *And fuck, wasn't it a sight to behold.*

"Goddamn, just when I thought you couldn't get any more beautiful, you do that."

Sliding my palm up her leg and around to the inside of

her trembling thigh, I spread her folds and gently rubbed her clit, eliciting a low moan from the back of her throat. Wanting to hear more, I slid two fingers into her slick channel, loving how wet she was for me. She jerked her hips forward, pushing my fingers in deeper and harder.

"I can't wait any longer. I need my mouth on you." I retracted my drenched fingers and slipped them into my mouth, sucking every bit of her off of me.

She watched in fascination, her blue eyes crackling with heat. "Good?" she asked, her voice low and husky and so sexy.

"Best damn thing I've ever had. I think I'll be moving on to the main event now," I answered with a grin.

I dropped my head between her lush thighs and plunged my tongue into her center. She cried out as I taunted and teased her with my mouth, bringing her almost to the edge and then backing off again. By the third time, she was panting and writhing with need.

"Declan, I need..."

"Tell me, Leah. What do you need?"

"Make me come. Oh God...I need to come," she moaned frantically.

"Beg for it. Tell me how much you need me."

"Declan, please. I need you, please."

Her silky tone, full of need, nearly sent me over the edge with its husky resonance. Sliding up her body, my mouth, still slick from her wet pussy, found hers and devoured it, letting her lick the taste of her own desire off my lips.

"I love it when you beg," I said against her lips.

My rock-hard erection found her dripping wet core

and I entered her in one hard thrust. Leah's nails raked down my back as she gasped for air.

"Again. Don't stop," she begged.

I lost it and drove into her with reckless abandonment, feeling like I needed to leave my permanent mark on her body forever. Stroke after stroke, she held on, her hands slipping down to grip my ass as I thrust into her like a wild man. When I felt her walls begin to tighten, I knew she was close. Her channel gripped me like a vise, and I thought I might die from the feel of it. I knew the moment she was about to fall. Her body began to shake as that sweet pussy of hers clamped down, and she started to scream my name. I quickly bent down and caught her screams with my mouth as I kissed her through her orgasm. She writhed and moaned against my mouth as I picked up speed again, needing to find my own release.

Pulling back from our kiss, Leah smirked, snaked a hand between our joined bodies, and gripped my balls as I fucked her.

"Oh shit," I groaned.

The addition of her hand stroking me was enough, and I came hard, losing myself in Leah's beautiful body.

It was then that I realized we hadn't used a condom.


LEAH

Still panting from what was probably the best sex of my entire life, I heard Declan let out a curse.

"Fuck!"

Alarm bells started going off in my head, and the insecure Leah —the one many people didn't know about —

came to the front of the line and started spouting off a million different reasons for that curse word. Like I had for the majority of my life, I tried to push her back and be rational about it. Most of the time I'd won, but sometimes, insecurity would still win out.

"What's wrong?" I asked, looking up at him.

We were still joined, his head lowered against my shoulder. Then, he leaned on his elbows, rising above me.

"We didn't use a condom, Leah. I'm so sorry...I wasn't thinking. I was careless, thoughtless. I just didn't think."

He gazed down at me then, and he looked so upset. He wasn't angry but wrecked, like he'd failed me.

"Hey, it's okay, Declan. I'm on the pill. I have been ever since I turned sixteen. I take it religiously, and I'm tested every six months. My last test was in October. You?" I asked nervously.

"November —right before I came out. I hadn't been with anyone in a few months, and I haven't slept with anyone else but you since," he answered.

Butterflies took flight in my belly. I wasn't aware I even had butterflies or that they could do that. *Declan had given me butterflies. Funny.*

"What are you smiling about?" he asked.

"Run out of women in L.A., Hotshot?" I joked.

"No, I just got tired of trying to replace you."

*Oh. I sure as shit didn't expect that to come out of his mouth.*

"Who the hell are you?" I whispered, tracing my fingers over his unshaven face.

"I'm the same guy I've always been, Leah. I've just

decided to be a bit more honest with myself these days. You should try it," he said with a cocky grin.

After several minutes of absolutely stunned silence on my end, I decided to change the subject.

"So, anyway...we are both clean, and I'm on the pill. So, we're fine. Nothing to worry about," I said, throwing a pillow at his head trying to drown out the laughter that was taking over his body. He knew I'd changed the subject on purpose, and he loved throwing me off my game.

"So, we could have been going without condoms this entire time?" he asked, grinning.

"Uh, I guess so."

"Well, shit, Leah! That would have been good to know. I hate condoms."

I giggled, and he pounced, tickling me and making me laugh harder.

"Sorry, it's not a typical conversation for me, like it might be for you, Hotshot!" I joked.

"Oh, it's most definitely not a typical conversation for me. I bag every time without fail."

"First, gross. Second, you've never..." I began to ask, eyes widening. I wondered if I'd just popped Declan's condom cherry.

"No, I mean...when I was with Heather, my college girlfriend, we, uh...didn't. But since then, every single time."

"So, why am I any different?" Right after the words fell out of my mouth, I hated that I'd asked. I really needed to work on the whole think-first-ask-later thing. It would save me so much trouble.

He leaned over, cuddling up next to my side, as he

draped his arm over my stomach, making patterns across my flesh with his fingertips.

"Do I really need to answer that?" he said.

Before I could ask him to elaborate, a loud knock came from the door of the trailer.

"Yeah?" Declan called out.

Someone from outside shouted, "Declan, you're needed on set! Five minutes."

"Damn," he said quietly before shouting, "Got it!"

He glanced at me and smirked, his eyes glowing a bright green with those flecks of blue and brown in them. He looked young and carefree, and I silently hoped it was a direct result of me.

At that moment, I knew I was in deeper than I'd realized. Fuck buddies didn't want to make each other happy or be the reason each other woke up in the morning. I felt like I was at a fork in the road with Declan. Our relationship was changing. I could turn left and let our fuck-buddy status continue, trying to keep him at a distance, until he moved back to L.A., or I could turn right and follow my heart even if it ended up in pieces at the end.

"You okay?" he asked, noticing my far-off look.

"Yep," I said brightly. "You better get dressed, soldier boy. I think they might come in for you next time if you don't get out there soon."

"All right, all right. I probably need to stop by hair and makeup. I'm pretty sure I need a touch-up or two after that," he said with a wink.

I looked him up and down as he hopped off the bed. He was so damn beautiful. He was sculpted like a piece of art, every single arch and curve seemed to be chiseled by masters. His hair was a disheveled mess, which was probably my fault. *Yeah, he'd definitely need to get that fixed.* The makeup didn't look half bad. It was supposed to make him look rough and dirty, and he still looked like that, but I was no expert.

He quickly redressed, and then he leaned over the bed to place a quick kiss on my lips.

"Rest if you want. We should begin filming again in twenty minutes if you want to watch. We are moving to the open field to the right of the cemetery though. It's the tail end of a battle scene, so a few extras will be on set."

I nodded, and he kissed me again before heading out.

*What the hell was happening?* Less than two weeks ago, we were simple, easy. We had gotten together, come together, and then gone our separate ways. *Wasn't that the way we'd both wanted it?* But then, things had begun to change, and I didn't know what to do anymore. This man —this arrogant, cocky man who I called Hotshot —was turning out to be more, and I didn't know if my heart could handle that.

After a while, I finally rose from our little love nest in the trailer. I slipped back into my clothes and returned to the land of the living. Opening the door to the trailer, I was met by the sun. While we were busy making love, the sun had woken up and made its appearance. It was still cold, and the air felt crisp, but the ground was covered in golden leaves. The trees, which were quickly becoming bare, looked beautiful, silver and statuesque against the landscape.

I began my journey toward the open field Declan had mentioned where they were now filming, passing by the cemetery that we had been in earlier. An old grave caught my eye, and I was suddenly mesmerized by the history surrounding me. The cemetery was still used, but this was the original section. The headstones here dated back to the Civil War and some even earlier. Without even thinking, I headed left, weaving my way through the old stones, looking at the names of those so long ago forgotten — mothers, fathers, brothers, sisters, and children...so many children lost. It had been a different time when the life expectancy was so low, and children had been cherished in a different way. Mothers had been grateful if their children made it to adulthood. Today, that was something we all took for granted.

When I helped deliver babies each day, the mothers I assisted were always scared but very rarely about whether their child would survive. They were always worried about if they were ready or if they would make a good mother. As soon as a child was dropped into the mother's arms, all those fears melted away when they saw that child for the first time.

Part of me hoped that if given the chance, I would feel the same way, but my life was different. I'd raised myself. My father hadn't been much of a father to begin with, but after my mother had left, he'd retreated into himself, and I had been left on my own from that moment on. *Wasn't I missing something because of that?* I always feared that if I became a mother and had that moment when my child was placed in my arms for the first time, my baby would know I was a fraud. That tiny bundle would look up at me and know I wasn't capable of taking care of something so precious.

I didn't know how long I'd wandered through the cemetery, but it must have been a long time because before I knew it, I'd ended up in the newer section, finding myself surrounded by new dates rather than old. Just as I was about to turn around to head back, I saw a familiar face coming toward me.

"Hey, I've been looking for you," Declan said, all decked out in Civil War regalia.

He pulled me into a hug, and he smelled like smoke and earth, like he'd been around a campfire. It must have been leftover from his scene they'd just filmed.

"Sorry, I was headed over. Then, I just started wandering and lost track of time," I said, a bit embarrassed.

"No problem. We have a break for lunch. I wanted to see if you wanted food," he said with a smug smile tugging at his lips. "Real food, I promise. Got to keep you fed," he joked.

"I could definitely eat, Hotshot."

I gave him a swat on the ass, which caused him to chuckle. He swung his arm over my shoulder, and we began to make our way back to the set when I stopped dead in my tracks, seeing a headstone to my right that squeezed all the air out of my lungs and nearly dropped me to my knees.

"Leah? Jesus...are you okay?" Declan asked, feeling my knees buckle, as he quickly moved to hold me up.

I couldn't even speak at that moment. I just pointed. His eyes followed my outstretched hand until he found the name that had left me speechless and unable to move from that spot in the cemetery.

"Lilith Jean Morgan," he said out loud, trying to make sense of it all. "Leah, is this your mother?"

"It was. We used to call her Lily," I said softly.

"I'm so sorry, baby," he said, pulling me into a tight hug. "I didn't know she had died."

I stared at the headstone, my eyes unable to pull away from it. "Neither did I."

DECLAN

"I should have stayed with her," I muttered into my beer, thinking no one would hear over the loud chatter of the sports bar we had picked for our guys' night out.

The bar was filled with men, eyes glued to TV screens that were showing a couple different college games. The group next to us, slightly younger, was loud and annoying, and I wanted to drop-kick them the moment we'd sat down.

"What did you say?" Logan asked between swigs of his O'Doul's.

I didn't know how he stomached that shit.

"Nothing...I said nothing. Shit, I don't know. Leah, man...she got all weird today in the cemetery. She found her mother's grave, and she's barely spoken all day."

His eyes widened, and he was quiet for a moment as he looked across the table to Garrett, who had actually managed to pull himself away from his desk for a change. The men exchanged some sort of silent conversation before turning back to me. Colin, apparently, had no idea what silent conversation had gone on between them either because he looked about as confused as I did while he continued to make progress with his Jack and Coke.

"What exactly is going on between you and Leah, Declan?" Garrett asked, giving me a hard look.

I would have gotten up to beat his ass if the look wasn't that of a big brother defending his sister. I appreciated the man for trying to take care of her.

"Fuck, I don't know. It wasn't supposed to get this deep. But now, I can't pull away now. She looked destroyed today. She said she didn't know her mother had passed. How is that possible?" I asked.

"Leah's mother left her and her father when she was seven," Logan said before taking a long draw from his drink. "She hasn't seen or heard from her mother since then."

"Damn it, I knew I shouldn't have left. She said she was fine. She basically pushed me out the door. She smiled and said she was going to call Clare and have a movie night."

Looking at Logan as he flinched, I figured out there was no movie night. I'd been duped.

The noise level of the group next to us rose to an epic level, and my jaw ticked in annoyance. Garrett turned in his seat, probably ready to tell the jackasses to shut the hell up. I kind of liked this kid.

As soon as he turned, one of the guys yelled, "Garrett fucking Finnegan! How the fuck are you, man?"

*Great, they were friends.* I pulled the cap tighter around my head, ducking slightly. So far, being in Richmond hadn't been a big deal. People here didn't expect to see celebrities in a sports bar. Therefore, they didn't look for them. In Hollywood, I could be spotted in two seconds flat. Here, it usually took a while, and if I kept my head down and didn't bring much attention to myself, I could usually get by without anyone noticing. They all knew a movie was being filmed here, but they figured we'd be hanging out in fancy restaurants and snooty clubs, not dive sports bars.

"Hey, Matt. How are you? It's been a while," Garrett responded, clearly not as excited as his friend was about the reunion.

"Damn straight, dude. Last time I saw you was at our high school graduation. You and Mia were smiling for photos, getting ready to leave for college. Hey, how's she doing by the way?"

Garrett looked ashen as he glanced down at his hands, suddenly very interested in his palms. "I wouldn't know. Never saw her after that day."

"What? Are you fucking kidding me? You guys were, like, practically already married in high school. You're telling me you let a hot piece of ass like that walk away?"

The last part was slurred, a by-product of the four empty glasses sitting in front of the guy, I was guessing.

Garrett's hands fisted together, and he was on his feet in an instant, towering over the drunken idiot. "Listen, Matt, we were never buddies, so I don't really give a shit what you think. But you are going to drop this. Right. Fucking. Now."

Not bothering to wait for an answer, Garrett stormed out of the bar, leaving Logan and me in stunned silence.

"What the fuck was that all about?" I asked, hoping Logan could fill me in on all the drama I'd just witnessed. *I thought chicks only had nights like these.*

"No clue. Absolutely no clue. Clare mentioned he'd dated someone in high school, but the way she made it sound, it was just a typical teenage crush."

"There was nothing typical about that," I said.

"No joke. I better go after him before he punches his hand into a wall or something."

"No, let me. You're too close to the situation. He won't want to be around you, man."

Logan nodded, and I walked out of the bar in search of his brother-in law. I found Garrett around the corner, stalking angrily back and forth in an alleyway.

"Hey," I said cautiously, "you want to talk about it?"

"Nope."

"Fair enough."

We stood in that alleyway for a while as he tried to calm his rage. I hung around, making sure he didn't do anything stupid. I knew what punching a brick wall felt like, having done so after Heather had left me, and it wasn't worth it.

"Can I give you some advice?" Garrett said, breaking the silence.

I nodded, not really sure what kind of advice someone almost ten years younger could possibly give me.

"I've known Leah almost my entire life. She had a rough upbringing. Growing up was no picnic for her. She might seem tough on the outside, but deep inside, she's just as insecure and unstable as the rest of us. She hides it behind sweet talk and offhanded comments, but she just wants what we all do in life."

"And what's that?" I asked.

"To be loved. She gives her whole heart to everything she does and everyone she lets into her world. She's the most selfless person I've ever met. If there is ever anything anyone needs, you can bet your ass, Leah is there, helping. But when she's hurting, she retreats —"

"And says she's fine as she pushes you out the door?" I finished his thought.

"Exactly."

"I've gotta go," I said suddenly, knowing where I needed to be.

"Good answer."


LEAH

Not even a night with *Pretty Woman* could budge my gloominess. After an hour of not being able to pay attention, I turned off the TV and stared at a blank spot on the wall instead.

She was dead. My mother was dead. I didn't know how to deal with that news. Did I mourn? Was I supposed to even care? She'd left me when I was seven. Should I care that she'd died over eighteen years ago?

Eighteen years...she'd been gone. My mother had died when I was ten, and I hadn't even known. Someone had obviously had a funeral for her since there was a headstone for her. The headstone almost made me laugh. Did someone think it was some sick joke? *Loving mother* and a date was all it said. Loving mothers did not walk out on their families. Loving mothers did not leave their children without ever looking back.

Was there something wrong with me? Had she looked at me, all those years ago, and decided I wasn't worth it?

Wetness splattered against my arm as I curled into a tight ball on the sofa, and I reached up, touching my cheek, to realize I was crying.

*Great, fucking great.*

The realization of tears apparently signaled more because it was like a dam broke, and I began sobbing uncontrollably. I didn't know why I was crying. For her...for me maybe...for the loss of what could have been if she'd just stayed.

In between my heaving sobs, I heard the front door open, and Declan suddenly appeared, sitting down next to me and pulling me tightly into his arms.

"What are you doing here?" I asked between sobs and really unattractive hiccups.

"What I should have done earlier —stayed with you while you grieved. No one should have to endure pain alone, Leah."

That sent me into another round of tears, hearing him be so kind and gentle. It was a completely different side to the bad boy I'd met months before. There were so many pieces to the Declan puzzle. I didn't know why I was surprised. The Leah puzzle was a masterpiece that required expert-level skill. It was no wonder not a single person had attempted to solve it yet.

I didn't know how long he held me, but he never complained. He just sat there with me curled in his lap like a child while I mourned the loss of a woman I both loved and hated. When I finally quieted down, he carried me to my room and gently laid me on my bed. He removed my slippers and covered me in a blanket.

When he turned to leave, I said, "Please stay with me."

"As you wish," he answered as he turned around with a little smirk.

He went around to the other side of the bed and slipped off his shoes, jeans, and then his shirt before slipping under the sheets.

"Come here, farm boy," I whispered, responding to his earlier *The Princess Bride* reference.

"See, I was paying attention."

"Yes, you were," I said, wrapping myself around him. I rested my head on his bare chest over the Celtic knot that forever rested there, letting my hair fan out over the lines and curves of his chiseled abdomen.

His warm body against mine relaxed me, but sleep still seemed impossible with all the thoughts running through my head. The same thoughts I'd had earlier raced through my mind.

Before I had time to think it through, I found myself blurting out, "Do you think there is a reason why she left?"

I hadn't thought about the fact that I could have just woken him up, but he turned to me, still awake.

"What do you mean?" he asked.

By now, I'd assumed that big mouths, Logan and Garrett, had filled him in on the gory past of Leah Morgan. The fact that he hadn't run out the door, screaming, was a plus.

"I mean, there has to be a reason. I always assumed it was me. There has to be something wrong with a child to make the mother want to leave. A mother is supposed to love her child no matter what, right? So, why did mine leave?" I felt weak because my voice broke near the end.

He shifted in the bed and turned on the bedside lamp before pulling me to a sitting position.

"Look at me," he said.

I couldn't. I just stared at the paisley pattern of my bedspread, the tears continuing to fall down my cheek.

"Leah, look at me," he demanded, grabbing my chin to bring my eyes level with his. "There is nothing wrong with you. Do you hear me? Nothing. If your mother left, it had nothing to do with you being inadequate. Do you understand?"

I nodded halfheartedly.

His hand left my chin, and then he grabbed the hem of my tank top and pulled it over my head. I looked at him. I was a bit confused. His eyes were shining in the dark, full of determined green light.

"Take off the rest," he instructed.

"But I —"

"Do it, Leah. Please," he said, whispering the last part like a prayer.

I stood at the edge of the bed and removed my pajama pants and panties before turning around to see that Declan had removed the rest of his clothing. Depressed or not, there was nothing better than seeing him like this. I was starting to believe he could heal all my wounds with one touch.

"Come here," he said softly.

I went without hesitation. I kneeled on the bed to meet him in the middle. His hand slipped slowly around my waist, and he bent down to kiss my collarbone, giving me chills.

"Turn around," he whispered.

I did as told, turning in his arms, so my back was pressed against his front. Both still on our knees, he positioned us on the bed, so we were facing the floor-length mirror sitting in the corner of my bedroom. His hands gripped me tighter against his body, and his fingers dug into my hips as his eyes found mine in the reflection.

"Do you know what I see right now?" he whispered.

Unable to speak, I just shook my head.

"Perfection. I see absolute perfection."

My breath faltered as he pulled me down onto his body, filling me completely in one stroke. My head fell back onto his shoulder as I savored the feel of our bodies connecting. As many times as we had come together, every time felt like the first time.

We moved together, slow and without urgency. His hands slid up and palmed my breasts, and our mouths found each other, our tongues mimicking the sensual rhythm our bodies were making. When I felt that familiar tightening in my core, Declan broke our kiss.

"Look in the mirror. I want you to see yourself when you unravel in front of me."

Looking at our joined bodies moving together in the mirror was the most erotic thing I'd ever seen, and it sent me over the edge immediately. My body broke apart in Declan's arms, and he followed behind with his own release. His hands gripped my flesh tightly as he came deep inside me, trembling, while he called out my name.

I sagged against him, looking at our glistening bodies in the reflection of the mirror. He leaned down and kissed my collarbone again.

He whispered in my ear, "See. Perfect."

I nodded, and he held my chin again, bringing my attention back to his handsome features.

"It's time to let this go, Leah. You are so much more than your past."

One last tear trailed down my cheek as we settled back onto the bed, holding each other like before. This beautiful man had told me I was perfect. He hadn't told me he was sorry, and he hadn't blown smoke up my ass, like most people would. He'd held me as I'd cried and told me I was perfection. I was the exact opposite, but hearing his determined words as he'd made love to me had made me feel close to it.

As I drifted off to sleep, the last image I saw was my mother's headstone, and I knew I wasn't going to let anything go until I visited the one man who might be able to give me some answers —my father.

# Chapter Nine

DECLAN

"Goddamn it, woman! Why the hell is your front door unlocked again?" I bellowed as I walked into Leah's townhouse.

It was around noon on Saturday, a week after discovering Lilith Morgan's headstone. I'd like to say that Leah had returned to normal after that night we'd shared, but there were still times when I could see the sadness in her eyes. I knew one night wouldn't heal her, but damn if I didn't want to erase it all for her. I hated seeing her in pain, and I only hoped time would heal what her parents had put her through.

"I left it unlocked for you," she answered, coming from her bedroom. She was wrapped in a towel, still wet from the shower.

"You mean to tell me that you were just taking a shower in an unlocked house?"

She shrugged. She just looked at me and fucking shrugged, like it was no big deal. She turned back around in her teeny-tiny towel, swinging that sweet ass behind her, as she retreated to her room.

Following, I exploded into a rant. "You drive me batshit crazy sometimes. We're stopping by the hardware store on our way out. You're going to get me a key, and from now on, you're going to keep that door locked. All. The. Fucking. Time."

"You're bossy today." She smirked while opening the top drawer of her dresser to retrieve a lacy pair of panties.

Coming up behind her, I pressed my body against hers, letting her feel exactly what the sight of her in that towel did to me.

"I just don't want any pervy men coming in here."

"Besides you?" she mocked.

"Exactly —hence, the key. Besides, you like me bossy," I countered.

I bent down to kiss the damp skin of her neck, and her head fell back onto my shoulders. I slipped my hands under the towel, pulling it apart, and it fell to the floor.

*Keys could wait an hour...or four.*

Suddenly, she turned in my arms and gave me a pointed look. "No."

She tried to look serious, but her slight grin had me laughing.

"No? Really? This again?" I faked a sigh.

"You're going to make us late."

"It's a Christmas tree farm. It's not like we have an appointment. We don't, do we?"

She laughed as she bent down to pull the panties up

her legs. I had to shift in my jeans to accommodate the bulge she'd created.

"I still can't believe you've never bought a live tree," she said, shaking her head. "And no, we don't have an appointment, but if we don't hurry, they will close."

"It's the middle of the day," I half-whined, trying to pull her closer to the bed with me.

Laughing, she resisted my advances. Then, she continued to pilfer through her drawers before pulling out dark slim jeans and a tan-colored sweater.

"It will take an hour to get there, assuming traffic isn't bad," she explained.

She swatted my hand away as I tried again to make a pass at her.

Grinning at our little game, I asked, "Why are we driving an hour out of the city when there are Christmas tree lots on every street corner?"

"Because, city boy, those trees have already been cut. Going out of the city, into the country, and chopping down your own tree? That's Christmas to me."

Pulling her close to me, I tilted her chin, so I could see those crystal blue eyes. "Well then, let's go get you a Christmas tree."


LEAH

"Oh! Turn here!" I exclaimed.

Declan took a sharp right onto the gravel road. "Are you sure?" he asked, briefly glancing my way with one raised eyebrow in disbelief.

"Yep. Positive."

"That's what you said the last four wrong turns, you know," he teased.

We had been lost out in the middle of nowhere for about thirty minutes. Siri had no idea where we were, and Google Maps seemed to be sending us in circles. The Virginia countryside was a virtual black hole to technology. I didn't have a map, and there were no signs. When we had seen the creepy scarecrow for the fourth time, we had known we were totally screwed. It would have been miserable with anyone else, but with Declan, it was just another outing. He didn't care that I'd gotten us lost. He'd just laughed every time we'd ended up at the same place where we'd started. He'd pointed out various land markings with a promise that he'd make a fire and build shelter if we never saw civilization again. *My hero.*

About fifteen minutes into our lost adventure, he'd asked how I'd managed to get us so turned around if I'd been to the place before. He'd assumed, based on our previous conversation, that this was a tradition for me. It wasn't.

I'd sheepishly answered, "I've never been here."

Rather than asking me to elaborate, he'd just grinned and said, "Well then, it's a first for us both."

When I'd said this was what Christmas was for me, I hadn't lied. In my head, this was exactly what Christmas should be. I'd always wanted to drive up to the mountains and cut down a tree. The years growing up when my dad had actually managed to remember it was December, we'd had a fake skinny green tree that was short, and the branches sagged when you tried to hang ornaments on it.

Whenever I'd visited Clare's house, they always had a live tree, and I had known the tree was up the minute I'd walked in the door because the smell of had filled the entire house.

Ever since childhood, whenever I had seen an ad in the paper for this Christmas tree farm, I'd wanted to come here. But what lonely single girl would come to the mountains and cut down a tree all by herself? That would be kind of pathetic. I'd shrugged it off, telling myself I hadn't cared, and usually, I hadn't bothered with even putting up a tree most years. I'd always spent the holidays with Clare and her family, so decorating a tree for my home had seemed frivolous.

When Declan had called me this morning, he'd said, "What do you want to do today? I want to take you somewhere. Name anything, and we'll do it."

I'd instantly asked him to take me here, and he hadn't even hesitated with the odd request.

"Oh, I think I see it!" I said suddenly.

Declan jerked the wheel in the direction of my outstretched hand signaling him to turn. Sure enough, there was a sign that said, *Lilac Greens Nursery and Tree Farm,* with an arrow pointing us to our long-awaited destination.

"Yay! We found it!" I said happily.

Declan laughed. "You're just glad you won't be eating squirrel for dinner tonight," he joked.

"Damn right. Those things get stuck in your teeth. Wouldn't mind seeing you in a loincloth though," I teased, wiggling my eyebrows in his direction.

"We could definitely make that happen. I'll even get into character and bang my hands on my chest before throwing you on the floor and taking you like an animal."

"Um..." *Yep, I had nothing. No witty comeback for that one.*

My brain was suddenly playing out that entire scene in vivid detail, and there weren't enough brain cells left to speak.

"Rendering you speechless and flustered has become my new life calling, I think." He laughed before putting the car in park and leaning over to kiss my cheek. "We're here by the way."

"Huh? Oh!" I said, finally taking in my surroundings.

There were trees as far as the eye could see. Adjacent to the parking lot, a log cabin stood with large glass doors and a sign that said, *Welcome*. There were red bows and fresh wreaths everywhere. Christmas lights were strung on the roof of the cabin, and the surrounding trees were lit up even though it was still daytime. It looked like a mini North Pole, minus the snow.

We ventured out of the car, and I noticed it was a hell of a lot colder in the mountains. We made our way into the cabin, which served as the store. It was a Christmas lover's paradise. There were handmade ornaments, tree toppers, garlands, homemade treats, fresh cider, hot chocolate, and apple doughnuts. *Oh my God. The apple doughnuts smelled like heaven in a pastry.*

I took one look at Declan, and he instantly smiled.

"Doughnuts?" he asked.

*This is a smart, smart man.*

We bought an entire dozen and two steamy cups of cider. Along with our lifetime supply of doughnuts, the grandfatherly man at the register gave us a saw and directions to all the various types of trees before telling us to have fun. We headed out the door, and Declan looked at me and then looked down at the saw.

"That dude just handed me a huge-ass saw and just sent us on our merry way!"

I just laughed. He really was a city boy.

We headed toward the firs first. I liked the way they looked better than the spruces, and I thought they would hold ornaments better —at least, that was what I told Declan.

My real reason? Clare's family had always had a fir, and I'd known if I ever had a tree of my own, I wanted one that reminded me of the evenings I'd spent at their house while growing up.

We huddled in our coats with our apple doughnuts from heaven and our cups of cider as we weaved through the trees. I lost count of the number of doughnuts I'd shoved into my mouth after the fourth or fifth one. Between the two of us, we polished them all off in less than fifteen minutes. In our defense, they had been small. And they had been so good, so damn good. I made myself promise I'd go to the gym more that week, knowing that would never happen.

The mountain landscape was beautiful. All it needed was a bit of snow, and it would be perfect.

After a brisk walk, we finally made it to the part of the farm that held the firs.

Declan turned to me with the giant saw in hand. "Well, my queen, which shall it be?"

Leah looked around, bundled up in her red peacoat with her tight jeans and boots. She wore mittens and a matching hat to keep the winter air out, and all I could think at that second was how damn beautiful she was. She glanced around the trees, appraising each one by one, before moving on to the next.

When she'd asked me to bring her here today, I'd thought it was an odd request, but I had been game. With Leah, I was game for anything. After we'd started on our adventure, I realized she'd never been here, and I put two and two together. Leah, in her own way, was letting me in by showing me one of her fantasies.

The little girl that Leah had never gotten to be wanted a real Christmas with a real tree and a decorated house, and she'd asked me to bring her here —not Clare, not Garrett. Me.

Two months ago, I would have run away, feeling overwhelmed with responsibility I wasn't ready to handle. Now, I wanted nothing more than to buy out the entire Christmas section in every major department store and deliver it to her house, so we could decorate every square inch to make up for each minute of her lost youth.

I hadn't always had the greatest childhood. My dad was a dick, and my mom was a bit of a pushover, but they had given me a childhood. They loved me as best as they could, and I knew they had done what they could to provide for me.

"That's a mighty big ax you've got there, mister." Leah

grinned before moving past me to check out another row of trees.

The scent of blackberries and vanilla from her perfume filled my senses as she drifted past, leaving me dizzy, and I quickly followed.

"That it is, ma'am...and I know how to use it. I think."

Leah turned, laughing at my confession. Hell, I had grown up with hired help and then moved to L.A. I didn't think I'd ever touched a saw in my life.

"This one," Leah said, stopping dead in her tracks.

Before her sat a perfectly shaped tree with dark green bristles and a straight round trunk. The man in the store had educated us on what to look for, and Leah had found one with all the checkmarks.

"How tall do you think it is?" she asked.

I walked up to it, comparing my six feet three inches against it. "Mmm...probably eight feet at the most. You've got ten feet high ceilings, so it will fit nicely."

She stood there, staring up at her perfect tree, not saying a word.

I closed the distance between us and whispered in her ear, "Is this what you want?"

Her breath caught, before her eyes found mine. "Sorry. What?"

"Okay, now, it's just getting too damn easy." I laughed.

She hit me on the shoulder, which only caused me to laugh louder.

"Are you saying I'm easy?" she asked, feigning indignation.

"Well..." I started.

She huffed as she crossed her arms over her chest, which only distracted me.

"I'll show you easy," she warned before taking off into a full run down one of the tree rows.

"Shit!" I cursed. Laughing, I dropped the ax and took off after her.

The trees were tall, and it was essentially like being in a giant green maze. I could see her head bobbing up and down every once in a while when she would turn directions. She might have been lighter, but I was quicker. I took a different turn, planning to cut her off. As she came around a corner, I caught her around the waist, making her squeal, as I lifted her off the ground.

"You have been a very naughty girl, Leah," I said.

She squirmed and giggled in my arms. Letting her body slide down mine, she froze as our eyes found each other. Still panting from our run through the trees, I gripped the back of her head and crushed my mouth to hers. She instinctively wrapped her legs around me as we kissed.

Breaking our kiss, she asked, "So, what is my punishment? Coal in my stocking?"

"No. After we take that tree home tonight, you're going to strip down naked and let me do whatever I want to you under it all night."

Her eyes sparkled. "Yes, sir."

After several wrong turns through the rows of trees, we found our way back to our ax, and I made my first attempt at cutting down a tree. I must have done a decent job because as soon as the sucker fell, Leah jumped me, telling me that was one of the sexiest things she'd ever seen.

As we dived into our second make-out session in the Christmas tree farm, I felt a tiny fleck of coldness hit my nose, chin, and then my forehead. I looked up just as Leah screamed in excitement.

"Oh my God, it's snowing!" Leah exclaimed.

As if her announcement were an invitation, the few flakes turned into a full-fledged winter wonderland, and snow filled the air. I picked her up and twirled her around while she laughed with her arms outstretched in the falling snow.

"Come on, snow goddess, we better get this tree back to the car. This weather is going to make getting back home interesting."

Making Leah drool again, I lifted the tree and lugged it down to the store. The man had some of the employees help us tie it down to the top of my rented SUV, and I went in and paid for it while Leah was distracted. I also picked up a fresh wreath and another dozen doughnuts for the road.

Our trip back to Richmond was uneventful, thankfully. By the time we got back to Leah's, there was an inch or two of snow on the ground, but the roads were still fairly clear. We hauled everything inside and spent the night decorating Leah's tree. We ate apple doughnuts for dinner, listened to cheesy Christmas music, and made the tree as tacky as possible. It blinked with every light bulb color imaginable, and it had some of the ugliest ornaments I'd ever seen. It was perfect.

When we finished, I looked over at a beaming Leah. "I

believe someone has a punishment to serve...an early Christmas present, I think?"

"Ah, yes," she agreed.

In front of our tacky Christmas tree, the woman I was falling in love with slowly undressed, and then she let me make love to her all night long.

# Chapter Ten



I knew I'd made a mistake in visiting him the minute I entered the house, but being the stupid woman I was, I walked in anyway.

"Dad?" I called out.

The house was messier than usual. Dishes were piled high with food so old that there was mold. I stopped breathing through my mouth as soon as the stench hit me. I knew better than to see him when he got like this, but I needed answers, and I was afraid I'd chicken out if I didn't go through with it then.

There was no answer as I continued through the kitchen. I made my way into the living room where I found him. Surprisingly, he was awake, sitting in the old recliner with a fresh drink in his hand. A half empty bottle of whiskey was in front of him on the floor. There was no coffee table. He'd never bothered replacing the one he'd smashed to pieces the night my mom left. He'd just left the living room with this big gaping hole, like a reminder of the hole we had been left with after she walked out.

"Dad?" I said again.

This time, he finally heard me. Turning his head slightly toward me, it took him a while before any recognition spread across his face. That meant he'd been drinking for some time, and that was my cue to leave...yet I stayed. *God, I was dumb.* I sat on the battered old sofa next to him, his eyes following my every movement as I picked up empty glass and garbage, but he didn't say a word.

"What do you want, girl? Did you bring me food?" he asked, his words sloshing together like the whiskey he was holding.

He loved whiskey. It was his god, and he worshiped it faithfully. He was the reason I, to this day, could never touch the stuff.

Girl —that was his name for me. He never called me daughter or addressed me by my first name. At this point, I wasn't even sure he would remember what it was. I'd been *girl* to my father for as long as I could remember.

"No, it's not Thursday. I'll bring you food on Thursday," I reminded him.

Without fail, I always brought him groceries on Thursday. He never remembered though.

"Well then, what the hell do you want?" he asked gruffly.

"I found Mom's grave the other day."

I watched to see his reaction, and there was none —no shock, no anger, no sadness. Nothing.

"Oh," was all he said.

"You knew," I whispered, squeezing my eyes shut, wondering how deep the depth of my parents' deceit had gone.

"Yeah, I knew," he said nonchalantly as he shrugged.

He took a long swig of his drink before picking up the bottle from the floor and refilling the glass up to the top. My father always did this. He refilled his glass constantly, never letting it get below half full. I think he was scared of ever seeing it empty.

"Did you ever think of telling me? That maybe I might want to know my mother died eighteen years ago?" My voice grew louder as I felt the anger rise from my chest.

The man I called father whipped his head back to me, looking shocked by my outburst. Fueled by alcohol, his shock turned to raw rage. It was a look I knew all too well.

"No, I didn't think of telling you shit. And why should I? Your mother was a bitch and a whore. Why would I ever waste a breath saying anything about that woman?" he spat.

I got to my feet, not wanting to hear anymore. I'd come here in search of answers, and the only answer I'd found was more proof that my father had no soul, which was something I'd learned long ago.

"Don't you turn your back to me, you little slut. You're just like her, pretty and willing to spread your legs for anyone," he said, his words slurring again, as he rose from the chair. He swayed a bit, but he managed to right himself fairly quickly before he came after me.

"Turn around and face me, girl," he yelled, yanking my arm and forcing me back around.

Pain raced up my arm as he jerked me around roughly. His shouting hurt my ears, reminding me of the nights I used to lie in my bed with my pillows above my head, wishing someone would come rescue me. My parents had been loud when they'd fought, and it had been endless, but no one had ever come. In our neighborhood, domestic disputes were part of the culture, and no one bothered getting involved in each other's business.

"Dad, I'm sorry I came. I'll leave now, okay? I'll be back on Thursday with some groceries," I said softly, trying to calm him down. My hands were shaking, and I could feel my heart beating like a drum in my chest.

Still holding my arm, he squeezed harder, causing me to wince.

"You are one ungrateful bitch, you know it? Do you know how much it cost me to raise you? Do you have any idea how many hours I had to work in that shithole of a factory to bring home enough money to feed you?"

"I know, Dad. I'm grateful, really."

I tried to pull out of his grip, but he just clamped down tighter, his overgrown nails biting into my skin.

"If you were really grateful, you'd bring me a bottle of whiskey with those shit groceries you bring every week, or you'd give me some money every now and then. God knows I paid enough of it for you over the years."

"I'm not giving you money, Dad," I whimpered, tears

running down my face, knowing I should have never come here.

My father yelled in frustration, and the blow to the head he gave me was the last thing I remembered.

DECLAN

The cryptic phone call was my first warning that something was wrong.

Leah and I had planned to watch a movie after my workday ended. It had been a long day of filming, but the director had listened to me, and I felt like I had actually learned and contributed to the film. Pulling me aside, he'd said I had a lot of promise and would even consider bringing me on as an assistant director for another project. It would be a much smaller project, but still, it was directing. It was a huge step, and I couldn't wait to share it with Leah.

When I'd called her, I could tell the minute she'd answered, something had been off. Her voice had sounded flat, and she'd tried to get me off the phone the second she'd answered, saying she didn't feel good and just wanted to be alone for the night. She'd said she came home early from work and just needed some rest. When I'd offered to come over and take care of her, she'd paused.

Then, she'd said, "Come on, Declan. We're not a couple. We don't do that."

*The fuck we don't.*

She'd basically hung up immediately after, and I had

been left wondering what the hell had just happened. *Had I missed something? Seen signs and feelings that weren't there?*

Panic stepped in as I'd begun to wonder if I had been walking down the same path I had years earlier, loving a woman more than she loved me. But then, I'd remembered the look of pure joy on Leah's face as we'd danced in the snow and later spent the night under our tacky Christmas tree, making love for hours.

*No. Something is wrong.*

And per Leah's usual methods, she was shutting everyone out.

*Well, fuck that.*

Twenty minutes later, I was unlocking her door with the new key we had made, only to find out the chain had been locked as well.

"Leah, it's me. Unlock the door."

I heard footsteps as she made her way toward the front door, but the chain stayed in place.

"Declan, I told you...I don't feel good. I just want to be alone. I'll talk to you later."

Her voice was rough and raw, like she'd been crying, and the words she said lacked conviction, like she was moving through the motions, but her brain had already checked out.

"Leah, this shit might work with others, but I'm not falling for it. You're not shutting me out. Unlock this door."

"I don't want to see you tonight. Just go away," she said softly.

Yeah...those words would have stung if I didn't know she was lying through her teeth.

"Open the fucking door, Leah, before I break it down. Don't think I won't."

The chain unlatched, and I plowed through the entrance. She turned and walked ahead of me. Dressed in her fuzzy robe and slippers, her hair was down and loose around her face. She always wore it up when she was home. She hated having it down when she slept.

"I'm going to bed. You can stay if you want. I'll see you in the morning if you're still around," she said, heading off to her bedroom.

She hadn't even looked in my direction since I walked in. Just as her bedroom door was about to click, I pushed it open and flicked on the light.

"What the hell is going on, Leah? You're acting strange. You won't tell me what's wrong, and —motherfucker!"

Just as I was delivering my speech, she turned toward me, and I finally saw her face. Her eye was nearly swollen shut, her beautiful cheek was now a mixture of blue and green, and her lip was cut.

I came to her, my eyes wild and frantic, as I started checking every inch of her body, parting her robe until it fell to the floor. My hands shook as I fought back the flood of emotions threatening to take me over as I noticed the hand-shaped bruise near a sprinkling of cuts that were clearly from fingernails. Suddenly, I saw red.

"Who did this?" I asked roughly.

She just shook her head, tears falling down her cheeks, until she collapsed on the bed with her face in her hands as she sobbed.

I didn't know what to do. I felt blinding rage flowing through my veins, and I didn't know where to direct it.

She wouldn't talk, and I had no idea if she was hurt anywhere else that wasn't showing.

*How would I know if she was damaged internally? Would she let me take her to the hospital?*

One look at her defeated form on the bed, and I knew I'd never get her to the hospital. But I needed to know. I needed to make sure every inch of her was okay.

Turning, I walked out of the room and headed for the kitchen. I pulled out my cell phone as I opened the freezer. By the time I found an ice pack, the call connected.

"Hello?"

"Logan, I need you. Now."

---

It was the longest twenty minutes of my life. When the soft knock on the front door finally came, I jumped from my seat by Leah's bed to answer the door.

Logan and Clare greeted me.

"Hey, thanks for coming. I didn't know what else to do. She won't talk to me, and I just...what if..."

"Hey, Declan, it's okay. I'll make sure she's okay," Logan assured me as we made our way to Leah's room.

When she saw all three of us enter, her eyes widened, and that was when all hell broke loose.

"You called them? What the fuck, Declan? I don't need a pity party!" she said, her voice rising louder than it had since I arrived.

Sitting next to her on the bed, I tried to be as gentle as possible. "Leah, you wouldn't talk, and I needed to make sure you weren't hurt anywhere else. It was either having Logan come here or taking you to the hospital."

"I'm not hurt anywhere else," she said, turning her head toward me.

I thought that was when Logan and Clare got the full view of the side of her face because Clare gasped, and I heard Logan curse under his breath.

"How do you know?" I asked Leah.

"He only hit my face. He only ever hits my face," she muttered.

"Who is he? And this has happened before?" My hands tightened, and I counted to ten, trying to keep a check on my raw hatred of whoever had done this.

"It was your father, wasn't it?" Clare asked softly from across the room. "This wasn't the first time, Leah? How long? Why didn't you ever tell me?"

Leah's eyes shot up to her best friend. "It wasn't all the time. I knew how to control it and avoid it for the most part. As long as I didn't antagonize him, I was safe."

"Jesus, Leah. You should have told me," Clare said, her eyes full of concern.

Leah must have read concern for pity because she retaliated. "Yeah, well...we all can't have perfect childhoods, Clare."

"I didn't mean it like that. I just...never-mind. I'm going to go wait out in the living room," she said, her eyes brimming with unshed tears.

Logan watched her walk out before taking a step toward Leah. "I want to examine your injuries, Leah. Will you let me?"

She just nodded, and I felt myself take a breath finally.

I wouldn't feel right until I knew she was okay or at least not hurting anywhere else.

"Do you want Declan here?"

Before she could even respond, I answered for her, "I'm not leaving."

She didn't protest, so Logan proceeded and asked to sit on the edge of the bed. He checked out her eye, which had already been cleaned up. The bruises and marks on her arm were looked at as well, and then the questions came.

"Leah, did he hurt you anywhere else?" Logan asked.

"No, I don't think so."

"You're not sure?"

"I blacked out after he backhanded me," she answered softly.

I bit back a curse but remained quiet. Logan just nodded and asked her to lie down, so he could check her abdomen for any signs of injury. When that appeared fine, one last question was necessary, and I felt my breath quickening, knowing Logan would have to ask.

"Did he...has he ever hurt you...sexually?"

"No. Never. The only thing that gets my father off is booze," she said with little to no emotion.

*Oh thank God.* I didn't know if I would have been able to let the motherfucker live for another minute if he had ever touched her. Even now, I wasn't sure how long his life expectancy was going to be.

Logan finished up and gave directions on how to care for the bruises and cuts. The directions were more for me than Leah since she obviously knew how to treat wounds with her medical background.

I walked Logan and Clare to the door and thanked them for taking the time to come over. I knew they'd had to drop Maddie off at Clare's parents' house in a rush to make it over here so quickly. I just didn't know what I would have done without their help.

"It's nothing, really. We would do anything for our family," Logan said, looking at me.

I nodded and pulled him into a brotherly hug.

Clare came next, and I whispered in her ear, "She didn't mean it."

She pulled back, smiling. "I know. Twenty plus years of friendship with Leah have taught me a thing or two. I'll get an apology call from her tomorrow."

After locking the door, I made my way back to the bedroom, finding Leah in the same position as before, curled in a ball on her bed. She looked so small and frail in her cotton shorts and T-shirt. Her robe was still in a heap on the floor where I'd dropped it. I picked it up and hung it on the hook where I'd seen her hang it so many times before. I padded to the other side of the bed. I removed my shoes and started to unbuckle my belt.

"You don't have to stay, Declan."

I finished undressing before lying down next to her. I pulled her around, so we were face-to-face.

"Look at me, Leah. That shit you throw out at others might work most of the time. Hell, your short tongue alone might send others running. But let me tell you something right now. I'm not going anywhere. I'm going to be here while you cry, scream, and let it all out...because all of us, even you, need someone to hold us when we cry."

The rest of the tears she'd been holding in while Clare and Logan had been here came spilling out. It was like the breaking of a dam. I held her until she cried herself to sleep, and then I held her while she slept, hoping my arms would protect her from all the harm life had shown her. While she slept, I remained wide-awake, gently stroking her hair, as I decided how to get rid of her father...for good.

# Chapter Eleven



I awoke slowly, covered in a warmth I'd grown accustomed to since Declan had come into my life. I smiled briefly, feeling his heated body flush against mine, as I listened to the even tone of his breathing. I felt peaceful...until my smile grew too big, and my lip started to split back open.

Then, the memories of the day before came roaring back —the trip to my father's house, the stupid trip when I'd asked questions I'd known I would never get the answers to. The trip had only proven what an even bigger soulless asshole my father was. And the anger...the anger was what I thought of the most. His eyes had glazed over and his rage was unleashed, as his nails had bitten into my delicate skin. I remembered the things he'd said. It wasn't the first time I'd heard them. My father loved to remind me of his sacrifices all the time. I'd like to share a few of mine with him, but I usually managed to keep my mouth shut.

Declan stirred a bit, and I turned so that our noses touched, and I could watch him sleep. He looked younger this way, vulnerable. What he had done for me last night...there were no words.

"Hey..." a groggy Declan said, bending his head down to briefly capture my lips.

"Hi," I answered quietly.

A still silence grew between us, and I knew he was waiting for me to speak, to say something. After yesterday, he deserved some answers. And for the first time in my life, I actually wanted to share them with someone. I took a deep breath and began to share a part of me I never thought I'd be willing to give up.

"It didn't happen all the time," I said slowly. "The...hitting. I was usually able to avoid it —well, *usually* being the key word. I was still a kid, and being me...I wasn't the greatest at keeping my mouth shut...at least in the beginning. Growing up with an alcoholic father taught me to censor what I said in front of certain people. And that certain person in my life was him."

"How many times, Leah?" he asked. "How many times has he hit you?"

Declan's eyes locked with mine, and I saw compassion, acceptance...and something else. It was something I wouldn't allow myself to think about.

"I don't know. It was enough that I lost track...but not so many that I couldn't pass them off as injuries or mishaps when I was at school."

His jaw ticked, and I could see him holding back the

anger brimming just below his calm facade. He was pissed. No man outside of my adopted family had ever wanted to protect me. My ex, Daniel, had left me when things got real. Seeing Declan react to my life without running away melted me to the core.

"The first time he hit me was a couple of weeks after my mother had left. Those first couple of weeks were the worst of my life. I wanted my mother back more than I wanted anything else in the entire world. My seven-year-old brain couldn't comprehend why she had left. I kept looking at the front door, expecting it to open up at any minute. I'd imagine her happy face walking through the door, and then she'd apologize and take me far, far away."

A single tear slid down my cheek, and Declan quietly brushed it away with his thumb. He bent his head to kiss my collarbone and then allowed me to continue.

"I became angry and bitter. It was a terrible way for a child to grow up." I briefly remembered the little boy in the hospital who had lost his mother. I thought about him often and wondered where he was and whom he ended up with. I hoped social services had found the family he was supposed to be visiting, and he was in a better place than I was after my mother had left. No child should go through that alone.

"When I tried taking my anger out on my father, I learned quickly that it was the wrong way to go. I ended up with a black eye, and I had to lie and pass it off as a soccer accident. After that, I learned how to be invisible and avoid most incidents. If I was quiet and just basically went unnoticed, I could usually escape bearing the brunt of his anger. There were other times when I wasn't as lucky, but I learned to dodge."

"And yesterday? What happened yesterday?"

"I should have never stayed. I recognized the signs as soon as I walked in. He'd had a lot more to drink than he usually does. He always has alcohol coursing through his veins, but this went beyond drunk. Usually, he's just numb and oblivious to everything around him. But sometimes, he drinks so much that it's like he wakes up and remembers everything. Then, he just gets angry...all over again."

"He took it out on you," Declan said. It wasn't a question.

"Yes. I asked him about Mom. I mentioned the headstone we'd found, and he lost it. He asked me for money, like he always does. I said no, like I always do. I bring him food and any other supplies he needs, but I never, ever give him money or alcohol. I know I can't do anything to stop him from drinking, but I won't support his habit."

Declan pulled me closer. Our bodies fused together, and I savored the feeling of his heated skin against mine. It was a cold morning, and feeling his warm hard arms and legs wrapped around me was blissful.

"What are your parents like?" I asked.

"My father is dead," he answered with little emotion.

"Oh, Declan." I leaned up on my elbows, so I could face him. "I'm so sorry. You mentioned that. I forgot." I remembered the conversation we'd had when he told me about his tattoo.

"We weren't that close. He was your typical stereotype of a wealthy man. He ignored his child, cheated on his wife, and acted like he was god when he was at work. It's no coincidence that he was friends with Logan's father. They were both from the same stock, although Logan had it far worse than I did."

"How did he die?"

"Heart attack. My parents were divorced several years before. My mother finally got the courage to ask for one, and he agreed. He hired the best lawyers money could buy though, and he left her with practically nothing. But she was free, and that was all she cared about. Years later, Karma caught up with him, and he was found dead in his penthouse by his twenty-two-year-old mistress."

"God, and I thought I was the only one with a fucked-up childhood."

His eyes flashed and grew intense. "No, Leah...what I went through was a soap opera compared to the shit you had to endure. What you went through was hell. What that man did to you..."

"Hey," I said softly, "it's okay. I'm okay."

When I cuddled back into the safety of his arms, I felt him relax again. Letting myself drift back to sleep, I thought I heard Declan whisper in my ear, "I'll make it all better, I promise."


DECLAN

I got the address from Logan. It wasn't that hard to find. The old neighborhood was well kept with dated houses that looked refurbished in an attempt at revamping the city.

Clayton Morgan's house stuck out like a sore thumb. It looked like it hadn't been painted since the original pale yellow had been brushed on decades ago, and the yard was covered in compacted leaves, now mushy and wet from the recent snow.

I pulled up to the driveway and felt my hands grip the steering wheel like a vise. Knowing this was the place where Leah had grown up while enduring years of misery at the hand of the man who lived inside did something to me. It brought out a side of me I hadn't known existed. I wanted to rush in there and rip him apart from limb to limb, making sure he could never lay a hand on her again.

And that was why Logan's car pulled up behind mine. When I called for the address, I also asked him to meet me here. I needed someone to keep me tethered, grounded, so I wouldn't do anything that could land my ass in jail for the rest of my life. As much as I wanted to end that motherfucker, I didn't want to spend my life behind bars, away from the one thing I was intent on protecting.

I killed the engine and stepped out of the car. I met Logan halfway between our two cars, and we silently made our way up the driveway. He didn't ask what I was going to do. He just stood by me.

A few months ago, when I had gotten his wedding announcement, I'd thought he was weak for feeling so deeply for another person. But here I was, standing side by side with him as brothers-in-arms...fighting for a woman I would do anything to keep. And yet, I was too chickenshit to tell her.

I didn't bother knocking. I just let myself in. I made my way through the dingy kitchen that had crusty dishes in the sink and empty pizza boxes on the counter. I tried not to picture Leah living in this hellhole.

We found the piece-of-shit lying on a couch in the living room with a drink in hand, watching a rerun of some sitcom from the eighties. His eyes were half-closed, and he looked like he'd already drunk half a bottle even though it was barely noon. It was a miracle, or a fucking curse, that the man was still alive with functioning kidneys.

It took him several minutes to notice the two large men in his living room. His eyes finally moved lazily from the TV to us, and then they widened in surprise.

"Who the hell are you? If you've come to rob me, you picked the wrong house," he said, his words meshing together in an almost comical way, like he didn't give a fuck.

"Get up," I said, venom running through my veins.

He eyed me suspiciously, looking me up and down, before apparently deciding that I meant business. He rose from the couch, looking at us warily.

"You gonna tell me who the fuck you are?" he asked.

"I'm the man who loves your daughter."

At my words, I saw Logan's head snap from Leah's father to me. It was the first time I'd acknowledged those feelings and said the words. It felt good. *Like really good.* I wanted to do cartwheels and shit. I didn't know when I'd get the courage to tell Leah how I felt, but at least I was being honest with myself now.

"Well" —he laughed —"don't get too attached, son. She's just like her mother —a tease and a whore. Find someone better and move on."

My fist flew so fast at his face that I didn't even process the fact that I'd hit him until his head snapped back. *Good mood gone.* I went at him again, but I was pulled back.

"Easy, man. Remember why you're here," Logan said.

*Leah —I am here for Leah.*

Breathing heavily, I tried to calm myself, even though every inch of me was now twitching with adrenaline. I watched as the fucker wiped the blood off his split lip. *At least he knew how it felt now.*

"Here's how it's going to go, jackass." I pulled out my checkbook from the inside pocket of my leather jacket and set it down on the counter, talking while I wrote. "You are going to leave town. I don't care where the fuck you go or what you do, but you are never coming back. From this day on, Leah doesn't exist to you."

I ripped out the check and handed it to him. His eyes focused on the amount and nearly bugged out of his head. I'd given him half a million dollars. It was more money than most people saw in a lifetime. I wanted to make sure he never came back.

"I don't care what the fuck you do with this. Go to rehab, or drink yourself to death. I don't give a shit. But one thing you will never do is come back here, asking for more. The second you do, Leah and I will report you for abuse and have you in jail so fast that your head will spin. The only reason you're not there now is because I don't want her going through a lengthy public trial, but don't test me. I will if I have to, and I hear child abusers don't get treated real well in the slammer."

He hadn't looked up at me since that check had been shoved into his hands.

I grabbed the front of his shirt to get his attention. "Do you understand?"

He nodded. "Yes. Don't come back ever," he said, grinning.

Whatever hope I'd had that the man might have a tiny bit of decency evaporated as I watched him worship that check. He now had a new idol, and it was money.

"One more thing, and then we're out. I want everything you have that belonged to Lily. Whatever is left of Leah's mother, I want it."

He looked at me then, puzzled, before saying, "Sure, fine. It's all in the attic. Take whatever. I don't care."

"Oh, and Mr. Morgan? Or can I call you Clayton?"

He drunken gaze found mine.

"There's one more thing." My fist came flying toward his face for a second time that day. This time, when I punched him, I made sure he didn't get up.


LEAH

I knocked on Clare's door and waited patiently. I didn't usually knock on the door, but after last night, I thought a bit of manners might be in order. Tapping my foot nervously while balancing the bags in my hands, I stared at the door, willing it to open. I thought about calling this morning and apologizing for my vicious behavior over the phone, but I decided she deserved this in person. And I brought backup.

The door finally opened, revealing Clare dressed in yoga pants and a pink thermal long-sleeved shirt. This was what

Clare called her morning wear —not pajamas but not dressed either. She'd said it was in between. It made her feel a little less lazy since she wasn't technically in PJs, and it was more comfortable than wearing jeans while doing house chores. I'd called it her whacked mommy logic because they were still pajamas in my book. I'd told her she'd do anything to get out of having to get dressed for as long as possible.

I held up my bags and travel tray filled with coffee. "I brought coffee and muffins. Phil says hey and that you should forgive me."

Her lip twitched as she tried to maintain her serious face.

"What kind are they?" she asked.

"Who the hell do you think I am? Do you think I would show up here with anything but double chocolate chip apology muffins?"

"All right then. You may enter," she said, her straight face turning into a grin.

Clare and I never stayed mad at each other for long. We'd had tiffs and disagreements over the years, the result of having two very different personalities, but we always managed to make up and move on quickly. We understood each other. I knew that she was kinder and gentler than me, and she recognized that I was sometimes gruff and outspoken, and I lashed out when I was hurting.

We made our way into the kitchen, and then Clare grabbed plates and napkins for our muffins.

"Where's Short Stack?" I asked, noticing how quiet the house was.

The house was never this quiet when Maddie was

around. It was usually filled with the sounds of running feet, giggles, or singing.

"Um, school? It's a weekday, babe."

"Right. School. I'm still not used to that."

"You and me both. Each day when we walk her to that bus stop, I feel like it's still pretend, like we're just practicing to go to school. But nope, she's in kindergarten. She likes to remind me every day. She's very grown-up, you know," Clare said with a smile.

We silently dug into our muffins, and I laughed when Clare made a slight moan that bordered on erotic after she had taken her first bite. Clare was addicted to sweets, and chocolate was her ultimate weakness.

"Phil is the bomb. How can I get Logan to learn to bake like this?"

"Make him gay, and name him Phil? I'm pretty sure that man is one of a kind."

Phil was a friend of ours who owned a cafe that Clare and I loved to eat at after our weekly yoga sessions. His muffins and pastries were orgasmic. I was fairly certain I'd asked Phil to marry me at least a dozen times now, only to be turned down each time because he was madly in love and taken.

"Yeah, you're right. But damn, if Logan could bake even half as well. That man can cook, but when he gets near sugar, bad things happen. I can't tell you how many cookies, cakes, and muffins he's burned since we've been married. He keeps trying though, being the sweet, foolish man that he is." She laughed.

I laughed with her as I picked a chocolate chip off the top of my muffin before popping it into my mouth.

Letting the silence settle between us, I looked down at the wood table and drew patterns with my finger. Finally, I glanced back up at my best friend, knowing it was time — time to apologize, explain, open myself up to someone again.

"I'm so sorry, Clare. The way I acted last night was wrong. I lashed out. I was embarrassed, scared, and angry...and I took it out on everyone who was trying to help. I know you were only there because you wanted to take care of me, and I'm sorry I didn't let you do that."

"After over twenty years of friendship, I know how you react in these types of situations. I understand, Leah. I just wish you would let someone in. It doesn't even have to be me, but you do need someone to listen."

"I know. I think I understand that for the first time in my life."

"Do you want to talk about it? We don't have to. I mean, we can talk about the weather, books, that hot guy from *Thor*...whatever. I'm here if you want."

"Yeah." I smiled. "I think I do want to talk about it."

Over coffee and chocolate chip muffins, I finally told my best friend about my real childhood, the one that I'd hidden from her for so many years. We cried together, and she held my hand. When she asked why I'd never told her, I honestly didn't have an answer.

"I don't know, Clare. I've always been so strong, so independent. I guess a part of me thought telling some-one, acknowledging it, would be admitting weakness. So, I learned how to avoid it for the most part. My childhood and teen years became a sick game of learning cues and signs of my father's drunken states so that I knew when to scatter or not come home at all."

"I just wish I had known, so we could have done something, Leah. We could have taken you away and adopted you for real. You know my mother and father would have done that in an instant. Hell, I think they even tried at one point. Had they known that, it would have been a lot easier."

"I know, and I love your parents more than I could ever put into words, but I'm stubborn as hell."

She gave me that no-shit look.

I continued, "But in the beginning, I was scared. I was scared it wouldn't work, then I'd be stuck with him anyway, and he'd be even angrier. Later on, I just figured I was almost free anyway, and I thought I could manage a few more years of dodge and weave."

She jumped from her seat and pulled me into a tight hug. "I love you, Leah. Never forget that. You are my sister, best friend, and partner in crime. Don't ever shut me out. Do you understand?"

I nodded against her shoulder, letting the tears fall freely down my cheeks. "I understand, Clare Bear."

"Good, because finding a new best friend would be really hard work, and I'm just too lazy for that," she said through sniffles. "Besides, you were with me when I bought my first vibrator. A bond like that is deep and unbreakable."

I couldn't help it. I laughed. The sobs and laughs mingled together as we held each other in her kitchen.

She pulled back and looked at me with devilish green

eyes. "So, what's up with you and Declan? Because what I saw last night was anything but casual."

I sighed as I sat back in my chair, resuming the demolishment of my muffin. "I have no fucking clue. One minute, we're super casual, and the next, we've blown past all other stages and landed on super intense. He makes me feel things I am too scared to admit. Loving him could complete me or destroy me. If I were to give myself to him and he left like Daniel, I don't think I'd ever recover."

"You know Declan is not Daniel, right?"

"No, he's not. He's a famous super-hot actor. That doesn't make it any better." I snorted.

"Daniel was a dillhole, plain and simple. When someone loves you, he stays —even when things get hard. When Ethan got sick and we all gathered together to take care of him, Daniel bailed. That shows you right there that he wasn't in it for the long haul. You can't assume Declan would do the same."

"You can't assume he wouldn't."

"Pessimistic much?" she asked.

"I like my glass half-empty, thank you very much."

"Well, I just don't want you to walk away from what could be the best thing of your life. Don't run away from love just because you've been hurt before."

"Love? I didn't say I loved him," I deflected. "Besides, isn't it a bit early for that?"

"Someone very wise once told me that there's no time restriction on love," she said with a wink.

"Very slick, using my own words against me. That's kind of evil."

"I learned from the best."

# Chapter Twelve

DECLAN

*I*'d been driving by Leah's father's house every day for the last week, making sure he didn't come back. The bastard didn't even bother closing up the house. He'd just hit the road, leaving the house wide-open to anyone who might pass by, including me. I'd gone in yesterday just to make sure he wasn't still there. I was being paranoid, but before I told Leah, I wanted to be sure he was gone —for good.

Could I guarantee he would never come back? *No.* The smartest thing would have been to file charges and have him arrested, but after that night of holding a battered and bruised Leah in my arms, I knew she would never make it through a trial against her father. It would be too much. It would have been too public with too many people asking questions. She could barely open up to Clare and me. How could we ask her to open up to an entire courtroom about the events that had haunted her for the last twenty years? I knew she would, and I knew she could if needed. Leah could do anything. She was stronger than anyone I'd ever met, but if I could keep her from pain, I would, no matter what it cost.

When I was sure the house was empty and he wasn't coming back, I told Leah I had somewhere to take her, something to tell her. She looked at me nervously and nodded.

*Shit, did she think I was breaking up with her? Could we technically break up?* I didn't even know what to call our relationship. We'd never put a title on it. That needed to be fixed. She was mine, and that fact needed to be made public.

When we pulled up to the curb, her head snapped over to me, her eyes filled with panic. "What are we doing here?"

Placing my hand on hers, I wove our fingers together before saying, "Do you trust me?"

She silently nodded, and I brought our joined hands to my lips before kissing each of her fingers.

"Then, you have nothing to worry about. Come on."

We made our way up the driveway, hand in hand, my heart beating hard in my chest.

*What if this wasn't what she wanted? What if, in some small recess of her heart, she loved this man, and I'd just sent him away?*

Sweat broke out across my brow, and I suddenly began second-guessing my decision, hoping I hadn't just destroyed the one good thing that had come my way before it'd even had a chance to start. We reached the front door, and I took a step forward. I grabbed the handle and ushered us in. I'd had a cleaning crew come in a few days after he left. I didn't want her to come back to a dingy house. There were enough memories here without the stench of alcohol and stale food to add to the mix. Pine-Sol and Windex now perfumed the air instead.

"What the hell? You cleaned?"

"No...well, yes. But that's not why we're here."

We walked through the kitchen and into the living room, the spot I assumed was where Leah's father usually was when she visited. When she didn't see him, she turned and looked at the vacant dinette and bar stools.

"Where is he?" she asked cautiously.

"Gone."

"Gone? What do you mean?"

"Well, he's not dead, if that's what you're wondering. At least, I don't think he is. But he's never coming back here, Leah. I made sure of that. You are free."

Tears brimmed her eyes, and she looked around the house again before circling back to me.

"But how? I don't understand. Are you sure? Did you do something illegal?" she asked, throwing out questions left and right.

"It doesn't matter how. Yes, I'm sure. And no, you're not getting rid of me that easily. No pending arrests," I said with a smirk.

"Shit. I'm going to cry again. Why do I cry so much around you?"

"I don't know, but I'll hold you every time you do."

She came into my arms then. It felt like I was whole, like my missing half was settling into place, and I knew I'd found exactly where I was supposed to be.

"Why, Declan? Why would you do this?"

I pulled back, knowing it was now or never. My heart raced. This time, it was for another reason. I still didn't know how she felt, and putting myself out there with no guarantee was the scariest moment of my life. It was scarier than when I'd asked Heather to move to Hollywood with me, and she'd said no. It was scarier than when I'd auditioned for my first movie and thought I'd throw up from the stress, and it was scarier than walking into Leah's bedroom and seeing her face covered in bruises.

"I love you, Leah Morgan. Since the moment I got off that plane, everything I do has been for you. You are so much more than you think you are, and I see you —all of you. You can push all you want, but I'm not going anywhere. I want every piece of you. No games, no going back. I —"

"Shut the hell up," Leah said.

She pulled my head down, so our lips could meet in a frenzied, passionate kiss.

"You better not hurt me, Hotshot, because everything you just said...I feel for you plus half a million other feelings I can't put into words. I love you even though you're arrogant and cocky and —"

"Shut the hell up," I mocked.

I kissed her again, and then laughter filled the air as I lifted her and spun us in the middle of her childhood home.

"Thank you," she said as I still held her in my arms.

"For what?"

Her eyes met mine, and she paused. "For everything.

But mostly, for this —for giving me one perfect, happy memory in the midst of hell."

Seeing her joyous face in the middle of what was once her prison growing up made me want to replace every terrible memory in her life with something better.


LEAH

I wiped the fog off the bathroom mirror that had accumulated during my shower. I stared at my reflection with a towel wrapped around my hair and body. My bruises and cuts had healed, and I was back to looking like me. Thanks to the miracles of makeup, I had been able to cover up most of the evidence, so no one had noticed at work. I was opening up, but that didn't mean I wanted the entire world to know every sordid detail of my life. I didn't mind talking to Trish about my new hot man-candy and how Clare and my family were doing, but I wasn't about to open up and bleed out all my secrets.

I pulled the towel off my head, letting my long blonde hair tumble down my back. It had been years since I'd let someone cut it more than an inch or two, and now, it was halfway down my back. It was naturally wavy and on the thick side. Being this long made it hard to maintain, but I just loved it. It made me feel so feminine and girlie. After noticing Declan's heated glances while watching me as I would brush and then braid it at night, I didn't think I'd ever cut it again.

"Declan James said he loves me," I said out loud to my reflection.

Just saying it brought a smile to my lips, and butterflies took flight in my belly. I touched my lips, remembering the kiss we'd shared in my father's house. *Well, his old house.* I couldn't believe he was gone. I'd spent so many years taking care of him, and now, it was all behind me. Like Declan had said, I was free.

I still remembered the years in college when I would work two jobs, so I could bring my father groceries, feeling guilty that he might starve if he didn't eat. I'd live on ramen for weeks just to keep him fed. He always blamed me for him getting fired from every job he'd worked, but we'd both known the real reason he couldn't hold down a job. Being drunk all the time didn't exactly fly with the bosses.

"Did I hear you talking to yourself in here?" Declan asked, peeking his head in the bathroom door.

He looked gorgeous in pajama bottoms and nothing else. His broad chest was bare and so delectable, displaying that tattoo I'd grown to love. I licked my lips as my eyes traveled down his body, loving the way his hips dipped perfectly into a V before disappearing under his flanneled waistband.

His lips upturned into a cocky grin as he sauntered into the bathroom before coming up behind me. His hands wrapped around my hips as his body pressed against me. I could feel him, eager and ready, against my ass.

"Seeing you look at me like that makes me hard...really fucking hard," he said, pulling our bodies tighter together to further emphasize his point.

A low moan rose up my throat as he ran his hands up

my arms. I savored the feel of his bare skin touching mine.

"Turn around," he commanded, his voice rough and sexy.

I did as I had been instructed. I slowly turned in his arms until we were face-to-face. His eyes had lost all hint of joking, and now, they were full of fire, transforming into the intense flecked green they became when he was turned-on.

"I think it's about time we lose this," he said.

My towel slowly slid down to the floor, exposing my naked body completely to him. He grinned slightly, taking an appreciative look at what he'd just unwrapped.

"Mine, all mine. I'm so fucking lucky," he said softly.

He took my lips in a searing kiss that left me breathless. I pulled back to see he was still sporting his cocky grin that I'd come to adore. He grabbed me around the waist and hoisted me onto the counter, sitting my ass right on the cold granite. I yelped in protest, and he laughed.

"Spread those beautiful legs wide for me, Leah, until one leg is on each side of the counter. Show me just how flexible my yoga-loving girlfriend is."

The man had told me he loved me, but hearing him call me his girlfriend reduced me to a love-struck teenage girl. I was mush, an absolute puddle of Declan-love goo. I lifted my legs, anchoring a foot on each side of the counter, with my knees bent. For support, I leaned back and let my hands rest on the countertop behind me. I was spread-eagle on my bathroom counter, and Declan looked like he'd just won the fucking lotto.

"Goddamn, that's a beautiful sight. I really want to take a picture of it."

"You want to take a picture of my snatch?" I asked, kind of amused. I'd never been told that one before.

"Are you kidding? I'd be fucking stupid if I didn't. Having that picture with me when we are apart…"

His words drifted off then, and he looked at me. We hadn't discussed what would happen after Declan finished his current project. We had decided to enjoy our time together until the time came. But we knew a decision would have to be made. A long-distance relationship between California and Virginia would never work.

Our eyes connected, and the lack of time we had left together suddenly seemed even more evident than before. His eyes heated again, and he came at me, burying his hands in my wet hair and kissing me like his life depended on it. Our tongues twisted and moved together like we were trying to fuse our bodies, defying the impending separation with our kiss.

"I need a taste of that sweet pussy first," he said against my lips before dropping to his knees in front of me.

Unlike other positions, I could watch him this time. Fingers spread my folds, and his mouth made contact with my core. I cried out in response, bucking against his tongue, as he licked me. From my spot on the counter, I looked down as he tongue fucked me with fervor, like he couldn't get enough. Just then, his eyes found mine. Those hazel eyes were now so vividly green, and I was done. I climaxed against his mouth as he watched and sucked, drawing it out to make the orgasm last longer. Just when the last quake died down, Declan's tongue slipped back into my channel, working my body like it was his to command.

"No, Declan, I can't. Not again," I said, panting, already feeling the orgasm beginning to build. *Holy shit, really?*

"You can, and you will," he answered.

He found my clit and flicked it with his tongue as his fingers slipped into my tight, slick core. When his mouth clamped down on my clit and sucked, I fell over the edge again, calling out his name. He rose then and slipped his slick fingers into my mouth as my hands found the waistband of his pajama bottoms. As I sucked on his fingers, licking off the taste of my own body, I untied the tie at the center of his waist and then let his pants fall to the floor. There, before me, was Declan —naked, turned-on, and mine, completely mine.

"Stay, just like that," he commanded, pointing to my legs, still bent up on the counter.

He slid me a bit farther to the edge, so I was nearly falling off, and then without warning, he slammed into me. I gasped at the sudden invasion, my body grasping his tightly, as he continued to thrust in and out. Our bodies crashed together as he kept up the relentless pace. I let my head fall back as I moaned and screamed out his name while he gripped my hips, so he could push farther into me.

"Say it, Leah. I need to hear it. Now."

"I love you."

"Say it again."

"Oh God," I moaned, feeling a third orgasm started to build. "I love you, Declan!" I screamed as trembled and broke apart.

I watched his eyes as I came, feeling my body clamp down on his cock while it pumped in and out of me. He gave one last thrust, and then he called out my name as he came.

He leaned down and kissed me gently. It was a complete opposite to the frenzied lovemaking we'd just shared. Yin and yang, sweet and spicy, the best of two worlds —that was Declan James.

"I forgot to tell you why I came in here," he whispered in my ear.

"You mean, it wasn't to fuck me senseless?" I teased.

"Well, that became my intent the moment I saw you in that towel."

"So, the reason?"

"Oh, right. Merry Christmas." He grinned.

I grinned back. I cherished the fact that I would be able to spend the entire day with all the people I loved, and I wouldn't have to spend a single second thinking about my father. And it was all thanks to Declan.

# Chapter Thirteen



"The doctor dude from Thanksgiving isn't going to be here, is he?" I asked, as we pulled into Clare's parents' driveway.

There weren't nearly as many cars here as on Thanksgiving, so I took that as a good sign.

"No" —Leah laughed —"just immediate family today, Hotshot. You really didn't like him, did you?"

"He was flirting with you —right in front of me!" I said defensively.

That only made her laugh harder. I gave her a scowl, and she pulled my hand in hers.

"You had nothing to worry about then, and you have nothing to worry about now. A million men could flirt with me, but I'm not going anywhere."

"Damn straight," I answered with a grin, leaning across the seats to kiss her.

Just as I deepened the kiss, I heard a tiny giggle and my eyes sprang open just in time to see a little girl's head appear in the car window. We pulled apart quickly as Leah turned and opened the door.

"Hey, Short Stack! What are you doing out here? It's freezing!"

Maddie's little nose was bright red, and she was bundled up in a puffy pink jacket with matching gloves and a hat. "I was waiting for you at the inside at the window, but you didn't get out of the car. So, Mommy said it was okay if I came out and got you."

"Well, we're ready to go inside. Think you could show us the way?" Leah asked.

Maddie nodded her head with enthusiasm. We got out of the car and all headed toward the house. I bent down and scooped Maddie up in my arms as she giggled. I was pretty sure it was the first time I'd ever picked up a kid in my life. *They didn't break easily, did they?* She seemed happy, so I went with it.

"Hey, you. I think you asked me a question about your Aunt Leah the last time we met. You remember?" I asked Maddie.

"Um..." She thought about it while scrunching her nose and lips together as if it helped her concentrate. "Oh, yes! I remember!" she said, getting excited as she looked at her aunt.

"You want to ask me that question again?" I chuckled.

She looked at her aunt, and Leah just shrugged in response, which caused Maddie to giggle.

"Okay, but first, I'm just going to say that you're silly."

"Duly noted," I said, straight-faced.

"Declan, are you my Aunt Leah's boyfriend?"

"Why yes, Maddie, I am Leah's boyfriend. Aren't I lucky?"

She just giggled again as we made our way into the house. I set her down gently, and she ran off into the house, announcing that Leah and her silly boyfriend were here.

"You're insane," Leah said, shaking her head.

"About you," I answered before kissing her cheek.

"God, that was awful. You need better pick-up lines."

I laughed. "Why? Who am I trying to pick up? I already got what I wanted."

"That was so much better. That one kinda makes me want to hump you right here."

"That can be arranged. I'm sure we could find a closet," I teased, remembering our almost indiscretion in the closet at Clare and Logan's house.

She grinned at me as we rounded the corner of the hallway into the family room where we found Clare and Logan huddled together in a tight hug. They looked up, and my heart fell. Clare had been crying, and Logan was visibly upset.

"Oh God, what's wrong? Please say it's not what I think it is," Leah said in a panic, gripping my hand tighter.

"No, no, I'm fine. Cancer treatment is exactly on schedule, and things look good, great even," Logan said.

Leah's death grip on my hand loosened a little, and I felt some of the blood rush back to my fingers.

"Oh thank God. So, what is it? Why are we upset? Whose ass does Declan need to kick?"

"Whoa, why I am being thrown into this?" I asked, throwing up my hands in defense.

"Logan's father called this morning." Clare said.

"Oh," we both answered in union.

That would explain it. Logan's father was like mine, only the upgraded model. He was richer, meaner, and crueler. His idea of love was sending checks on birthdays and graduation. He hadn't spoken to Logan since the day his previous marriage went public in a very embarrassing way and he'd made no attempts to meet Logan's new family since he'd married Clare. He'd never spent one second of his life caring about his family, and Logan had spent his feeling like a shunned outcast.

There was only one reason Mitchell Matthews would be calling.

"So, how much is cancer going for these days?" I asked.

"A quarter of a mil apparently," Logan answered absently.

"So, the man called you up, after years of nothing, only to offer you money because he'd heard that you have cancer?" Leah asked.

"Yep, pretty much."

"So, did you take the money?" I asked, grinning.

"Declan!" Leah scolded.

I brushed it off. Logan and I were friends for a reason. We thought the same way, and I bet he was thinking the same thing I was.

Logan grinned back and nodded. "Yep, sure did. It's being wired on Monday. I will then take his guilt money and donate it anonymously to as many cancer societies as I can find. My family and I will spend the rest of the holidays in New York with my mother, knowing his money is going to hundreds of other families in need. It's a win for everyone."

I probably would have thrown in something with a little more vengeance, like sending out a party invite with my father's address to the entire population of Facebook and then watching from afar as they all descended on his house. But that was where Logan and I differed.

"It's still pretty messed-up that your father calls only to send you money. Did he even ask about your wife and child?" Leah asked.

"Nope."

"Well, I'm pretty sure the motto we used for these situations back in high school still works," I said.

He chuckled, nodding his head in agreement.

"What motto is that?" Leah asked.

"Fuck 'em. Fuck 'em all."

LEAH

I'd spent Christmas with Clare's family for as long as I could remember. Years ago, ever since Clare's mother had asked about my plans for the day and I'd sheepishly mentioned my father having to work, I'd been here. I thought she had known it was a lie, but she never asked. She'd just opened her home and family to me, like she always had...like she did this night with Declan.

Christmas Day for the Finnegan family was for family only. Where Thanksgiving was a come-one-come-all event, Christmas was small and intimate. Having Declan with me felt special. It made it more absolute to me that he was actually here, holding my hand, whispering, "I love you," in my ear. Sharing him with my family made our love real to me.

Clare said nothing about our obvious new commitment to each other, but I did see her wipe away a tear or two when she overheard one of Declan's endearments whispered over the course of the night. By the way she was reacting, she must have really thought I was going to die a spinster.

Mrs. Laura Finnegan, or Mama as we all called her, was completely enamored with my new boyfriend. Not only was he a Hollywood star in one of her favorite movies, but he was also charming, sweet, and hot as hell —her words, not mine. When she'd uttered those shocking syllables, I'd about choked on my stolen cookie in the kitchen. Mama Finnegan did not usually use such language.

As we waited for dinner to cook, we all debated on what to do. When we were kids, we would all beg to open presents, which Maddie had already tried and failed at, but we were adults now, and we had restraint. Plus, we'd already asked. We were shot down, just like the kid. Some things never changed. So, we'd moved on to card games.

"Uno!" Logan yelled triumphantly.

We all groaned.

"Okay, that's it. I'm not playing with him anymore. Remind me not to play against a Harvard-educated doctor anymore. It's just not fair," Garrett lamented, who'd arrived shortly after us.

"Ah, come on, I didn't win every game, did I?" Logan asked.

We all nodded at him.

"Sore losers," he grumbled.

We all laughed. I relaxed into my seat on the sofa and sipped on my hot apple cider. Clare was snuggled up next to me, sharing a blanket. Both of us had wisely opted out of the card games, having played with Logan before.

"Logan seems very comfortable with your parents now," I commented.

"Well, he did put a ring on it," she joked, holding up her beautiful antique wedding set.

"Hand job?" I asked quietly.

"What?" she feigned innocence. "No! I can't believe you...okay, fine, you got me."

"Nice. Nothing relaxes a man like a little hand action before meeting the parents." I laughed.

"And Declan?"

"Blow job."

"Right on."

We high-fived each other before giggling into our cider, which eventually turned into roaring laughter. The men finished cleaning up their cards and looked to us for entertainment.

"Okay, so what do we do next?" Garrett asked.

There was a strict no-TV rule on Christmas.

"Oh, I know! Let's look at photo albums!" Clare exclaimed.

Both Garrett and I moaned.

"I think that sounds like an excellent idea," Logan said, looking over at my soon-to-be-dead boyfriend.

Declan was laughing and nodding his head.

*Traitor.*

Almost immediately after saying it, Clare returned to the family room with a ton of photo albums, nearly skipping in her purple sweater dress and heels.

"Come on, everyone gather together! Let's see how cute I was!" she beamed.

Logan joined her on the floor in the middle of the living room. He pulled her onto his lap, and she began to sort through the albums. I rose from my seat on the sofa and begrudgingly planted my ass next to them on the floor, next to my traitorous boyfriend who was still on the floor from getting his ass kicked in Uno. He was currently leaning over to sneak a peek at whatever Clare was looking at.

Garrett, seeing he had no choice in the matter, also made his way down to the floor, lying down next to his sister, as she started on the first album. Clare's father sat behind us in his ancient recliner, chuckling as Clare flipped through the pages. I could hear her mother humming away in the kitchen as she prepared dinner. As much as I'd groaned, it was nice to sit here, flipping through happy young memories. All of the good parts of my childhood were in these pages, under this roof, and with this family.

"Here's one of Leah from...oh, junior prom!"

Before I had time to grab it, Declan snatched it up in his hands.

"You were just as hot back then," he said with a smirk before frowning. "Who's the dude?"

"Oh, uh...Scott Evans. We dated for a few months that year. He was the quarterback, and I was a cheerleader. Looked good on paper, but it was a disaster in real life."

"Looks like a moron," Declan said.

"Are you jealous of a boy I dated over ten years ago?" I was seriously amused.

"No," he grunted. "Yes."

I laughed and squeezed his arm. "If it makes you feel better, he flunked out of college and works part-time at a shoe store in the mall. Oh, and he still lives with his mom."

"Marginally better, thanks." He grinned.

We looked through more high school pictures and then got to college. Clare's hand stopped when she found a picture of her and Ethan from their first Thanksgiving. Their beaming young faces were mushed together in an exuberant hug. He looked happy, healthy, and full of life —exactly like I always wanted to remember him. Ethan, like me, hadn't had a place to call home, and he'd spent all his holidays with us after he started dating Clare. The Finnegans had opened their home to many people over the years —taking me, Ethan, Logan, and now Declan, it appeared, into their family. They were the very best kind of people.

Logan's fingers wrapped around his wife's, and he held her, knowing that even though she was happy in his arms, the man she'd lost would always be close to her heart.

"You okay?" he asked.

We all watched on, ready to help her through the grief if needed. She nodded as a single tear ran down her cheek. Then, she placed the album down and moved on to another one.

"I'm fine, really." She smiled softly. "Thank you," she said quietly to Logan.

He nodded and placed a gentle kiss on her cheek.

"Let's find some pictures of Garrett, why don't we?" Clare said.

We all agreed and began looking through the piles of albums. I hit pay dirt first when I cracked open an album to be greeted by the familiar face of a younger, more innocent-looking Garrett.

"Hey, there's the Goober I remember!" I looked up to the present-day Garrett and then back down to the high school version preserved on the pages of the album.

We all gathered around as I flipped through photos of Garrett in high school. It was then that I realized how much he really had changed. He'd had a light in his eyes then that didn't reach his eyes now.

"Okay, dinner's almost ready!" Laura called from the kitchen.

I skipped a few pages and made my way to the end of the album. I was eager to see if that genuine Garrett smile was still there. I was trying to pinpoint when it had disappeared. Then, I landed on graduation pictures. There was eighteen-year-old Garrett, posing with his high school girlfriend, their eyes brimming with excitement and youth.

Garrett visibly stiffened next to Clare as his emerald eyes locked on the picture.

"Hey, I remember her," Clare said, "Mia, wasn't it?"

Garrett just nodded. Clare was sitting next to him rather than across from him, so she didn't have the view I did. She couldn't see the look of absolute devastation on his face.

"What happened to her?" Clare asked.

"She left me," was all he said before getting up and exiting the room.

Based on the look on his face just now, I'd bet that shadow of a smile he carried showed up the day she walked out of his life.

# Chapter Fourteen

DECLAN

"So, this is your idea of fun?" I asked as we walked hand in hand into the retirement home.

Leah gave me a shy smile before greeting the lady sitting at the front desk. "Hey, Alice. How's it going?" she said.

"Well, good morning, sugar. Is it Wednesday already?"

Looking down at the calendar with many papers and schedules scattered on her desk, the older woman, who reminded me a little of Betty White, nodded.

"Well, I guess it is. Always glad to have you Miss Leah. And who's this handsome gentleman you have with you today? You didn't have to bring me a present, you know?" she said with a wink.

Leah laughed and introduced me to the rather randy secretary. "Alice, this is my boyfriend, Declan. He was curious why I kept disappearing every Wednesday afternoon, and when I told him this is where I went, he had to see for himself." She took a sideways glance toward me and smiled, clearly remembering our conversation from earlier that week.

"You volunteer at an old folks' home?" I'd asked.

"Yep. And they really hate when you call it that."

"But last week, didn't you say you volunteered at an after-school program?"

"Yeah, I do that occasionally, too." She'd just shrugged.

And that was when I'd told her I had to see it to be sure. *How could one person do that much?* I could count the number of volunteer hours I'd given in my life on one hand. *What was her motivation?* I had to see her in action, see this other side of the woman who had captured my heart.

And so, a few days later, we were here, about to spend the afternoon with the elderly. I suddenly regretted that decision when we signed in and took a left down the hall into the dining room where I saw the residents for the first time.

*What the hell was I supposed to do? What would we talk about?* I didn't have anything in common with an eighty-year-old. As if sensing my anxiety, Leah squeezed my hand, gave me a reassuring smile, and pulled me into the dining room.

"Want to grab a piece of pie? They make amazing pie," she said.

"Sure." Pie sounded safe. I'd do anything to delay the awkwardness.

I should have chosen a different activity for the afternoon. My grandparents had died when I was young, and since then, I hadn't had any contact with anyone older than my parents. *Would she be disappointed if I sucked at this?*

We grabbed our pie, coconut for her and lemon meringue for me, and then we took our seats next to a couple at a round table near the center of the room. Leah had explained this retirement home had all levels of residents. Some were highly functioning and had come here because they simply hadn't wanted to live on their own anymore. Others required constant supervision. Leah's volunteer duties were simple. She was there to be a friend.

The couple we sat next to recognized Leah in an instant, and they greeted us warmly. They appeared to be part of the higher-functioning group Leah had described. They were both well-dressed and presentable. The woman looked like she'd thrown her entire jewelry box on. She was wearing several gold necklaces around her neck, four or five clunky bracelets, and a ring on every perfectly polished finger.

"Hello, darling!" the woman said. "How are you?"

"Good, Millie. How have you been this last week?"

"Can't complain. Still breathing," she said with a wink. "Now, who's this? You've never brought a friend with you...and such a handsome one, Leah!"

Her husband let out a huff, and Millie placated him by placing a hand on his shoulder and giving him a loving smile. He looked a little worse for the wear than she did. He was thinner, his expensive clothes hanging a bit on his frail body, and his skin appeared to be a few shades paler than it should be. When his eyes locked with hers, he smiled, and it was like the whole world disappeared.

I turned away, feeling like I was intruding on a very intimate moment.

Leah smiled as she turned away briefly, too. When she looked back toward them, she said, "This is my boyfriend, Declan. Declan, these two lovely people are Millie and William Taylor. They've been residents here for almost a year."

"It's lovely to meet you, Declan. You look very familiar," Millie said, looking at me a bit closer.

"I just have one of those faces, I guess," I said with a shrug, giving Leah a knowing smile. I wasn't about to out myself in an old folks' home.

We talked over pie, and I found it easier than I'd thought to speak with them. They were just people, and I could understand why Leah would come here. They were kind and loving. They treated Leah like a friend rather than someone coming in to check on them, and Leah did the same to them. She honestly enjoyed returning every week, visiting with the residents and learning about the different paths their lives had taken them on.

In our conversations, I learned William, or Willie as he liked to be called —it took me a minute to get over the fact that they were Mille and Willie —had been diagnosed with Parkinson's disease. I noticed the small shaking in his hand as he brought the fork to his mouth and when he tried to hold his coffee cup.

"When we found out, we had many options. We could have had a live-in nurse, but I didn't like the idea of having someone in our space all the time. The doctors said I could have moved Willie to a facility and stayed in the house by myself." She gave her husband a meaningful look. "But I knew that would never be an option. I couldn't leave him. So, we decided to sell our house and make the move together." She gave her husband a small smile as she held his hand. "No matter what life might throw at us, we're in it together until the end."

"Always," Willie said, his voice shaking. He carefully brought his wife's hand to his lips.

I looked at Leah, and at that moment, I knew I needed to figure out a way to close the gap between our homes because I would not lose her over something like distance. I would not lose her, period.


LEAH

"You're amazing. You know that, right?" Declan said as we made our way to the car.

We'd had an enjoyable afternoon with the Taylors. We'd spent a few hours with them, eating pie and then taking a short walk through the halls since it was too cold to do so outdoors. Eventually, we'd said our good-byes, and Millie had made me promise to bring Declan next week. He'd happily agreed.

"Why? Because I hang out with old people once a week? That hardly makes me amazing," I scoffed.

"It's more than that. You do so much, and you don't even see it. You are constantly taking care of others and putting the needs of everyone around you first, and that makes you amazing."

"I don't do it to be amazing. I just do it because that's who I am," I argued.

"I know," he said softly, stopping as we reached the car.

He turned and wrapped his hand around my waist, curling his fingers in the belt loops of my coat, as he pulled me close. I could see his breath flowing out of his mouth, the signs of winter evident all around us.

"That's what makes you amazing."

"I think you're starting to abuse the word *amazing*." I laughed.

"I could use other words, like fascinating, stunning, breathtaking...beautiful."

"Shut up." I ended his verbal praise with a scorching kiss.

He pressed me against the car, a growl escaping his lips, as his hips dug into mine.

"Careful what you start, Leah," he purred, pulling back to challenge me with his fiery hazel eyes.

"You were nervous today, weren't you?" I asked, changing the subject.

He laughed, knowing I would back down to his challenge. I was kinky, but we were in a freaking parking lot in the middle of the afternoon.

"Yes, a bit."

I gave him a hard look that called him out on his bullshit, and he relented.

"Okay, a lot. It sounds stupid, but I suddenly became very panicked that I would embarrass you, that I would be unable to speak to them. I was afraid I wouldn't have anything useful to say, and you would be disappointed. I had never done anything like that. Not too long ago, my life was going from one party to the next, and my biggest concern was which club I was going to visit next. Before and after Heather, I made it a point to make my life as shallow as possible. Having a meaningful chat with an elderly couple about the trials and joys of their lives is a bit heavier than I'm used to."

"You did great. You need to give yourself a bit more credit, Hotshot. You're more than just good looks. And if you stick around me long enough, you'll find a whole world of fun outside of those clubs and bars...not that I don't enjoy those, too," I answered.

"Well, tomorrow is New Year's Eve. Why don't we do a bit of both? I'll take you out for a bit of fun my way, and then afterward, we can have a bit of fun the Leah way. What do you think?"

"You have no idea what you've just gotten yourself into."

After asking him for the hundredth time where we were going, only to hear him answer for the hundredth time that he wasn't telling me, I asked him if he would at least give me a hint on wardrobe. He just smiled and walked away. Then, I could hear him whistling as he made himself a sandwich in the kitchen.

I couldn't remember the last time Declan had spent the night in his hotel room. Part of me tried to feel bad for whoever was still paying for the expensive room he was supposed to be staying in, but every night when I would be lying in his arms, the smidgen of guilt seemed to drift away as I fell asleep.

When the sun fell and Declan informed me that it was almost time to go, I let him grab whatever he needed out of my room, and then I kicked him out, sending him across the hall to the guest bedroom to change. I'd told him a girl needed privacy when getting ready for a fancy date.

"How do you know it's fancy?" he'd joked. "I could be taking you to a country bar with peanuts on the floor."

I stuck my head out my bedroom door to find him standing in the middle of the guest bedroom. He didn't have a shirt on, and his jeans were unbuttoned. I thought my brain shorted out as drool hit the floor. *How could his body still make me go idiotic after all this time?* I thought it would at least stabilize a little...but nope. If my eyes saw even one inch of naked Declan, I would turn into a drooling sex fiend.

"Were you going to say something, babe?" he teased, slowly sliding his jeans down his ass.

No boxers today —he'd gone totally commando. *Damn him.* I turned around and slammed the door behind me, hearing him burst into a fit of laughter.

"You better not be taking me to a country bar! You know I hate country!"

Declan suddenly came through the door, still gloriously naked. He stalked toward me, grabbed my ass, and pulled me against his tight, lean body. His eyes were bright, heated, and his smile lit up the room.

"I'm not taking you to a country bar. Put something sexy on but not too fancy. We're not going to a ball. Do it fast before I change my mind and just throw you on the bed and fuck you till morning. Got it?"

I barely had the chance to nod before he slapped me on the ass, and then he was gone.

*Well, this could be fun.*

Searching through my closet, I found my black leather jacket, something I hadn't pulled out in a while. Declan wore his like a second skin, so I figured he'd lose his mind seeing me in one. I danced happily over to my dresser where I grabbed the tightest pair of skinny jeans I owned. They required me to lie down on the bed and do several awkward positions and squats to get them on. That was not sexy at all, and it proved another good reason for kicking Declan out. After the jeans, I found a sexy white tank top that barely touched the waistband of my jeans. I finished off the look with high-heeled ankle boots.

*Yeah, he's done for.*

I redid my makeup, applying a bit more eyeliner and some light eye shadow. I kept the eye makeup on the light side because I had plans for my lips, and I didn't want to look like a hooker with too much. Makeup rule number one —when going big on the lips, keep the eye makeup understated, and vice versa. Nothing said, *For hire*, like a woman with four layers of cheap makeup on.

Finishing my eyes, I dusted a bit of bronzer on my cheeks and pulled out the lipstick. It was the perfect red. It was a classy matte and reminded me of old Hollywood. I took my time putting it on, making sure it was exactly right. I didn't usually wear much lipstick. It got in the way of kissing Declan, but tonight, I had evil plans, and they involved lipstick.

I took a look in the mirror as I brushed my hair, and then I headed for the living room. Declan was standing there in dark jeans that hugged his ass. I could see a dark green long-sleeved Henley peeking out of the leather of his coat. He turned around when he heard me come in, and seeing his face was priceless.

"Hey there, stud," I said, quoting *Grease*, another favorite movie.

"Well, fuck me sideways. Where the hell did you get that?"

"I've had it for a while actually."

"And why is this the first time I'm seeing it? Jesus, you in leather —why did I not think of that?"

"Don't know, but here I am. I think I was promised a hot date."

"Right. We better get on that before I change my mind."

His eyes lingered down my body, giving me chills. Suddenly, the idea of staying in for the holiday sounded much more appealing, but I was curious about where he was taking me.

"So, you gonna tell me where we're going yet?"

"Hope you're prepared for some liquor, babe, because we are going to do an old-fashioned Richmond pub crawl."

*Oh Lord.* I was pretty sure I could hear my liver whimpering in protest.

# Chapter Fifteen

Being the responsible adult that I was, the limo I'd rented pulled up just as we were locking Leah's front door.

"You know, I didn't know a limo was part of a traditional pub crawl," Leah teased.

I swung an arm over her shoulder and walked with her toward our transportation for the evening.

"Yeah, well, I decided to throw a bit of Declan flair in there for style...and safety," I added.

"Responsible and sexy —how did I get so lucky?"

She fanned herself as I rolled my eyes.

I held open the door, and she bent down and made her way into the car. My eyes followed her tight ass as she crawled across the seat. I followed, giving the driver directions, and then I raised the privacy screen, so we could enjoy our twenty-minute drive into downtown alone.

"So, that privacy screen...is it soundproof?" Leah asked, her brow arching.

She gave me a look that had my entire body coming to full attention. My eyes were immediately drawn to her full red lips. I wasn't used to seeing her with lipstick on, and every word she said just drew my eyes to her lips, making me want to suck, lick, and devour every inch of them.

"I don't know. Do you want me to ask?" I challenged, trying to see how serious she was.

"No!" she exclaimed. "I mean...we can just be quiet," she said softly.

I scooted towards to her, closing the distance between our bodies. "What exactly do you have in mind, little temptress? We only have twenty minutes."

"That's enough time for what I have in mind." She grinned. "I see you've noticed the lipstick."

"Hard not to. Your lips are making me hard every time you speak."

"Well, in a few minutes, they're going to be making perfect red rings around your dick, so think about that."

*Fuck. Me.*

"Is that why you wore the lipstick?" I asked, trying to remember how to form words.

She just smiled as she reached for my belt buckle. She didn't waste any time. She freed me from my jeans and boxer briefs in a matter of seconds. She knelt down in front of me and took my hard length in her hand, giving it long, firm strokes up and down, as I groaned. With her other hand, she reached up to shrug out of her jacket, but I stopped her.

"Don't you dare. The leather stays."

Kneeling between my legs, she bent her head toward me. She gave one long lick to the head of my cock before running her tongue down the side and then back up again. She threw me a sly grin before she went down, taking all of me into her mouth, leaving a perfect red ring at the base of my dick.

"Shit, Leah!" I cursed.

She worked me in and out, sucking and hollowing out her cheeks as she went. My fingers curled into her hair as I thrust hard into her mouth. She moaned, gripping her fingers under my ass, as I fucked her mouth.

"Fuck, Leah, I'm gonna come. Suck me harder. Don't stop," I begged.

She did exactly as I'd asked. She sucked harder, faster, and deeper. I came hard into her mouth, and she took it all, moaning, as she swallowed every drop I gave.

"Jesus, woman. Where did you learn how to do that? No, wait...on second thought, don't tell me."

She crawled up my body and straddled my waist as she grinned. "Silly man, no one taught me that. We just have a natural inclination at some things."

"Well, thank God that's one of yours."

She laughed, resting her head against my still racing heart. "You were really loud," she said.

"I really don't fucking care. At least you were quiet. I don't want anyone hearing those moans but me," I said, giving her ass another slap, which caused her to yelp.

We managed to get ourselves back together by the time the limo pulled up to the first bar. We could choose from actual routes for tonight, depending on what type of pub crawl we wanted to do. I picked one of the more traditional crawls, picking establishments that had been around for years. I liked their vibe more than the upscale clubs. I also figured I had less of a chance of getting noticed in a more casual type crowd as well. The limo didn't help, but I wanted it to be special for Leah, so I took the chance. For her, I would do anything.

The first place we stopped at was known for great food, so we ate a late dinner, enjoying some of the best burgers in Richmond. We drank and talked about work. She told me about her coworkers and the deliveries she'd helped with over the last week. I updated her on how the movie was progressing and how much I enjoyed helping the director. We agreed our brains were fried, and we were both in need of a serious vacation.

"Hey, I'm supposed to attend a movie premiere in two weeks. I originally said no because I never attend them. But we could go if you want to?" I suggested.

"You're asking me if I want to go to a Hollywood movie premiere with my hot boyfriend?"

"Um, yes?"

"Are you insane? Of course I want to go. And why the hell didn't you tell me you had a movie coming out?"

"Oh, um...it didn't come up. It's not a big deal...and well, there's a sex scene."

"Oh," was all she said.

*Yeah, I probably should have brought this up sooner.*

"I wasn't sure if you'd want to see that. But we can sneak out before then if you want to go."

"No. This is what you do, and I need to support you, no matter the circumstance. We'll go, and I will be with you the entire time, holding your hand."

Stunned, all I could say was, "Okay, I'll make all the arrangements."

"One quick question, and I'm gonna kick myself for asking, but I need to know going in. Did you, um... by chance, sleep with the actress you did the sex scene with?"

"No. Fuck no," I answered.

She exhaled a breath she must have been holding for several seconds, judging from the amount of oxygen leaving her lungs.

"I've made it a personal policy to never sleep with coworkers. I've seen that shit blow up in people's faces way too many times. Plus, she drove me insane."

Finishing our dinner, we moved on to another bar, and by the third bar, we'd switched from beers to shots, wanting to celebrate the evening in style. That was when Leah had the brilliant idea for a drinking game.

"Let's play Never Have I Ever!"

I groaned. "No. Hell no."

"Come on! It will be fun," she begged, her voice accentuated by the buzz of alcohol running through her veins and her eyes bright. "You remember how to play, right? I'll say, 'Never have I ever,' and then I'll follow it up with something I've never done."

"Yes, and if I've done the deed, I take the shot."

"Yep. Sounds like fun, right?"

She gave me that pretty-please look that always won me over.

I groaned. "Okay, but I'm warning you...this could get messy."

"Nah, it's going to be fun!" she exclaimed.

We ordered a line of shots and set them in front of us on the table.

"Okay, I'll go first. Never have I ever..." She looked at me, a devious smile spreading across her lips, before she said, "Shaved my balls."

I nearly choked on my own tongue, as laughter rolled out of me. I gave her a hard stare and took my first shot.

"I knew it!" she said proudly. "It was either that, or you were sneaking away for ritual waxing sessions. I didn't want to have to go kill a bitch for touching your junk. Thank you by the way. My girlie bits really appreciate the effort," she said with a wink.

I shook my head, laughing, before firing off my question. "Never have I ever...laughed so hard that I peed my pants."

It was cruel, but she had just called me out on my manscaping in the middle of a bar, so I figured she deserved some payback. I already knew the answer to the question, having heard her and Clare laughing and reminiscing one night over a bottle of rum.

She gave me a look and took her shot. "That's so not fair. I'm pretty sure guys can't even do that."

"I wouldn't know since I can hold my bladder," I teased.

"It was college, and I was drunk!" she said defensively.

I nearly fell out of my chair, laughing. "Maybe we should cut you off then!"

"Oh, I have one! Never have I ever been arrested," she said with a cocky grin.

I took a moment, letting her sweat it out, before grabbing the shot and letting it burn down my throat. She stood and did a little dance of triumph, squealing, before sitting down.

"Every bad boy has to have a back story, so spill it, Hotshot."

"It was only once —disorderly conduct at a party. I was in high school, and my dad got me out without much fuss. It was all very uneventful. But it did make me quite popular for a few weeks." I grinned. "Does it make me sexier, Leah?"

"Well, it would have been hotter if it were a bar brawl or something, but it will do."

I shook my head, chuckling. "I'll try harder next time. Okay, my turn. Never have I ever experimented with someone of the same sex."

She hesitated for a second before saying, "It was only once," and then she downed the shot.

"Holy shit...I want details. Now."

"College. Clare and I had a third roommate our sophomore year, and one night, when we got a little too drunk, we...well —"

"What? You, what?" I asked, hanging on every word.

"Oh my God, Declan, I'm fucking with you." She laughed. "It was worth the shot though."

"You're going to pay for that one," I promised.

"Can't wait, Hotshot. My turn," she said.

"Nope. I get to go again because you cheated."

"Okay, fair enough. Go ahead."

"Never have I ever...TP'd a house."

She quickly took her shot and then said, "Seriously? They didn't TP houses in your uppity neighborhood?"

"Nope."

"Well, shit. I just figured out what we are doing for the Leah part of the evening!"


LEAH

The cashier at the twenty-four-hour grocery store gave us quite a look when we checked out with two entire carts filled with toilet paper and nothing else. We tried not to laugh, but I was sure she suspected our devious plans. She didn't say a thing though as she quietly rang up our purchase.

We wheeled our two carts to the limo and loaded the back. The limo driver never said a word. He just opened the trunk, and when that was packed full, he helped us throw packs of toilet paper in the backseat with us. I hoped Declan would tip him well for putting up with our drunken madness. We sat in the back amidst the piles of toilet paper as I gave the directions to our victim's house. We spent the car ride unwrapping each roll, so they would be ready to go. We made sure the driver parked across the street before we pulled up near the house. No lights were on, and no cars were parked in the front, making me think the owners were out enjoying the night's festivities.

"Whose house are we at anyway?" Declan asked as we finished unwrapping the toilet paper.

The floor of the once pristine limo was now covered

in plastic wrappers and pretty white rolls of toilet paper. *Classy.*

"My ex-boyfriend, Daniel. This is the house he bought with his wife, the woman he started dating a week after he left me. I've always wanted to do something really juvenile to him for walking out when Ethan got sick, so this is the perfect opportunity."

"Do you want me to just punch him instead? Because I'd be really happy to do that. We could just save the toilet paper. I'm sure we could stockpile it in the event of a nuclear war."

"No, this will be way more fun. Besides, if he hadn't left me, I'd probably be out somewhere with him, listening to his boring stories about his job or what he did at the gym. He did me a favor," I said.

"That might be true, but I'd still like to kick his ass," he agreed before bending his head to place a tender kiss on my lips. "Well, why don't you come help me cover his house in ass paper instead?" I whispered.

"Gladly."

We quietly exited the limo, making sure to close the door as softly as possible. The driver, Max, actually volunteered to help us. He was a pretty cool guy. He was in his late fifties with salt-and-pepper hair and a Harley Davidson attitude that didn't quite match the suit attire he was wearing for the evening. We thanked him but declined, not wanting him to lose his job if we got caught.

Daniel and his wife, Mindy, might not be home, but that didn't mean their neighbors weren't. I zipped up my jacket, trying to ward off the cold and cover up the white tank I had on underneath. Luckily, we had both worn dark clothing, so we faded into the night fairly easily. January was cold on the East Coast, and New Year's Eve was no exception. I could see my breath puffing out in front of me as we made our way across the street, our arms loaded with rolls of fluffy white toilet paper. The frosted grass crunched under our steps.

"So, is this a crime? Could we get tossed into jail for this?" Declan asked quietly.

"Mmm, I don't know," I whispered back.

"That would be an interesting headline —Hollywood Actor Arrested for Vandalism. Weapon of Choice? Toilet Paper."

When we got to the middle of Daniel's front yard, we dumped our load, and I started giving directions. "Okay, let's do the trees first. You need to give yourself a bit of a lead, pull some out...there you go...and then chuck the roll over the limb."

We both hurled our rolls over the tree branches and watched them land on the other side. Giving each other goofy grins, we raced to the other side and grabbed our rolls to repeat the process. In a matter of minutes, we had the trees covered in white. It was the worst re-creation of a white Christmas ever.

For Daniel's beautifully decorated bushes, I stuffed wads of toilet paper in between the branches, like little paper flowers. Those would be a bitch to pull out in the morning, especially if they got wet and frosted over. I might have snickered a bit as I hopped from bush to bush. Last was the house. I really wanted to get the rolls on the house, but I didn't think I could throw that far.

"Hey, do you think you can throw a roll over and clear the house?"

Declan gave me a look that said I should never doubt him as he grabbed a roll and took a few steps back. He let it sail, clearing the house and leaving a brilliant white streak over the top of the roof.

"Yes! Now, do that twenty more times!" I said quietly, jumping up and down.

He silently laughed, doing as I'd asked, taking every last roll we had and throwing them over the roof. Just as the last roll cleared the roof, I heard a nearby house explode in an array of voices, all chanting, at what must have been a party as they started counting down.

"It's almost midnight!" I said excitedly.

"Well then, you better get your ass over here and kiss me."

I ran to him and jumped into his arms, wrapping my legs around him, just as the voices got to one.

Everyone at the party nearby yelled, "Happy New Year!" at the same time my lips met Declan's.

His fingers curled into my hair as he devoured me. Every part of me was freezing, but my lips felt like they were on fire the minute they'd touched his.

I could have stayed like that forever, ringing in the New Year in Declan's arms, but as I did, I noticed the voices from the party starting to grow louder. Declan must have heard them as well because he pulled back. We looked around and saw the neighbor's party was spilling out onto the lawn. A few of them were pointing to our toilet-paper masterpiece.

"Oh shit! We better go!" I said, laughing.

We ran to the limo, and Max took off just before Daniel's neighbor made it across the street. We were both laughing so hard, and I couldn't breathe.

"Well, there is one thing I am absolutely sure of. Life with you will never be dull."

"Right back at you, Hotshot."

Now, if we could just figure out how to rearrange the states, so Virginia and California shared a border. Then, we wouldn't have a single care in the world.

# Chapter Sixteen



"Not only have you ruined me for other men, but you've seriously ruined flying for me as well. I'm not going to be able to fly anything less than first class from now on." I snuggled into the oversized leather seat as I pulled the plush blanket tighter around my lap.

This was how flying should be. No one had stepped on my feet, knocked my elbows with a cart, or kicked the back of my chair. It was bliss.

"I've ruined you for all other men?" Declan grinned.

"Shit, you weren't supposed to know that."

"Really? Why? I'm very happy, knowing you're inevitably ruined for all eternity for all other men but me," he bragged.

"See? Exactly. You're already too cocky as it is. Too much more and your head will explode. Then, where will I be?"

He gave me a lopsided grin and leaned over to kiss my shoulder, which was very much looking forward to seeing the sun for the first time in months. While it wasn't hot in January in California, it definitely wasn't winter-coat weather. Declan had promised to take me to the beach and the Walk of Fame. He'd even said he would take me shopping in Beverly Hills. Dating a movie star definitely had its perks.

When the flight attendant came on the intercom and announced our final descent into LAX, I squealed like a schoolgirl. I'd never been to the West Coast. Hell, I'd barely made it out of Virginia. Staying across the country for a few days was definitely the most adventurous thing I had ever done.

"It's a shame you're not excited," Declan teased.

I stuck my tongue out at him, and he laughed.

"Shut up. Give me a moment, and I will go back to calm-and-collected Leah. I promise that I won't embarrass you when all your adoring fans meet us at the gate."

"I'm afraid TV and movies have lied to you a bit on that. For the most part, rabid fans and paparazzi don't hang out at the airport. It's a waste of time to sit around, hoping a celebrity will come in on a flight. They go where the tips are, so we should be able to cruise in without a problem."

"So, I get you all to myself for a little longer?"

"Yep," he answered, grinning.

"Good."

I leaned over and kissed him far too deeply for public, but I didn't care. Everyone in first class was either asleep or too wrapped up in his or her own business to pay attention to us. I wanted nothing more than to enjoy the feel of Declan's lips on mine.

A few minutes later, our plane landed smoothly, and we did the first thing everyone does nowadays when the wheels hit the pavement. We both reached down to our stowed bags under our seats and immediately turned on our phones. I looked around, and every single person was doing the same thing. Checking out from the world for several hours should seem like a present, but we'd all grabbed our phones like our lives depended on it, making sure the world was exactly the same as we'd left it.

My iPhone finished booting up, and I had a funny text from Clare and a few emails. Declan's phone beeped. I saw him pull up several text messages, and then he cursed.

"What is it?" I asked, concerned.

"Looks like I've been outed on the Internet by someone who saw us on the plane. My publicist says a few cameras are waiting for us at baggage claim. Sorry, babe. It's not quite the quiet introduction to Cali you were hoping for."

"It's okay. It was bound to happen anyway. Might as well dive right in. Do you want me to hang back and let you go first?" I asked, not knowing how this whole press thing worked.

I didn't know if he wanted us *out* or not. I was honestly fine with either. I didn't know the life he had to deal with, and I didn't want to cause further stress by forcing him into something.

"What are you talking about? You will walk with me, always with me. Got it?"

I nodded, watching him bring my hand to his lips in a sweet gesture, before we had to exit the plane. We made our way off the plane and through the gate. A few fans were waiting for him. Apparently, passengers from other flights had found out about Declan's arrival. He immediately wrapped his arm around me as he greeted them, making his taken status very obvious. Even when he leaned over to sign a few autographs, he still held my hand.

We made our way through the rest of the airport and down to baggage claim. Just as we were about to leave the security area, he gave me one final look.

"You ready for this?" he asked.

I nodded, and he grinned.

"Welcome to the jungle, babe."

He wasn't kidding. As soon as we were off the escalator, they were on us —three or four cameras with men shouting questions. Declan was as cool as a cucumber. With his arm around my waist, he greeted them politely and answered a few questions.

"Hey, Declan, welcome home. Who's the blonde?"

"Thanks, Eddie. This lovely lady would be my girlfriend, and it's her first trip to L.A., so I would appreciate you gentlemen giving us a bit of space while I try to show her a good time," he said with a wink.

They laughed and gave us some room as we grabbed our bags. We headed out the door, and they followed, of course, asking a few more questions and flashing pictures of us. The driver Declan had hired loaded the car, and I made my way inside.

"Hey, Declan, give us a kiss, will ya? Something for the papers?"

"Sorry, guys. I'm not pimping my woman out for your paycheck. Have a nice day."

He joined me in the car, and we were off.

"Oh my God, is that what this place is like for you all the time?"

"Hmmm...not all the time, but yeah, pretty much."

I was shocked, completely shocked. His life was totally different. In Virginia, he'd been recognized a number of times when we'd been out, but for the most part, we had just gone about our normal lives. He had even gone to the grocery store with me.

"And you were so calm about it," I said.

"I've had a lot of practice by now, but enough of that. You've gotten your first paparazzi mob out of the way now." He grinned. "What do you want to do now?"

"I want to go to the beach! No, wait! I want to see your house!"

"Well, you're in luck. I can grant both of those wishes in one stop."


DECLAN

I never knew why I bought this big house until I heard Leah scream in glee when we pulled up to the driveway.

"Are you fucking kidding me right now? You live on the beach? Why did I not know this about you?"

I just shrugged. Since I'd bought it a year ago, I'd probably spent less than half that actually living here.

"Well, don't just sit here. I want to see this place!"

The driver carried our bags inside, and then I handed over a large tip, thanking him for his help. When I returned, Leah was in the foyer, looking out the floor-to-ceiling windows at the panoramic view of the Pacific.

"Holy shit. It's breathtaking. Can we have dinner right here? We can eat on the floor. I don't want to move from this spot."

"The master bedroom has the same view," I said passively.

Her eyes turned to me, and she looked around until she located the stairs. She took off and ran up them so quickly that I could barely catch up. She made a beeline for the guest room, but then she passed it by and went straight for the master. Decorated in steel gray, tans, whites, and various shades of blue, it matched the view perfectly. It was like an extension of the beauty nature had on display outside.

"So, I may not know a lot about actors, but I'm fairly sure that a house like this isn't cheap. I'm also pretty sure it is probably in the salary range of someone a bit more, um..."

"Famous?" I guessed.

"I was going to go with established, but yeah. Seriously, Declan, what gives? I know you've got to make good money, but this is stupid money rich. Unless they paid you twenty million for that sex scene I'll have to suffer through tomorrow, I really am at a loss here."

"It's called inheritance."

"Really?"

"Yes. My father, the jackass that he was, left his entire net worth, which was a lot by the way, to me. Since he was divorced from my mother at this time, she didn't get a cent, and he made sure of it. But the will didn't prevent me from giving over any of my inheritance to her, so I split it with her."

"And you still had enough to buy this house from Brad Pitt?" I joked.

"First of all, I didn't buy it from Brad Pitt. It was Will Smith's, and secondly, yes, plenty more."

Her eyes bugged out so fast that I couldn't help but laugh.

"I'm kidding...about the Will Smith thing. You were about to go all fangirl on me, weren't you?"

"Don't kid when it comes to celebrities."

"You know, I'm a celebrity," I said smoothly.

"Yeah, but I've heard you pee, and now, all the mystery and allure is gone." She shrugged.

"You have not heard me pee!"

"Have to. You pee with the door open at night, and guy pee is really loud."

"This conversation has taken a really weird turn."

"Just trying to make sure your head doesn't blow up, Hotshot." She grinned.

"You're so sweet."

I came up behind her and wrapped my arms around her as we watched the waves crash into the surf. This beach was privately owned, so only a few people were scattered along the shoreline, mostly runners and walkers. Surfers usually took to the waves in the early morning.

"You got your gigantic inheritance and bought a huge house, so you'd have a swanky place to bring home the ladies?"

I gripped her waist and swung her around until we were nose-to-nose.

"Is that your not-so-subtle way of asking whether you're the first woman I've brought here?"

"Maybe. Now, I'm starting to regret asking it because that bed looks so comfortable, and I really don't want to ruin it with an image of another woman rubbing her skanky body all over it."

"Leah..."

"Hmm?" she said, looking at the bed like it suddenly sprouted horns and bat wings.

"I've never brought anyone here but you."

Her head snapped back to me. "Promise?"

"Promise," I assured her.

"Oh, thank God," she squealed, leaping out of my arms and onto the bed.

"Ditched for my own bed. That's a first."

"You could join me, you know," she said suggestively.

I jumped on top of her, causing her to laugh.

"So...why? I mean, I'm beyond relieved, but I'm not dumb enough to believe that you've been a saint since purchasing this house, so I've got to know why you wouldn't use your bachelor pad for...well, bacheloring."

"Honestly, it's kind of a dickhead reason. But you asked. If I were to take a woman home, she would know where I lived, and then she could track me down. I didn't want any ties or strings with anyone...until you." I smiled. "It was easier to keep where I lived out of it."

"Wow, you were kind of a douche, Declan James."

"I'm a reformed douche," I amended.

"Yes, a reformed douche. Now, why don't we take this

bed for a test ride? Then, you can take me on my romantic walk on the beach."

I slowly unbuttoned her shirt to be greeted by a sheer pale pink bra that left nothing to the imagination as I agreed, "You've got yourself a deal."

# Chapter Seventeen

LEAH

There were so many light bulbs.

They flashed and flared, memorizing our every move from the second we arrived, and their reign over the event seemed endless. I didn't think I'd be able to see straight for years.

Declan and I had spent a magical twenty-four hours in Los Angeles. We had taken a moonlit walk on the beach where I'd dipped my toes into the Pacific Ocean for the first time. *Holy fuck, it was cold. How did people swim in that water?* When Declan had threatened to throw me in, I'd sworn that I would never wear lipstick again. That had ended the water threats in a heartbeat.

He had woken me up with breakfast in bed, bringing me an omelet with fresh avocado and a side of strawberries from a local farm. I'd understood why California was known for their produce. It was amazing. When I had felt pleasantly stuffed, he'd taken me shopping on Rodeo

Drive. I'd felt like I'd stepped into a scene from *Pretty Woman* —minus the fact that I was not Julia Roberts or a hooker.

But the shopping had been similar. He wouldn't let me look at any price tags, and he'd told me the sky was the limit. He'd sat back and let me play dress-up for him for hours. Never once had he gotten bored. He'd watched me come out of the dressing room, wearing each dress, and his eyes would darken and flare with heat. I hadn't known shopping could turn a man on so much. In fact, at one point, he'd asked the woman assisting me for a few moments alone, so he could help me decide, and instead, we'd gotten busy in the dressing room. Yep, I'd had sex in a dressing room on Rodeo Drive. I was such a classy slut.

And now, one dress, a pair of ridiculously expensive shoes, and a professional hair and makeup session later, we had arrived to an actual Hollywood movie premiere.

All I could think was, *Don't fall, don't fall.*

As if sensing my nervousness, Declan leaned his head toward mine as his arm wrapped possessively around my waist. "You look breathtaking. You'll be fine. Just smile, and I'll do the rest."

I nodded, and to my surprise, he gave me a tender kiss before we entered the press area where the vultures would descend.

First, I felt actual pity for celebrities because they had to stand for that long and smile. It was agonizing. My face felt like it was going to cramp, and of course, we had to endure even more attention and scrutiny because Declan had never, ever brought someone to an event. He apparently very rarely ever showed up to events at all, so this was big news.

The last twenty-four hours had really opened my eyes. I knew, in the back of my head, that Declan was famous, that he was well known. This had been confirmed every time we had walked down the street or had been stopped in a store. But people in Virginia were different about it. They were polite, shy even. When they had approached him, they had been hesitant as if they couldn't really comprehend it was him right there in front of them.

Here, people held nothing back. Cameras were in his face whether they were held by a news crew, paparazzi, or fans. People wanted pictures with him everywhere we went. And, oh my God, the screaming —I couldn't get over the screaming. As soon as we exited the limo, women cried out blood-curdling screams. It was deafening.

We made our way through the flashing lights, stopping every so often to smile and pose again. Declan never strayed from my side. His arm was firmly fastened to my waist. He was announcing our status loud and clear, and I liked it —a lot.

As we walked by the screeching fans, yelling things like, "Marry me, Declan," and other things I'd rather not say, I might have slid my hand resting on his waist a bit lower, slipping it into the pocket of his suit pants over his firm ass. Declan looked over at me, giving me an arched brow, and I just smirked.

"Being a little evil tonight, aren't we?" he seductively whispered in my ear.

"Just making sure they understand you're taken."

"Well then, you should do it properly."

Pulling me to him, he slowly kissed me, wrapping his fingers from one hand around my neck while the other hand went around my waist. I swore I heard the crowd sigh. He turned back to the puddle of goo that used to be the crowd and flashed his award-winning smile as he gave a wink.

"Sorry, ladies. I just couldn't help myself. Love does crazy things to a man."

And just like that, the previously rabid fans were now the charter members of the Decah Fan Club.

Giving me a smug grin, we made our exit from the crowds and walked toward my most feared part of the night —well, besides the sex scene —the interviews. *What if they asked me shit, and I sounded stupid? What if I embarrassed Declan?*

He squeezed my hand in reassurance as he told me that I was doing fantastic, and we took the last few steps to his first interview. An overly made-up woman started firing off questions, and Declan handled her like a pro. The first were a series of questions about the movie, so I relaxed a bit.

This movie, *Crossroads*, was about a love triangle, and Declan had explained that he was not the chosen one in the end. The heroine, trying to decide between her bad-boy neighbor and her long-lost love, finally comes to her senses in the end...but not before she shakes a few walls with my boyfriend. *I was totally looking forward to witnessing that.*

The interviewer asked why Declan had chosen the movie and how he enjoyed his costar. He was polite and said she had been a delight to work with. I hid my smile, remembering him describe her as a pain in the ass.

Finally, running out of relevant questions, the woman looked to me. "And I see you've brought a date, Declan! Care to introduce us to the new woman in your life?"

He looked at me and grinned. "This is my lovely girlfriend, Leah, joining me tonight."

And then came the question Declan had prepared me for. "And what are you wearing, Leah?"

Apparently, this was the most important question of the evening, and Declan had told me to be prepared to repeat it over and over again.

I answered quickly, remembering the designer of my gorgeous floor-length, mermaid-style red dress that fit me like a glove and made my ass and boobs look like a million bucks. This was the dress that had Declan attacking me in the dressing room.

The interviewer smiled before saying I looked beautiful, and then she wished us a lovely evening.

*Holy shit, it was over.*

Until we had to go to the next one.

But I made it through all of them without tripping over my words. I'd even managed to answer a few questions outside of my wardrobe. It had gotten easier, and I'd learned to ignore the camera —for the most part.

"Who the hell are you?" Declan said as we made our way into the theater.

"What do you mean?" I asked, suddenly concerned I'd done something wrong.

"That was amazing. You were smooth, cool, and

collected, and you had those interviewers eating out of the palm of your hand. It was fucking hot."

A sly grin spread across my face. "Did you learn a thing or two, Hotshot?"

"Let's not get ahead of ourselves, babe. Don't want your head to explode."

Once inside, Declan saw someone he needed to have a word with, and he asked if I'd be all right for a minute by myself. I assured him that I would be fine, and I was a big girl, so he ran off to talk shop for a minute. I took the opportunity to run to the ladies' room to touch up my makeup and use the restroom. I had no idea how long it would take to wrestle out of this dress.

After finishing my business and managing to suck my body back into the dress, I was touching up my makeup when the restroom door opened, and I was face-to-face with Melody Quinn, Declan's costar and the woman I'd have to witness him having fake sex with in a matter of minutes.

She looked regal and elegant in a dark blue gown that made her sapphire eyes shimmer against her ivory skin. The long black ebony hair she was known for was cascading down her back in perfect waves. I suddenly felt inadequate next to all of her upscale sophistication.

"You are Declan's date?" she asked, showing off a dazzling smile.

"Yes, his girlfriend actually," I corrected.

"Girlfriend? Oh, please, honey. Is that what he told you? He told me the same thing when I fell into his bed, and then he left me just as fast. That man doesn't even know the meaning of the word."

My heart started racing, and I felt light-headed. I looked at her as she placed an arm on my shoulder, giving it a light squeeze. She gave me a sad look as she tried to comfort me.

"Oh God, I see I've upset you. I didn't mean to be so blunt. I didn't know you were so attached. Oh, sweetie, here...let me help you get a cab. We'll get you out of here before he even knows you've left!" she said brightly.

I nodded absently, walking with her, as we exited the bathroom. Everything whirled around me, and I couldn't seem to focus. *Did he lie? Why would he lie to me about something like that?*

And just like that, I stopped.

I looked at her again, and her eyes were bright and shining, like she had just won a prize. She was a good actress, but she wasn't that good.

"You know, I'm pretty sure I would have realized if Declan had slept with someone like you," I said coldly.

She started to realize that her little plan wasn't working out quite the way she'd hoped. "Oh, and why is that?"

"Well, his man parts would probably have shriveled up and died by now just from the contact. And since he's still hung like a horse and fucking me several times a day, I'd say you're lying through your teeth. So, why don't you go find some other naive newbie to play around with, bitch?"

If her eyes got any bigger, they were going to pop right out of her Botox-filled head. She turned and stormed off, like I'd just taken her favorite toy away in the sandbox.

Laughing silently to myself, I realized I was in the

exact place where Declan had left me. He came sauntering up, looking hot as ever in his black Armani suit.

He leaned in and gave me a kiss on the collarbone, completely oblivious to the verbal fight I'd just had. "Sorry it took so long. We good here?" he whispered.

I just smiled back. "Yeah, we're great."


DECLAN

If I wasn't convinced before, I was now one hundred percent sure that Leah could do anything, hold her own anywhere, and master any situation. I had basically just thrown her into the lion's den, and she had come out completely unscathed. Right around the last turn into the event, as the limo had pulled into the front, I had seriously started to doubt my sanity in bringing her here.

We had been happy in our own secluded little part of the world, away from my crazy life. Why would I willingly bring her here? She knew me and loved me the way I was in Virginia, but here, it was a completely different world. What if she panicked and couldn't handle the life I had? I could lose her in an instant.

But, like so many times before, I'd underestimated this amazing woman I'd fallen in love with. I could tell she had been feeling nervous. I could see it in her eyes and the way she had constantly kept fidgeting with her hands, but she'd stepped up and took charge, learning the twisted game as we went. Every step we had taken, she'd become more confident, more sure of herself, and I had fallen even more in love with her. She had taken my crazy, chaotic life and had run with it, holding my hand as my partner. It was humbling.

I'd even felt confident to leave her for a few minutes, stepping away so I could talk to a director I'd been hoping to get a word with. Those few minutes had paid off, and I thought I had my chance to get a very important foot in the door. As I'd returned, Leah might not have noticed that I had seen her putting my costar Melody in place, but I had. I'd worked with Melody for a few weeks, so I knew her various faces and moods, and I knew when she was pissed. I didn't know why Leah hadn't wanted to share her run-in, but from the smile on her face, I could only guess that she had been the victor, which didn't surprise me. Leah could hold her own —I had no doubt about that.

With my arm on the small of her back, I ushered her to our seats just before the lights dimmed. I was nervous. I hated seeing myself in films. It was weird, and I constantly criticized every move, action, and word, wondering if I could have done it better, different. It was maddening. Plus, this film included my first sex scene, and to add to that, I'd brought the woman I loved.

*God, I was an idiot. I should just go now.*

"You okay, Hotshot?" Leah whispered as the opening credits began.

I nodded, but she leaned in further.

"You're nervous." It wasn't a question.

She weaved her fingers through mine, and I savored the warmth of her delicate skin. Taking a deep breath, I tried to calm myself as the movie began.

I was a secondary character, and I didn't come into the storyline until about midway, so watching up until that part was easy. My foot bounced in anticipation, knowing my scenes were coming up soon.

When Melody's character went to her next door neighbor's door and knocked, I appeared, and I wanted to throw up. *Fuck, I needed to leave.* This was why I usually ducked out when the movie started or why I wouldn't show up at all. Maybe this was a sign that I hadn't been made for acting. When I couldn't even sit in the same theater and watch my own film, hating every word I said, every gesture I gave, perhaps it was a clue that I was meant for something else.

Her eyes never leaving the movie screen, Leah's hand ran down my thigh as she whispered in my ear, "You look so fucking sexy."

It was exactly what I needed to hear to break the tension running through my body. Her voice was the calm that helped me come back down from my epic freak-out. Relaxing, I countered, "Yeah, how sexy?"

"So sexy, I'm wondering why we've never watched one of your movies before. That could be fun."

"We'll put that on the schedule, babe."

Watching the movie with Leah as she whispered in my ear and ran her hand down my thigh made the minutes go by quickly, and before I knew it, we were at the part I had been dreading. I recognized it immediately when Leah's entire body tensed. Her fingernails dug into the fabric of my pants, and she gasped. Just as Melody and I were about to go at it, Leah's eyes darted down from the screen, and her breathing increased. It wasn't a warm, gentle love scene. I was the side road the heroine took on her way to true love. We fucked, and for everyone in the theater, I was sure it was hot. For the two of us though, it was torture.

Leah was shutting down, and I didn't blame her. Movies today did a very good job of making love scenes look real, and in her mind, all she could picture was what was on that screen and how authentic it appeared.

"Hey."

No answer.

"Leah, look at me," I whispered.

She blinked, looking at me finally.

"Close your eyes, and shut it out," I said gently. "Focus on my voice, and on the feel of my hands. I'm here with you, no one else."

Eyes still closed, she nodded and took a steady deep breath.

"You are the only woman I want. You and I are real. I could do a hundred scenes like this, and none of them would ever change the way I feel about you. You're it for me. I love you, Leah —only and always you."

She opened her eyes, finally catching my gaze, no longer focused on the movie. Everything else disappeared —the theater, the people around us. It was just her as she said the four words I would spend the rest of my life making her never regret.

"I love you, too."

## Chapter Eighteen



We skipped the after-party, taking our leave shortly after the ending credits. I thought we'd both had enough socializing for the evening.

Seeing Declan on the big screen wasn't a new experience for me. I'd seen every movie he'd done. But that had been all before I actually knew him, before he'd walked into that bar so many months ago and completely changed my life.

Seeing him act now was completely different. I knew his mannerisms, his smile, and his laugh now. I knew every expression he displayed, and now, when I saw his movies, I could tell he was acting. It was Declan in the movie, but it wasn't him. Because of this, while watching him on the big screen now, I'd felt an overwhelming sense of pride. I could see the talent and power he had when he acted, knowing he wasn't just regurgitating lines but actually taking on his character. It was completely engrossing, and I'd gotten swept away when watching him.

Until the sex scene. I had been so invested in my sexy conversation with Declan and watching his character on the screen, that the love scene had completely blindsided me. I didn't know why. It wasn't like it had come out of left field. It had quite the normal buildup.

*God, it had been awful.* It had felt like walking in on my boyfriend doing it with another woman, except I'd gotten to see it in twelve different angles with perfect lighting as it was set to music. It had been a horrid experience.

When Declan had turned to me and told me to tune it all out, I had. I'd shut it all off, focusing on his voice and the feel of his touch. He'd brought me back to reality, reminding me that in the real world, he was mine. When I'd tried to apologize for freaking out on him, he'd covered my mouth with his, ending my attempts before they could even begin.

In the limo ride home, Declan said he was starving, and I agreed. I hadn't wanted to eat before the event. I had felt too scared that I wouldn't fit into my dress. So Declan had the driver take us to this hole-in-the-wall Mexican place. I raised my eyebrows when we pulled in. He just laughed, gave me a quick kiss, and said he'd be back in a few minutes. I was just glad he wasn't making me go in. I'd look a little ridiculous ordering tacos in my ruby red ensemble. After about ten minutes of putzing around on my phone, Declan popped back in with two bags of food, and then we were on our way. We got back to his place, and a few minutes later, he was spreading out the food on the coffee table in the spacious living room overlooking the ocean.

I looked down at my dress before taking another glance at the food. I needed to change, but I was so damn hungry.

"Declan, can you unzip me?"

"Yes. The answer to that question is always yes," he joked.

He came over and slowly unzipped my dress, placing a sweet kiss on the sensitive skin of my neck as he did so.

"Thank you." I turned and shrugged out of my dress, letting it fall to the floor.

Wearing nothing but a lace thong since my dress came with a built in bra, I headed over to the coffee table and sat down on the floor. Declan stared at me, dumbfounded.

"What?" I asked innocently.

"You're seriously going to eat like that?"

"Well, you didn't think I was going to eat greasy tacos in a three-thousand dollar dress, did you?"

"That's an excellent point. I shouldn't be eating tacos in Armani either."

He made quick work of his jacket, shoes, socks, pants, and shirt. He left nothing on but a black pair of boxers that hung low on his hips. I bit my lip when he turned, and I saw the top of his rock-hard butt cheek peeking out of his waistband. *The jerk probably did that on purpose.*

"So, shall we eat?" He grinned.

"Absolutely." I smiled. I couldn't wait to see who caved first.

"So, why did we stop by a Mexican joint in a limo, sporting formalwear?"

"This is not just any Mexican food. This is the best Mexican food ever."

"Um, okay. That's some serious passion about Mexican food. You know we have Mexican food in Virginia, right?" I argued.

"No, no, you don't. You have food that pretends to be Mexican food. This? This is the real deal."

"Okay. You sound a bit crazy, but I'll try it."

He was right. It was better. The smug bastard laughed, too, when I moaned after biting into a taco. Of course, that moan was also his undoing, and I threw a couple more in there for the fun of it. He lost it and tackled me to the ground, the food completely forgotten. We rolled around, kissing and laughing, until suddenly, Declan sobered. He rose above me, his eyes full of passion and purpose.

"You drive me crazy —all day, every day. I can never get enough. You are my first thought when I awake and the last as I drift off to sleep. I can't imagine how I existed without you, Leah, and for once in my life, I don't want to be alone anymore. Don't ever leave me. Please."

"How can you leave your own soul, Declan?"

He kissed me then, an earth-shattering, love-defining kind of kiss that shocked my very core.

"Make love to me," I begged.

He stood, picked me up, and carried me in his arms, heading out the double glass doors onto the wide deck facing the ocean. It was dark, but we could still hear the waves crashing against the shore.

He placed me on a chaise lounge and laid his warm body on mine. Rising to his knees, he slid my panties down my hips and dropped them to the ground. Needing to feel all of him, I peeled away his boxers, loving the way the moonlight highlighted the toned muscles of his body.

"I love you," he said softly as our bodies became one.

"I love you," I answered back.

Then, he kissed me fiercely, claiming me with his body and heart.

We made love under the stars, loving each other's bodies for hours. Afterward, I lay in his arms, enjoying the sounds of the ocean and the beat of his heart.

"I'm going to sell my house," Declan said, breaking the silence.

"What? Why?" I asked, panicked, rising to face him.

"Because I'm moving. That's what people generally do when they move."

"You're moving? Where? When?"

Panic started to seep into every molecule. *He was moving? Where? Why didn't he tell me?*

"Leah, I'm moving to Virginia —permanently."

"What? How can you do that?"

"Does it matter? My life means nothing if you aren't in it."

Tears blurred my eyes, and I felt them falling down my cheek. *Why did this man always make me cry?* "But what about directing? Your career?"

"I'm figuring it out. I've got a couple of things lined up. One thing I do know is that they have these fancy inventions called planes, and I can fly here if I need to. Plenty of actors and directors live outside of L.A., and they do perfectly fine. I can, too."

"Oh my God, are you sure? You have to be sure...because I'm not giving you back," I said, unable to believe this was happening.

"I've never been more sure of anything in my life."

"Okay, but one thing…"

"Anything," he answered, chuckling.

"One, don't sell the house," I pleaded.

"Why?"

"It's too pretty. I seriously love this house. Let's keep it as a winter house or whatever the hell you want to call it. You'll need some place to stay when you fly in anyway. Just don't get rid of my view…I mean, the view."

He laughed but agreed. We spent the next hour making plans of when, how, and what he would move. I'd never lived with a boy before. *That would be fun.*

We made our way inside and started getting ready for bed even though it was bordering on morning now.

"Hey, can I borrow a sweatshirt? I'm freezing from being outside for so long."

"Yeah, second drawer."

He continued to talk about his moving plans as I rummaged around in his drawer, getting caught up in all of his old sweatshirts —college sweatshirts, team sweatshirts. He even had a Planet Hollywood sweatshirt, which I found adorable. I chose that one and pulled it from the bottom of the stack, making a mess. Stuff spilled out of the drawer, and I bent over to pick it all up.

Several photographs fell during my epic mess-making, and I gathered them up before stuffing them back into the drawer, but the one on top caught my eye as I was shutting the drawer. The face —I recognized it. I pulled the photo back out and stared at it.

She was beautiful with long light brown hair and bright eyes. She looked younger than when I'd seen her. *But where did I recognize her from? And why would I recognize someone Declan had a photo of?*

"Hey, Declan. Who's this?"

"Oh, that's Heather, my ex-girlfriend from college," he answered, joining me from across the room.

I stared at it a second longer as Declan watched me. I was sure he was worried that I was going to go all jealous girlfriend on him, but I couldn't figure out that face.

The photo was haunting, and I couldn't place where I'd seen that face before.

*The photo...*a memory started to surface at the edge of my mind.

*The boy...the boy in the hospital...the photo he'd had in his hand...the one from the fair of him and his mother.*

The mother that had died. It was her.

Heather was dead, and I needed to tell Declan.

An image of the boy's eyes flashed through my memory, and I suddenly felt sick. I remembered sitting with the boy, thinking his eyes looked so familiar.

I turned and looked into Declan's eyes —the eyes I'd stared into a million times, fallen in love with, and memorized, so I could dream of them when I slept.

*Oh God, they were the same.*

"How long ago did you break up?" I asked, feeling my hands begin to shake.

"Uh, hmmm...well, I was twenty-four, so about eight years ago, a little less maybe. Why?"

Just then, he saw my hands shaking and my panicked expression.

"Leah, what is it? You're freaking me out here."

"I think you have a son."

DECLAN

I would have thought it was some sort of joke, but Leah looked destroyed as the words tumbled out of her mouth.

"What are you saying? I don't understand," I asked, taking her shaking hands in mine, trying to make sense of the fright and panic in her eyes.

Her chest was heaving so hard, I thought she might hyperventilate. I pulled her into my arms and sat us on the bed as I stroked her hair while tears fell from her eyes.

She took a deep breath and began her story. "It was the night you came back into town. I was just getting off my shift at the hospital. Logan called me and said there had been a horrible accident, and the woman driving had died. Declan, it was her. It was Heather. I didn't know at the time, but I recognize her now from this picture."

I hadn't seen Heather in eight years, but hearing she was gone killed me. "How?" was all I could manage, my voice coming out rough and gravely.

"Trucker fell asleep at the wheel and veered off into oncoming traffic. Heather didn't have a chance. She tried to save them, but she ended up driving head-on into a tree."

"Them? It was more than just Heather?"

"Declan, she had a child with her —your child."

"I do not have a child. I would know," I said adamantly. "I haven't seen or heard from her in eight years. She would have told me, came to me, included me."

Leah looked at me with such sad eyes as she placed her hand gently on my cheek. "He had your eyes, Declan. He was seven, and he looked like you."

"No," I whispered. "No!" I shouted, rising from the bed, needing space.

"I'm so sorry, Declan. I'm so sorry."

I couldn't deal. I started throwing on clothes and shoes, not having any idea of what I was doing. I needed out. There was too much to process —Heather's death, a son. My mind shut down, and I ran. I tore down the stairs to the bottom level and out the sliding door to the beach where I kept running. I ran until my lungs burned, and my face was numb from the constant wind. When that wasn't far enough, I ran farther.

Finally, after what seemed like forever, I stopped. I looked around, but nothing looked familiar. I must have run for miles. I didn't even have a watch or cell phone on me to see how long I'd been gone. Leah must have freaked out with my psychotic departure. I owed her an apology, but I just needed out, and I needed a bit of time alone — time to grieve, time to wrap my head around my new reality.

*Heather was gone. And I was possibly a father.*

Saying both by themselves was difficult, but saying both together was nearly impossible. I hadn't been in love with Heather for a long time, and I'd lost my anger toward her several years ago. Even at twenty-four, we had been young. I'd wanted more, and she hadn't. I'd asked her for a new life together, and she hadn't been ready, so we'd gone our separate ways. It was one of the hardest parts of my life, but I'd gotten over it. Had it not happened, I would have never found Leah, and she was the life I wanted.

But knowing Heather's life was over hurt, and I didn't know how to grieve for someone I barely remembered — especially after learning she could have borne my child and never told me. *Why would she do that?* I had been nothing but caring, loving, and dedicated with her. I would have stayed with her, given that child everything I could, but I hadn't even been given a chance. *Why?*

I was a father. *Was I?* Leah had seemed to think so, but I needed to know for sure. If that child was mine, I needed to know.

Finding my way back to the house, I quietly entered the back door and made my way up the stairs from where I'd fled hours earlier. Leah was curled up on the couch facing the panoramic window that opened out to the ocean. She had fallen asleep after probably waiting up for me. I bent down, pulled her body into mine, and carried her upstairs to our bed.

She stirred as I laid her down. Her eyes fluttered open, and she immediately pulled me into a tight hug.

"I'm so sorry. I'm so sorry, Declan." She sobbed into my shoulder.

"Shhh, it's okay. I'm sorry I scared you. I just needed to process everything, and I bolted. It was a jackass thing to leave you here."

"No, it's okay. I understand. Are you okay?"

"I don't know. I don't really know what to think right now. You said they were both in the accident? Was he injured?" I asked, realizing I'd naturally assumed he was okay until this moment.

"He was unharmed. He just had a few bumps and bruises from the seat belt."

I nodded before pulling her body against mine, needing the physical reminder of her love.

"What's his name?"

"Connor."

"Leah?"

"Yeah?"

"I need to find him."

# Chapter Nineteen



We cut our trip a day short. Neither one of us felt like frolicking on the beach after the bomb I'd dropped the night before. Declan had let me sleep most of the day, and then we took a red-eye flight out of LAX, leaving in the dead of night with little notice. It was a good thing, too. When we arrived in Atlanta to catch our connecting flight, Declan grabbed us some coffees while I stopped at a store in the airport to pick up a magazine, and then I saw my own smiling face staring back at me.

We were everywhere. The news that Declan was in love had made the front page. Suddenly, the up-and-coming bachelor actor was the source for hot gossip again.

*People* magazine had us front and center with the caption, *Declan James Finds Love in Virginia!*

The photo showed us in our elegant evening wear,

close together with our foreheads touching, as we shared a private moment —a private moment that was now everywhere. It was a beautiful picture —one that I would have normally loved to frame and display on the mantle of our fireplace, so we could see it every day as we cuddled on the couch, watching movies or eating take-out at the coffee table.

*Our fireplace. Declan was moving in with me. We were going to live together.*

*Oh God, he was still moving in with me, wasn't he?*

*What if he had changed his mind? What if what I told him last night changed everything?*

He hadn't said anything against it. But he hadn't mentioned it since either. I suddenly felt panicked over my future —a future that, not twenty-four hours ago, was secure and bright with so many possibilities. Now, I saw nothing but murky waters and uncertainties.

As much as I'd wanted to dispute that I could have been wrong, that the child could have been anyone's, I knew. Looking back, I remembered those eyes and the way I'd felt when sitting with Connor. He'd seemed so familiar, and I couldn't place it at the time. I had spent six months desperately trying to forget Declan, so it was no wonder I couldn't place the face at the time —not that it would have done any good. I didn't know Heather. I didn't know their history like I did now.

"Hey, are you ready? They just called our flight," Declan said, coming behind me as I paid for my purchase.

I nodded, and we made our way to the gate. Keeping our heads low and hats snug, I felt like a criminal trying to escape prison. But I also didn't want a scene, especially now. Declan was putting on a good face, but I knew he was a wreck inside.

He hadn't slept since I'd told him about Connor, and I was afraid if he didn't sleep soon, he would crack. He was tense and edgy. Besides travel arrangements and other superficial questions, he hadn't spoken. He was retreating into himself, and I didn't know how to help. I felt useless and guilty —guilty because I had been the cause of everything. Yes, he'd deserved to know, but I was still the one who had told him, the one who had completely altered his life.

We boarded the plane and found our seats. After stowing our bags, he didn't say a word as he lifted the armrest separating our seats. He pulled me closer, wrapping his arms around me like a lifeline. We sat like this for I didn't know how long, clinging to each other, as the plane took off, taking us away from our little oasis and back to reality...a completely unknown reality.

"How do I find him, Leah? I don't where to start."

"I'll help you. We'll find him."

"How?" he asked, sounding desperate.

"Logan said they were on the way to a friend of the family's house. That was why they were in Virginia. Did she have any friends who lived in Virginia?"

"No, not that I know of," he answered.

"Sarah? Does that name mean anything to you? When I was with Connor, he said he was going to see Sarah."

"Heather's best friend's name was Sarah. She lived in New York though...or at least, she used to. Her last name was Weaver."

"Maybe she moved?" I suggested.

"Maybe. But how would I find her now?"

"Hotshot, you have heard of Facebook, right?" I asked, raising an eyebrow.

"Mmm, yes, I've heard of it, but I don't have an account."

"What? Yes, you do. I see you post all the time."

"That's a fan page. My publicist runs it. I do not have a Facebook page on purpose. It's too easy to track me, and I would prefer to remain a bit of a mystery," he said, giving a slight smile. "So, you could find her on Facebook?"

"Yes, I think we could, assuming she has an account. Want me to look?"

He nodded, and we spent the next half an hour, thanks to the Wi-Fi on the plane, stalking Sarah Weaver on Facebook. I started off by looking up Heather, and I found her with the help of Declan. Her account was pretty well secured, only showing a small photo of her, but her friend list was still accessible. We went through it and found a Sarah Keane who lived in Williamsburg, Virginia. From there, it was as simple as looking Sarah up on Google.

"You found him," Declan said, completely astonished.

"Assuming he's still there."

"He's there. They were best friends, and Heather didn't have any other family. I don't see Heather leaving him with anyone else," he said.

I knew he was trying not to be angry with Heather because of the fact that eight years had gone by and she'd never once bothered to let him know that he had a child.

"It's okay," I said. "We'll make it right. He'll know you now."

He agreed, and for the first time in twenty-four hours, he rested his head on my chest, closed his eyes, and slept.

DECLAN

We arrived home early. It was one of the perks of taking a red-eye. Of course, my body had no idea what time it was, considering the time change and the fact that I hadn't slept more than a few hours since the night of the premiere. Stepping off the plane in Virginia, I felt like I was coming home. Even though my home, the one I owned, was in California, Virginia felt like my real home now. Leah was here, and there was no other place I wanted to be. It turns out that someone else was here, and I needed to find him —as soon as possible.

Father, dad, daddy, papa —none of those words registered in my brain. For now, he was a child I was connected to, but I still didn't feel like anyone's father. A million thoughts raced through my head as we made our way out of the airport and onto the interstate. Williamsburg was less than an hour from the airport, so I had very little time to gather my thoughts. It was like trying to pluck bits of dust scattering through the air. They were everywhere and fanning out in a million directions.

*Did Heather tell him anything about me? Did he know my name? What if he hated me already? Worse, what if I didn't exist at all? Was I ready to be a father? Did I want to be? If he was living with Sarah and her new husband, he should stay there...right? That was what Heather had wanted. But what about what I wanted? What did I want?*

*Fuck.*

Thank God Leah was driving. I didn't think I saw any of the scenery the entire way there. It was just endless trees passing by in a blur. Leaving L.A. a day early had given us an entire twenty-four hours of free time. Neither Leah nor I had to work, and rather than wait and try to put this off, we'd thought it would be better for both of us to just go now while we had the time and the courage. I needed to know if that child was my son, and I needed answers that I was hoping Sarah could give me.

The crunching gravel pulled me out of my trance, and I looked up to find us in the driveway of a Colonial brick house. It looked new, but the architecture was fitting of the historical town and surroundings. It was well kept with a porch swing and potted plants, and it looked like the perfect place to raise a child. I suddenly felt like an intruder. The boy had just lost his mother. He was probably adjusting to a new life, and here I was, about to screw that all up.

*What was I doing? I shouldn't be here.*

I turned to Leah to see her eyes were on me. She was trying to appraise the situation. Apparently, my freak-out was evident.

"I can't do this, Leah. I can't do this to him."

"Declan..."

I didn't respond. My head went to my knees, and I felt like my lungs were caving in. This was too much, too real. I was an epic fuck-up. No one deserved a father like me. Jesus, Leah's face was plastered everywhere this morning from one night out in Hollywood with me. *What would happen when the papers found out I had a secret child?* It could destroy a kid.

"Declan, look at me," Leah said firmly, causing me to turn my gaze upward. "You need to calm the fuck down. You're starting to hyperventilate. I know this is hard. I know it's a lot, but I'm here, okay? We're in this together, and whatever happens, you owe it to yourself and that little boy to get out of this car and try. Do you understand?"

She squeezed my hand, and I felt my pulse begin to slow. Her touch always calmed my nerves.

"God, I love you."

She smiled, and we eventually made our way out of the car and down the long walkway. Leah knocked on the door. It was a weekday and just past noon. If anyone were home, it wouldn't include Connor. Leah and I had figured it would be best this way, talking to Sarah first, rather than showing up, unannounced, with Connor in the house.

A few seconds passed by before a familiar brunette opened the door. It took her a minute, but the recognition appeared, and she pulled me into a tight hug.

"Declan, it's so good to see you!"

"You, too, Beanpole. How are you?"

"I hate that nickname! And as you can see, I'm not quite a beanpole anymore!" she said, wiggling her hips as she led us inside.

"No." I laughed. "You look great, Sarah."

"Turns out having a baby will work wonders on a figure if you have none."

"Congratulations are in order, I guess," I said warmly.

"Thank you. Her name is April, and she's ten months. She's down for a nap, but she should be up soon." Sarah smiled and then motioned for us to sit down in the family room. It was large and filled with baby stuff —a rocker, swing, toys.

As I looked closer, I saw a few older toys lying around —an iPod, some sort of hand held gaming device in the corner, and a few action heroes. *Connor was definitely living with them.*

"So, what brings the Hollywood star to my door today and who have you brought with you?" she asked sweetly.

I introduced Leah and they exchanges pleasantries, complimenting each other on their outfits and shoes, and all the other shit women did when they met.

"I heard about Heather," I said, trying to get to the point.

"Oh, yes, we lost her a few months ago in a car accident. She was like a sister to me, you knew that. Even after Devin whisked me away to Virginia a few years ago, we always remained close. I miss her every day."

"I'm so sorry, Sarah. I know you were like sisters. I still remember how you used to raid each other's closets and finish each other's sentences. I always envied that closeness you had."

She blinked back tears and nodded silently. "Thank you, Declan. I really appreciate you coming by to pass on your condolences. You didn't have to come all the way here to do it though."

"Well, I'm moving to Virginia permanently, so I wanted to come by and say how sorry I was. Leah's a nurse in Richmond. She works in labor and delivery."

Sarah looked a bit confused, but she smiled. She asked if we'd like anything to drink or to snack on but we politely declined. I was getting a tad annoyed with Sarah for avoiding the topic at hand. She had my son, and she was obviously going to make no attempt to tell me.

"I was lucky enough to meet Leah through my good friend, Logan. You remember Logan, right? My childhood friend? I mentioned him a time or two in college."

She nodded and started to reply, but I just continued, "Anyway, he lives in Richmond now with his wife and daughter. He's an ER doctor. He works on all sorts of trauma cases...including car accidents."

She saw my eyes narrow in on the action figures on the coffee table. Her eyes widened, and tears began spilling over.

"I'm sorry, Declan. She made me promise not to tell you, and I was just trying to be a good friend."

"Why, Sarah? Why would she do that? I deserved to know!" I roared.

"She went to visit you after she'd found out she was pregnant," Sarah said quickly.

"What? No, she didn't," I argued.

"Yes, she did. She flew to California. She said L.A. was completely different than any other place she'd ever been to, but she managed to find where you lived. She saw you coming out of your apartment. There was a woman with you, and Heather said you basically gave the woman the toss. Told her you had a great time and sent her on her way."

My jaw ticked, and I cursed under my breath. I hadn't gotten over Heather well. Getting over the heartbreak had been what had ushered in the new phase of my life where I'd spent years moving from one woman to the next, never allowing myself to get too close. I'd been too afraid that I would get hurt again.

"So, she left? Without talking to me?"

"You have to understand, Declan. She had a baby on the way, and she was scared you weren't the same man. She had to make a choice, and she chose to protect her child."

"She chose wrong, Sarah. No matter what was going on in my personal life, I would have done anything for him, anything."

"I tried to change her mind," she said.

I picked up the action figure and held it in my hand, wondering what he looked like when he would play with it. I wanted to know everything about him. What kind of music did he like? Did he like Mexican food? Did he like watching movies?

"I want to meet my son, Sarah."

# Chapter Twenty



Unfortunately, Declan didn't receive the answer he had been hoping for. But he hadn't gotten a no either. Sarah had said she would need to discuss it with her husband, who was currently away on business, and he wouldn't be returning for a few days. She'd promised she would call us soon and give us a decision. She'd seemed open to the idea, but having never met her husband, Devin, I really didn't know how things would go.

We had other options. Declan could prove his paternity and fight for visitation, but he would much rather go this route, believing it would be easier on everyone involved. The last thing we needed was the press getting wind of this and having Connor's picture all over the headlines. Sarah would never let Declan see him.

As we were leaving, Sarah pulled Declan aside and whispered something in his ear. He looked at her and silently acknowledged with a slight nod. I didn't know what was said until we were in the car and about to leave Williamsburg.

He said, "Could you take a right here? There's somewhere I want to go before we leave."

Five minutes later, we were at a cemetery.

"Sarah said this is where they buried Heather. Since custody of Connor was given to Sarah and Devin in the will, they decided it would be best to have her final resting spot closer to where he would be raised. I wanted to..."

"Go," was all I said. I knew he needed this —to say good-bye, to grieve for a life he had never had the opportunity to have.

I followed close behind as we quietly walked through the old cemetery. It was nearly empty, only a few people wandering around due to the cold. I pulled the belt of my coat tighter and carried on. Just ahead, we found it. The headstone was new and gleamed against the sun, proudly displaying the name Heather Brooks. Declan didn't have any flowers, but he knelt to the side, careful not to disturb candles and notes.

One in particular caught his eye, and he hesitated a bit before picking it up.

It had *Mom* written across the front, and on the inside, it simply said, *I miss you*, in messy little boy handwriting.

Declan stared at the words for a moment, rubbing his thumb over them, before placing the note back exactly where it had stood earlier.

"I don't know how to do this," he said. "I don't know what to say."

"You don't have to say anything if you don't want to.

It's just you and me, Declan. Say whatever you want or say nothing at all."

"I'm just so...I'm just so angry with her. Eight years, Leah. Eight years went by, and she couldn't have picked up the phone and bothered to mention that I had a fucking son?" His voice turned harsh, and I could hear the raw hurt.

Something had been taken away from him, and he had no one to blame, no one to be angry with, except for a headstone.

"I wanted so desperately to ask Sarah if I could see a photo of him just to see what he looked like. But then I thought, *What if they say no? What if I never get to meet him?* Then, I'd have an image of him for the rest of my life, and nothing to go with it. Nothing. Just a ghost of what could have been if Heather had just chosen to do the right thing."

I knelt down and wrapped my arms around him. He fell back into me, and we sat down on the dirt together, me cradling him as he let go. All the pent-up anger and tense disposition he'd been holding on to gave way, and he sobbed. He turned in my arms, so he could bury himself into me as he released everything he'd bottled up.

I could do nothing but stroke his hair and be there for him. When women cried, they wailed and moaned. Hearing a man cry was agonizing. When men cried, it was ugly and raw. It was guttural and visceral, like someone was ripping them into two. It was like they were both fighting and giving in to the emotion all at once.

He clung to me like his life depended on it, gripping

the fabric of my coat so hard that his fingers were turning white.

"Do you think I'm ready to be a father?" he asked when his tears had finally dried up and his breathing had slowed.

"I think you are one whether you are ready or not," I answered.

"Never in a million years would I ever be ready for something like this."

"I think you can do anything," I said against his ear.

"Let's go home, babe," he said, giving me a ghost of a smile.

We made our way back to the car, hand in hand, wandering silently down the path.

"You know, you really suck at pet names," I said suddenly.

"What? What's wrong with babe?"

"It's totally unoriginal."

"Well, I guess I'll have to work on that then, honey buns."

"Nope, try again."

"Sweet bottom?"

"No!"

He laughed, and it was the first laugh I'd heard in what felt like years. It was like music to my ears. He threw an arm over my shoulder as we walked.

He kissed my head. "Thank you," he whispered.

I didn't ask why. I knew he meant for this, for the last two days, for being in that hospital that night. As hard as this discovery was, I had known he needed to know, and I knew he would be better because of it.

Five long agonizing days —that was how long I had to wait for a phone call back from Sarah. I'd gone back to sucking at work, and I was once again known as the diva asshat on set. I'd fucked up my lines and cussed out a PA for getting in my way. I was a disaster.

Patience was not my thing. I hated waiting for anything. By day three, I was pacing the floors like a fucking psycho. By day four, I was convinced Sarah had brushed me off and would never contact me. Leah had done her best to prove to me that Sarah and Devin were just taking their time, and it would all happen eventually, but I was a pessimist to the core, and I'd already convinced myself of the worst.

When the call actually came in, I was on break at work. I answered the call on the first ring, seeing Sarah's name show up on my phone.

"Sarah?" I answered.

"Hey, Declan," she began.

Her tone was even —not energetic, not sympathetic. I didn't know what to think.

*Was it good news or bad? Give me a damn clue!*

I got up from my seat at the small table in my trailer, and I started to pace, only to realize I couldn't pace in there unless I counted walking two steps and turning around to go back and do it all over again.

I headed out the door, opting for someplace less confined. If she were about to tell me no, I needed some damn fresh air and someplace to scream.

"How are you doing?" she asked.

"I'm all right, a bit anxious. I really want to see him, Sarah." I tried leveling with her. I was sick of pussyfooting around the subject.

"I know, and that is why we have agreed."

"What? You have?" I let out the breath I'd been holding for the last five days. I finally felt like my lungs were functioning again.

"Yes, but we have some requirements first, Declan."

"Anything, Sarah. Anything."

"First, we believe it's a good idea that, initially, Connor be introduced to you as a friend of Heather's. We're afraid introducing you as his father might overload him."

"Okay, I agree with that as long as you understand that he will eventually know me for who I really am."

She sighed before saying, "Yes, I understand that, Declan. We aren't trying to keep you from him. I only tried to do what Heather had wanted. I know it was wrong, but she was my best friend, and now, I'm trying to make it right. Having him here with us...we're doing the best we can, but it's difficult."

"What do you mean?" I asked, furrowing my brow in concern.

"When Heather asked us if we would agree to take Connor if anything were to ever happen to her, we agreed wholeheartedly. We had just gotten married, and we didn't have any kids of our own. We never once believed that anything would ever happen. When it did, our lives were very different. We have a baby, and now, all of a sudden, we have a very angry and sad seven-year-old. He is having a hard time with finding a place in our family. As much as I love him, he needs something more than me.

I'm willing to admit that. If that is you and you can give him what he so desperately needs right now, then I am more than willing to open up our home to allow that to happen. But just know that I am taking a risk here. We are not going to social services. We didn't hire a lawyer. This is between us —as friends."

"I understand. Is there anything else?"

"Yes, one more thing —your girlfriend. How close are you two?"

"What do you mean?"

"Connor is in a fragile state right now. We don't want to introduce anyone into his life who might not be there in a few months. We don't want him to form attachments to people who aren't committed to being in his life for the long haul. He's already suffered a major loss, and I can't stand to see him lose anyone else."

"Leah and I are together for life. You have nothing to worry about," I said without hesitation.

"I'm happy for you, Declan. You deserve happiness. I've been worried about you for years. It's good to see you finally in a good place."

"Thank you, Sarah," I answered as I paced back and forth between the trees lining the film's location for today.

"So, when do I get to see him?" I asked.

"Does tomorrow sound good?"

"It sounds perfect, Sarah. Thanks."

In less than a day, I was going to meet my son.

# Chapter Twenty-One



"Seriously Declan, stop fidgeting," I said, for the fourth time. He'd been a mess ever since he'd come saying Sarah and Devin had given permission for the visit. One minute he was excited, super pumped and happy, dancing with me across the room and laughing. The next he was a ball of nerves, scared out of his mind. We'd already made three separate trips to the store so he could pick up a gift for Connor. The second trip was because he thought the first gift was too small and it needed to be bigger, so we exchanged it for something larger. As soon as we got home, we had to turn around because the gift was suddenly too large and he didn't want to look like he was trying to hard, so after three tries we were back to the original gift.

I tried to explain to him that he didn't need a gift, but he was insistent. I think he was afraid he wouldn't have anything to talk about and at least the toy would be an ice breaker.

"Hot Shot, you're going to be great," I encouraged as we drove down the interstate once again, making our way back to Williamsburg. Sarah and Devin had given us the entire afternoon with Connor. We had four hours with him alone. We asked if they were sure, and they said yes. They thought it would be better for Connor to get to know us without them around, and they trusted us with him.

I was humbled by their generosity. I know what they must have gone through the last few months couldn't have been easy. Becoming parents for the first time, and then becoming parents again to a broken seven year old. I remember what I was like when my mom left and at times it seemed like no amount of love would ever be enough to replace the void left in my heart. A mother's love is irreplaceable, and to lose it so suddenly, and so young...there are no words to describe what that does to a child.

"Do you think he'll remember you?" Declan asked.

"I honestly don't know. We spent such a short time together. I hope so," I said, smiling softly. I'd thought about Connor quite a bit over the last few months, not realizing who he was or what he would come to mean to my life. He'd left his mark on my heart because I'd felt for him, being a child who'd lost someone at a young age. I don't know if that was reciprocated. His life had just been turned upside down that night, and in retrospect, that entire night could be a complete blur.

Pulling into the familiar driveway, Declan put the car in

park and we made our way to the front door. Sarah opened the door just as I went to ring the doorbell and we all said our hellos as she invited us in. Just inside the front door was a tall, regal looking man with gray framing his face glasses that made him look very scholarly. It fit the professor stereotype I'd had brewing in my head ever since Sarah told us he taught History at the College of William and Mary.

"Hi, I'm Devin," he said, offering his hand to Declan first, before turning to me.

We all finished our introductions and made our way to the living room. Declan took a look around, and I know he was looking for Connor.

"We thought we'd talk to you for a moment privately before we brought Connor in, if you don't mind," Devin said.

"Absolutely not. Like I told Sarah, we're willing to do whatever is necessary to make this work. I spent the last seven years unaware of his existence. The only thing I want right now is to know him." He weaved his fingers in mine as sat down across from Sarah and Devin in the living room.

"As Sarah told you, Connor's had a bit of a rough time since Heather died. No one blames him for this. It's normal and necessary, I think. He's grieving, and I know with all the other changes in his life, it will take time for him to adjust. We're doing everything we can, but he's still in so much pain."

"And he will be, forever. It will never go away," I chimed in, suddenly embarrassed by my outburst.

"Sounds like you're coming from experience Leah?" Sarah said.

"Yes and no. My mother left me when I was seven. So the loss I can relate to. The circumstances are different, but the loss similar and I can tell you it never goes away. It's a festering hole that never completely heals. You can find ways to cope...ways to move on, but it will always be there. A dull ache in your side that reminds you of the immense loss."

"How can we help him then?" she asked quietly.

"Honestly? Just be there for him. When I was growing up, the one thing I wanted, begged God for every night was a parent who would just hold me at night while I cried. Pretty soon the pain will dull and he'll be able to wake up in the morning and her face won't be the very first thing he thinks about, maybe the second or the third...and eventually he will be able to go on with life. But until then, all you can do is let him talk when he needs to and hold him when he'll let you."

Declan squeezed my hand in silent support and leaned down to kiss my cheek. As he did, he whispered ever so softly, "I love you" in my ear. My sexy bad boy who wore leather and whispered sweet endearments in my ear. He really was my perfect match.

After that, we went over a few housekeeping things about Connor. He was allergic to peanuts and hated fish. So seafood was out. He also had a serious movie obsession, and loved reading. Declan's ears perked up at the mention of movie obsession, wanting to know what types.

"Um, all sorts really. He loves old black and white films, campy eighties movies, and anything with Ironman of course."

Declan laughed, and shook his head like he couldn't quite believe he had something in common with his child. Just wait until he saw him.

"Well, Declan...are you ready?"

He glanced at me and I gave me a small encouraging smile. "Yes, we're ready."


DECLAN

There were certain moments in life when I felt like I needed to hold my breath and close my eyes, so I could properly capture the magnitude of what I was experiencing.

I wished I'd fully captured the first time I saw had seen Leah —, sitting in that bar, her eyes meeting mine. I'd had no idea how much my life was about to change. If I could have bottled up that memory, savoring it for eternity, I would have.

When Sarah moved to the bottom of the stairs and called Connor's name, and I heard him running to the top of the stairs, I knew this was one of those moments. I'd had so few in my existence, but I knew this was a big one. I wished I could freeze-frame everything —the emotions, the feel in the air, and the anticipation —so I could always know what it felt like in this exact moment. The only other time I'd felt like this was when I had stood in Leah's father's kitchen right before I'd told her I loved her.

My heart hammered in my chest, and I felt like I could pass out from how fast my breaths were moving in and out of my lungs. In the next few seconds, I knew that my life would change.

It sounded like a herd of elephants were coming down the stairs, and it made me smile. My mom used to scream at me for stomping down the stairs when I was a kid.

I turned just in time to see him round the corner, and my heart froze in my chest. *His eyes...shit, Leah was right.* Even from a distance, I could see the resemblance to my own. It was like looking in a mirror. Everyone had always said my eyes were so unique...but not anymore. They had been cloned in this kid. The rest of him was like staring at a mash-up of Heather and me —or at least, what I remembered of Heather. He had my hair color, but his skin was fair like Heather's. I was always on the tan side, but Heather had always been light in complexion. He had several features that came from Heather, but overall, it was like looking at a younger version of myself.

He stopped dead in his tracks when he reached the living room. He gave us an appraising look. He looked me up and down, trying to figure out my place in his world. His eyes then shifted to Leah, and recognition registered across his small features.

"Hey, you're that nurse from the hospital," he said, allowing me to hear my child's voice for the first time ever.

He sounded so grown-up yet young at the same time, reminding me of his age. He was seven, going on eight. I'd missed the years where he'd learned to talk and said his words wrong. I'd missed him going to school for the first time, learning to read and write. Anger at Heather threatened to take over my calm demeanor, and I reminded myself that he was here. I'd found him. Leah had found him, and every day forward, I would be here.

Leah smiled at Connor's recognition of her. She bent down slightly, so she could be at eye level with him.

"That's right. I'm Leah, and this is Declan. He used to be a friend of your mom's. We thought you might like to spend the day with us. We were headed over to Colonial Williamsburg and thought you might like to join us."

"Well...Sarah took me there a few weeks ago...but I could be, like, your guide or whatever."

"That sounds great. Doesn't it, Declan?"

"Sounds perfect. Let's go!" I said.

<hr>

Colonial Williamsburg was almost sectioned off from the rest of Williamsburg. It was about ten minutes from the newer area where Sarah and Devin lived. I followed the signs to the main gate, but Connor stopped me.

"You know, you don't have to buy tickets. You can see almost everything without having to buy a ticket."

"Really?"

"Yeah, Sarah told me so. She says the tickets are cool if you want to see reenactments or go into the buildings, but if you just wanna walk around, shop, and eat, you can just park and go in," he said.

"Well, glad we have our own tour guide to show us the ropes then," Leah said.

I saw Connor smile shyly in the rearview mirror.

We headed back to the street and found a lot to park in. It was a cold winter day, and there weren't as many people here since it wasn't tourist season, so parking wasn't an issue.

Getting out of the car, I pulled Leah to me and asked, "Did you know the thing about the tickets?"

"Of course I did. I've been here a gazillion times."

"Were you ever going to tell me, snuggle bear?"

"Mmm...nope. I love reenactments. Guys in colonial uniforms are hot. And snuggle bear? Seriously? That's gross."

I laughed. It really was awful, but I just couldn't resist. "It was worth a shot, and there will be no checking out anyone in a uniform...unless it's me."

"Yes, sir," she teased. "So, Connor, since you've been here, where's a good place to eat? I'm starved!"

Connor, being a child, suggested one of the pubs where everyone dressed in period clothing and said, "Ye," a lot. Luckily, the food was good, and we stuffed ourselves on bread and stew. After an hour-long meal though, Connor still hadn't spoken much. He'd stirred around his stew and pulled off pieces of his bread, but that had been it.

I gave Leah a look that basically said, *Am I doing something wrong?*

She gave me a look back that was soft and warm as she held my hand under the table, giving it an encouraging squeeze.

After leaving the restaurant, we strolled around the dirt streets and visited several shops. Around the third one, Connor was busy, looking at a toy sword, when I came up next to him, trying to figure out what to talk about. Then, he beat me to it.

"How did you know my mom?" he asked quietly as he fiddled with the swords.

"She was, uh...my girlfriend for a long time," I answered honestly.

I briefly thought about just saying that we had been friends, but I didn't want to start out my relationship with my son on a lie. I was already lying about who I was. We didn't need any more deceit. I would do my best to always be truthful with him, especially with the things that truly mattered.

"But you broke up?"

"Yes. We realized we weren't right for each other, and I moved to California while she stayed in New York."

He was quiet for a long time after that as we made our way through the gift shop. He returned back to the swords several times. He'd pull one out and hold it in his hands like a little knight. I suddenly remembered I'd never given him his present. It was still sitting in the trunk of the car, and now, seeing him with that sword in his hand, it seemed unimpressive.

I found Leah by the jewelry as she was looking at a small silver necklace.

I asked, "Hey, would you mind walking with him to go get some hot cider while I get something real quick?"

"Sure," she answered, taking one last look at the necklace before gathering up Connor in search of cider.

I picked up my two purchases quickly and tucked the small one into my pocket. Then, I went in search for Connor and Leah and found them at a small stand selling hot cider. I came up, pulling the toy sword out of the bag as I approached. Connor turned and saw the sword, his eyes going wide with excitement.

"Every soldier needs a sword," I said, bending down to hand him the sword with a bit of flare. *Might as well put those acting skills to good use.*

He took it in his hand and looked up at me in wonder.

"Thank you, Declan," he said.

It made me both happy and sad at the same time. It was the first time I'd made him happy, the first time I'd made him smile, and the first time he'd said thank you to me. But it had all been done under the false pretense that I was just another guy. I was just an old boyfriend of his mother's. I wasn't anyone special to him yet. I was just Declan.

I wanted that to change.

I still had one more gift to give.

I knelt down to Connor. "Hey, think you could help me out with something?"

He nodded enthusiastically. I was glad to see him happy even if it was temporary or wasn't quite the way I'd wanted it to be. He was happy, and that needed to be celebrated.

I pulled out the small box and handed it to him before motioning to Leah. He nodded, giving a half smile. He took the few steps to Leah and held out the box to her.

"What do you have there, Little Man?" she asked.

"It's from Declan."

"It's from both of us," I corrected, which made his half smile turn into a full smile as he held the box higher.

She gave me a cheesy grin and opened it, finding the silver necklace she'd been eyeing in the store. It really was beautiful. A lot of the things sold here were inexpensive and cheap. This was actually made by one of the silversmiths employed here, and it was a work of art, something not seen often in modern jewelry stores.

"Well, aren't you two charming?" she said.

Connor turned around, and I gave him a thumbs-up.

Leah bent down and gave Connor a quick kiss and a hug. He went into her arms easily. It was a familiar place for him, having been held by her the night of the accident. Seeing the woman I loved holding my child did something to me. It made my heart feel like it was too large for my chest.

Leah looked up at me with Connor's head tucked under hers as she mouthed, *I love you*

I wanted them. I wanted both of them. This was my new reality, and I actually felt ready for all of it. Leah had said I was a father whether I was ready for it or not...and I was.

# Chapter Twenty-Two

LEAH

"So, you leave for a few days, and manage to become an overnight celebrity? Seriously, it's weird seeing your picture in the grocery store...Oh and Declan's a father and he's moving here?" Clare said, as we sat down inside Phil's for coffee and freshly baked scones.

"Mmhm," I said, taking a sip of my mocha as I settled into the flowery cushioned chair with my late breakfast.

"Is there anything else?"

"Ahh, nope. I think you got it all," I answered, taking another sip of my hot coffee. The liquid instantly warmed my body, warding off the chill from the outdoors.

"Wow, well...let's see. I got a new sweater while you were gone. Oh, and I went to the dentist, no cavities by the way, and Maddie attempted to braid my hair. I had knots for days. So, I mean...that's totally the same, right?"

"You let Maddie braid your hair?" I laughed. "I wouldn't let that crazy child near my hair for all the conditioner in the world. She's like a tornado with a brush."

"True that, but enough about my non-exciting life. Tell me everything!"

I did. We spent hours talking, and eating. When our coffees and food ran out, we ordered more. Phil kept our coffee table full of goodies and our coffee cups hot.

"I just can't believe you were with Connor that night. Can you imagine if it had been someone else Leah? Declan would have gone on for probably the rest of his life never knowing he had a child out there. What an amazing gift you gave him," she said.

I leaned my head back on the chair, remembering those first few days. "It didn't feel that way in the beginning. There were times when I thought I might lose him. It was just so much for him to take in all at once, I was so scared he was going to crumble under the pressure. But, the minute he saw Connor, he was different."

Clare gave a knowing smile, "He became a parent."

"Yes, I guess so. He just became so much more focused. Before we got that phone call that we could see him, he was all over the place...up, down...positive, negative. But seeing him finally meet him, he finally relaxed. I know we have a long road, and so much more to go through...hell, at this point Connor doesn't even know who Declan really is, but right now, it's enough for him."

It had been a week since that first visit with Connor. It had gone better than either of us had expected. Our time in Williamsburg had been short, but I think we made an impact on him. I know he made an impact on us. I could see the toll grief had taken, but there was still a bit of a kid left in him that so desperately just wanted to play and have fun. But when something so tragic happens to someone, at any age, it's hard to decide when it's okay to smile again, to play and enjoy simple pleasures again. Are you allowed to feel happiness when you're still missing someone every minute?

I wanted so desperately to teach him it was okay to feel joy again, to allow himself to be a kid again. We both did. I just hoped he let us.

"Do you think Declan will eventually want more?"

"He hasn't mentioned it, and I honestly don't know," I admitted.

"Have you thought about it? About if he did eventually want custody?"

"Yes..no...I don't know. Less than two weeks ago, I was still trying to adjust to the fact that I was in love, and now I'm having to suddenly having to readjust to this. My head is spinning."

"Would you support him?" she asked.

"What? Of course I would. I would never get in the way of him and his son," I answered adamantly. After having the childhood I did, I could only hope that other children could grow up with as much love as humanly possible. I'd never stand in the way of Connor having the opportunity to be raised by his father if that is what they wanted.

"And would you stand by him?"

"Of course I would!"

"Okay, well then your head can stop spinning now, because you've answered all the questions you need to know. Whatever happens, whatever he decides, you are there for him. That's all you need to know.

"God damn, you are fucking smart! When did that happen?"

"I've always been smart. You just don't pay attention."

"Well, I am easily distracted."

"That's an understatement. So, does Declan get to see Connor again anytime soon? Is there a schedule? Do I get to meet him? Ooh, we could set up a playdate for him and Maddie. That would be adorable!"

"First, no more coffee for you. You're practically vibrating in your seat. Second, yes...we have another visit set up in a week. Declan is finishing up filming this week, and then he's officially unemployed. Well, for now. He has a few other projects he's hoping might work out, but we're waiting on those. In the meantime, he's working on having all of his shit moved out here."

"Leah and Declan. Shacking up together. I'm so proud of you!" she said, before she threw her arms around me, practically jumping into my chair as she sat on my lap.

I laughed, hugging her back, "He just doesn't know what he's getting himself into. I'm a royal pain in the ass."

"Oh, I'm pretty sure he's aware. We all are. We just love you despite it," she grinned. "So, where are you two taking Connor for date number two?"

"Well, if your father was a movie star, where do you think he would take you?"

"Neiman and Marcus so he could buy me a diamond studded pony?"

"No, dork. We're taking him to the movies, of course."

We chose a theater that was slightly out of the way, and we picked a matinee. Sarah and Devin had graciously allowed Connor to spend the night with us in Richmond. Even though I was still just a family friend to him, I didn't want to screw this up.

*My son loved movies.* I couldn't get over that. It was my passion and chosen career, and he was obsessed. It was something we had in common, and I couldn't wait to share it with him. A new Marvel Comics movie was showing, and Sarah had mentioned that Connor really wanted to see it. As soon as Leah and I had picked him up that morning, we'd headed back to Richmond, going straight for the theater.

With my baseball cap pulled tight to my bowed head, I bought our tickets at the electronic kiosk, avoiding as much person-to-person interaction as possible. After the pictures of Leah and me had been plastered all over the tabloids a few weeks ago, we were a bit more recognizable now.

Turning, I found Leah standing in line at the concession stand. She was bent over while talking to Connor. She had a slight smile and nodded before laughing. I couldn't help but grin. She was radiant. It didn't matter what she wore, did, or said...I always wanted her. She had me. I was a goner, and I'd never been happier. Our life was completely crazy and uncertain, and I didn't care because I knew everything would be fine with her by my side.

*Jesus. I'd turned into Logan. No wonder the man walked around with cancer and still grinned like a damned fool.*

This, seeing her, made me feel invincible.

Sliding my way past a few people in line, I caught up with Leah and Connor, who were talking about their favorite movies.

"I like *Iron Man*," he said.

"Which one?" Leah asked.

"All of them. Iron Man is way cool."

"And way hot," she shot back.

"Say what?" I asked, raising my brow.

"But not as hot as you," she amended, giving me a quick kiss on the cheek.

"Better." I slapped her on the ass as we moved up in line, causing her to yelp.

Connor looked back with a confused expression, but he just gave a shy smile.

"What's your favorite movie?" Connor asked me as we came to another stop.

*It was the longest line ever. Thank God we'd gotten here early.* I'd suggested skipping the concession stand altogether when we arrived, but Leah had given me the death stare, stating she would not enter the movie without Milk Duds, so we waited.

"Hmmm...that's a hard one. Someone just introduced me to *The Princess Bride*," I said, giving Leah a wolfish grin. "But I'd have to say *Casablanca*."

"What's that?" Connor asked at the same time Leah nearly shouted, "Liar!"

"What do you mean, liar?" I asked her.

"*Casablanca* cannot possibly be your favorite movie.

That is just what you tell people to make yourself sound artsy and smart. Come on, Hotshot, what is it? It's got to be embarrassing —otherwise, you wouldn't have pulled the *Casablanca* card."

*I seriously hated this woman sometimes.* She could call me on my bullshit in two seconds flat. *Casablanca* was absolutely a lie. I appreciated it from a directing and film perspective, but movie favorites were not based on that. They were based on emotions and what moved someone. What made that person keep coming back time to that specific movie? It was something special.

"*Twilight?*" she guessed.

I choked out a laugh, "No. Hell no,"

"*Weekend at Bernie's?*"

With my shoulders still shaking, I shook my head.

"*Austin Powers!*" she nearly squealed.

"Not even close."

We got to the concession stand before she could guess again, and she ordered her Milk Duds. I got some popcorn and a Coke for Connor. We then took a right to the hallway that led to our movie. Giving our tickets over, we waited until the pimpled teenager ripped them in half and handed them back. His eyes widened a bit when he looked up at me, but I quickly turned away before he could say anything.

"Hey, I need to visit the ladies' room," Leah said.

"We'll wait for you," I said.

She disappeared into the restroom, and Connor and I wandered the hall, looking at movie posters. Connor froze in front of one, and it took me a split second to realize why.

"Is that you?" he asked.

*Crap, I'd forgotten I had a movie out. How does one forget he has a movie in the theaters?* Well, I had a lot of shit going on, and whether or not my movie was doing well had been the least of my worries over the last few weeks. I hadn't even taken my agent's last few calls. Moving across country and finding out I had a son kind of took precedence.

"Ah, yeah...that's me," I answered awkwardly.

"You're a movie star?"

"I don't really like to use those particular words, but I act, yes. Well, I did. I'm trying to direct now."

He looked at me then, and I didn't really know what else to say. Most kids didn't have fathers who were movie stars. Of course, most kids knew who their fathers were.

*God, this situation was fucked-up on so many levels. Would he treat me differently?*

I hadn't told him what I did because I didn't want him to treat me weird or act strange around me. When I would finally tell him who I actually was, I just wanted to be his dad —not Declan James, actor. I didn't want to be anyone but someone who would love him.

"Do you know Iron Man?" he asked very matter-of-factly.

I grinned. "Yep, I've met him a few times. Pretty cool guy."

"Awesome."

And that was that. I was cool —but not as cool as Iron Man.

I could live with that.

# Chapter Twenty-Three



"I'm seriously not going to tell you," Declan said as we lay in bed early the next morning.

Our movie adventure had been a success. The new Marvel movie was awesome. It wasn't as awesome as *Iron Man* according to Connor, but I was beginning to think not many things made it Iron Man cool for that particular seven-year-old.

"You know the longer you don't tell me, the worse it gets in my head," I said.

"Still not telling, so you might as well get your ass out of bed and make me breakfast."

I laughed as he pinned me beneath him. He was shirtless, and his muscles flexed as he held my arms above my head.

"How exactly am I supposed to do that when I'm like this?" I asked softly, slowly rolling my hips under his, reveling in the way my body affected him.

"I think I've changed my mind," he announced before claiming my lips in a searing kiss.

His tongue rolled with mine as our mouths fused together. His hand that had been pinning my hands slithered down my arm before cupping my breast through my tank top. My nipples instantly pebbled at his touch.

I moaned, and then like a bucket of ice water, I remembered. "Declan, we aren't alone. Connor is across the hall! What if he wakes up?"

"Do you hear anything?" he asked.

I shook my head.

"Babe, it's barely six in the morning. I realize kids are known for waking up early, but I don't hear anything yet, and I really, really need to fuck you."

The last part was whispered seductively in my ear, and that was all it took. I was a goner. I melted against him again and kissed him frantically, like we were on borrowed time.

"We need a bigger house," I said as I quickly shed my top and panties.

"With a room for Connor down the hall, not across," Declan agreed, pulling down his pajama bottoms in one swift motion. "Fuck, you're hot," he said before thrusting inside me.

Trying not to cry out, which was my usual method, I buried my head in his shoulder.

He chuckled. "Having a bit of a hard time keeping quiet, Leah?" he whispered in my ear, slowly sliding in and out like we had all the time in the world. "You are quite the screamer. Let's see what happens when I do this."

That was when the motherfucker pulled all the way out, tilted my hips just at the right angle, and then slammed back in, causing my eyes to nearly roll back in my head. I bit down on his shoulder to keep myself from screaming like a banshee.

"Shit," he hissed, turned on now more than ever.

He let go, pounding in and out of me as I orgasmed around him again and again. My body shook as he finally came, and then he collapsed on top of me in a mindless heap. He readjusted to lie by my side.

Still breathing heavily, he said, "Holy hell, that was hot. You've never bitten me before."

"You've never pissed me off before." I grinned. "Were you trying to make me scream and scar the kid for life?"

"Just wanted to see how far you'd go to keep quiet. Apparently, pretty damn far." He laughed.

"You're an arrogant ass."

"Yeah, I know. And you're a pain in the ass. We're a perfect pair."

We settled back into bed, enjoying the last few minutes of morning, before we heard some rustling, and then the door across the hall opened. The guest bathroom door creaked and shut, and that was our announcement that Connor was up.

"Time to make us men some breakfast," Declan said with a wolfish grin, rising out of bed to get dressed.

I took a few moments to admire the view, loving the way his ass looked as he slid back into his pajama bottoms. He slipped on a shirt, turned, planted a quick kiss on my lips, and went to go find Connor.

After slipping into a robe and fuzzy slippers, I entered

the living room, and I heard them talking. They'd pulled out the Xbox that Declan had bought for this very week-end, and they were currently trying to blow up aliens. They laughed, and explosions boomed through the speakers.

I made some coffee and started the griddle for pancakes. A few days earlier, I'd picked up everything to make them from scratch. I wanted to make Connor a special breakfast while he was here. I knew Sarah prob-ably had done all sorts of special things for him, but it was the first time we had him with us, and I wanted it to be perfect —for both of them.

A few minutes later, bacon was sizzling, and pancakes were cooking. I got out butter and maple syrup and set the table. I piled a plate high with chocolate chip pancakes, my favorite, and then I sandwiched the bacon between layers of paper towels to soak up the extra grease.

"Okay, boys, come and get it. The food is ready!"

They'd been so involved with their game that I didn't think they had even realized I'd been cooking. It was an adorable sight, seeing them huddled together on the living room floor, playing video games in their PJs.

But as soon as I'd said food, they were up and running. Declan snagged a piece of bacon from the plate as he sat down, and I scolded him as I poured orange juice. When I went to grab myself another cup of coffee, I realized then that Connor hadn't taken a seat. I turned and saw him frozen in the kitchen, staring at the plate of pancakes, like they were infested with maggots or something equally hideous.

"Connor, what is it?" I asked, rushing to his side.

"My mom used to...I hate pancakes!" he shouted, running from the room.

The guest bedroom door slammed, and I looked up, locking eyes with Declan.

"What did I do?" I asked, feeling the tears stinging my eyes.

He came to me and pulled me into his arms. "You didn't do anything. Let me go talk to him, okay?"

"I just...I didn't know."

"How could you, Leah? We are going into this blind. We are learning as we go, and we can do this one day at a time. Just think about everything we've accomplished with him so far. He's still recovering, and we're going to have setbacks."

"Please tell him I'm sorry," I begged.

"He knows. He's not mad at you. He's mad at the universe. Someone was taken away from him, and he doesn't understand why."

I nodded, and he gave me one last kiss on the forehead before heading to the guest room. I watched him walk away, and it was the first time I saw him truly as a father. I didn't know how to be a parent.

*Could I be the woman he needed me to be?*


DECLAN

I knocked on the door and took a step in. Connor was curled into a ball on the large bed, reminding me of how young he really was. He put on a bold front, acted tough and aloof, but he really was only seven. He was a second grader who had lost his mom on the way to visit a family friend. He was only a child who had to leave his entire life behind to move to another state while he wondered why his mommy was never coming back.

"Hey," I said, sitting on the edge of the bed next to him.

He didn't say anything, but I could hear sniffling, indicating he was crying. His head was buried into his knees, and he had his arms wrapped firmly around his legs. I remembered taking this same position on several occasions when I had been his age and older.

"I remember your mom used to make the best pancakes. Blueberry, right?"

His head shot up, and his face was red and splotchy. There were marks from fresh tears, and his flannel pajama bottoms were wet from where they had soaked up other tears.

"Whenever I'd have a bad day, she'd always say, 'Why don't I make you pancakes?'" I looked into the eyes of a child I hadn't known existed, but somehow, I felt like I'd loved him his entire life despite it. *How else could I possibly describe the depth of love I felt for him?*

"She used to make me birthday pancakes, and she'd stick a candle in the stack. She'd tell me to make a wish...I should have wished for her."

My heart nearly exploded as he launched himself at me, wrapping his arms around my torso, as he sobbed. I pulled him in tight and gently rubbed his back.

"You couldn't have known. And you can't let your happy memories of your mom be ruined because of what happened. She wouldn't want it that way."

"But how do I remember the good stuff when it hurts?"

"You take it one memory at a time, one day at a time. But if you stopped doing all the fun stuff you and your mom did together, you'd miss out on a great life."

"Does Leah hate me now?" Connor asked, still leaning on my shoulder. He crumpled up his Iron Man T-shirt and wiped off his eyes. They were still red and puffy, but at least, they were dry now.

"No, absolutely not. Leah thinks you're a pretty cool dude. She could never hate you."

His eyes flashed up to mine at those words, and I was momentarily stunned again by how much his eyes mirrored mine. They were green with flecks of blue and brown, but now, they were a bit greener as he smiled shyly.

"She's really pretty."

*What is this? A crush?*

"Yes, she is." I grinned. *Yep, definitely my son.*

"Do you think she'll still let us eat pancakes?"

"Let's go find out."

We walked out together and found Leah on the couch, still in her bathrobe and fuzzy slippers. Whenever she wore them, I remembered that night when I'd shown up here, trying to sleep with her. I'd thought I would be able to get her out of my system, nice and easy. I had been fooling myself. She was an addiction I never wanted to cure. She was my Hollywood happy ending, and I couldn't wait to spend every moment of our lives together making real-life movie magic.

Leah jumped from the couch, fiddling with the tie of

her robe. She looked nervous and devastated. I hated seeing her this way. I knew she felt guilty for upsetting Connor, and I understood. I would have felt the same way, but we couldn't keep the bad from happening. We couldn't shelter him from his feelings. I knew she'd been through something similar, and I knew the pain she had gone through. Part of her just wanted to bottle him up and keep him safe from everything, and I loved her for it. But the realistic side of her understood that he had to face his fears and learn to live life without Heather, no matter how hard that would be.

"I'm so sorry, Leah," Connor said before giving her a long hug.

She looked at me before bending down and embracing him. "No problem, Little Man."

"Okay, okay...that's enough hugging, Casanova," I said, grinning. "She's mine. Go find someone your own size."

I ruffled his hair as we made our way to the kitchen again.

"What do you want for breakfast, Connor?" Leah asked.

The table had been cleared, except for the plates and juice glasses. I saw a light on in the oven, and I figured she'd stuck everything under the warmer. Connor glanced over at me, and I gave him a slight encouraging nod.

He took a deep breath and said, "I think I'll have some chocolate chip pancakes."

"You sure?" Leah asked quietly.

"Yep, one memory at a time. Right, Declan?"

"That's right, Little Man. That's right."

Leah pulled out the pancakes and bacon from the oven, and we settled at the table. I told a story about one of my first auditions in Hollywood, causing them both to laugh. It had been for a horror movie, and the part had been for a victim who got attacked in his car. I hadn't gotten it. Apparently, my screams weren't so good. Leah about choked on her chocolate chip pancake when I said that, remembering our game from earlier in the morning.

We made it through breakfast, and Connor managed to polish off three pancakes and a pile of bacon.

He smiled down at his empty plate and looked at me. "Thanks."

"Anytime, dude. Let's go kill some aliens now."

And just like that, he made it through to the other side, unscathed and stronger.

Pancakes and hugs —they were miracle workers.

# Chapter Twenty-Four



"Logan, next time you have cancer and get a clean bill of health, can you do it in the fall?" I joked, sweeping a bead of sweat as it trickled down my temple as we all stood around in Logan and Clare's backyard.

It was summer. Months had passed by since Declan had moved in. We'd had so many happy days. I didn't think life could get better.

Until last week, when a hysterical Clare had called me, saying the words we'd prayed for. Logan was officially in remission. No signs of cancer could be found. The chemo and radiation had done their jobs. He would still have to go back in for checkups, but other than that, he was better.

I'd collapsed in the bedroom when she told me, crying tears of joy for my best friend and for a man I'd come to love. Logan had saved Clare. He'd loved her when she had needed to be loved so desperately. Knowing he was going to okay...I couldn't explain it. I felt relief, joy, elation. It was overwhelming. Knowing what the alternative was, remembering the feeling of losing Ethan, I'd cherished that moment. We'd hung up, and I'd told her I'd call her soon.

Declan, of course, had rushed into the bedroom, ready to kill whoever or whatever had harmed me, but when he had seen me smiling, he'd calmed and asked me what had happened.

"Logan...he's in remission."

Declan's eyes had closed tightly as he'd braced himself against the doorframe for a moment. I hadn't realized how worried Declan had been until then —when I'd seen his visible relief for his longtime friend.

He'd opened his eyes, and slowly, he'd smiled. His eyes had crinkled a bit, giving him that boyish look I loved so much.

"I think we need a party," he'd suggested.

And that was how we all ended up at Logan and Clare's a week later. We'd offered to host it, but since we hadn't found a house we both could agree on yet, the party had been moved here for space. Our townhouse, although spacious, just couldn't hold more than a few people comfortably. This party was only for immediate family and us, but it still would have been cramped. We really needed a new house.

Logan grinned at my snide comment. It really was damn hot though. Summer was the one season I both loved and hated. I loved it when I was able to lie near a pool and sunbathe. I hated it when I was required to wear clothes, and jumping in water wasn't an option. Virginia in the summer was hot and sticky and made my hair do hideous things.

Connor and Maddie chose that moment to run by, laughing, making a beeline to the swings. They had become fast friends, which had made Clare and me swoon as we envisioned an adorable wedding in twenty years. The men had just shaken their heads at our crazy plans.

Connor had made tremendous progress. Between all of us, including Sarah and Devin, we had helped him through the roughest months and the strongest memories. He'd learned to recognize that memories of his mom were good things and should be celebrated. Declan and I had taken him to an ice rink, and we'd all gone ice skating, which was something Connor had always done with his mother. We'd made a new tradition of eating our ice cream with the cones flipped over in a bowl because that had been the way his mom used to give it to him. We didn't want him to lose her, but we also didn't want him to live in the past. We tried to bring new adventures to his life as well, so he could create new memories.

The fact that Connor still didn't know who Declan was killed him. Declan wanted to tell him, but Sarah and Devin had asked for six months. It was difficult on Declan. He was developing this amazing relationship with his son, but it was based partially on a lie. By the end of the summer, we would fulfill the time requirement, and then we could tell Connor.

"Hey, where's Goober?" I asked, noticing Garrett's absence and the obvious void in our little family.

"He said he had something for work, so he couldn't make it." Logan shrugged.

"On a Saturday afternoon?"

"I don't know. He does work a lot," Clare answered.

"I'm worried about him. I don't think he's had a date in months, if not years. He doesn't do anything but work, and it's beginning to show. He looks tired and worn out all the time."

Clare nodded in agreement. "I know. Me, too. I've tried to talk with him, but he brushes it off, saying he needs to put in the time to move up. He says he'll have time to do everything he wants to do later when he's higher up the ladder."

"I don't think it's a career choice. I think he's purposely avoiding something. Work is just a happy accident that keeps his mind occupied," I said, holding up my glass to my face in a vain attempt to cool myself down.

*Backyard cookout in the summer? Whose dumb idea was this?*

*Oh yeah, mine.*

"But what could it be though?" Clare asked.

"I don't know, and I doubt he'll tell anyone. Keep an eye on him, and if it gets worse, let me know. I'll force it out of him if I have to," I said.

The men wandered over to the grill, pretending to cook, as they drank beer and laughed. Clare and I took a seat on the patio where a fan had been plugged in, and we sighed as the cool wind blew in our direction.

"Guess what?" Clare said before sipping her sweet tea.

I didn't know how she stomached the stuff. I knew I was born and raised in the South, but I couldn't stand it. It tasted like simple syrup with a bit of tea thrown in for color. *Yuck.*

"You really do think I look fat in this dress?"

"No!" She giggled. "You look gorgeous as always. You need to take it down a notch and give the rest of us a fighting chance."

"Oh, please. Do you see the way your husband keeps looking over here? He's staring at one of us, and it's definitely not me. I'd say you have it going on and then some."

She smiled as she quickly glanced across the yard, catching Logan's heated gaze. His hair had mostly grown back, and it was back to his messy signature style.

"You were going to tell me something before you started eye-fucking your husband?" I teased.

She blushed and laughed. She tore her eyes away from Logan and focused back on me. She was the color of a cherry red tomato, and she probably would be for the next five minutes. No amount of embarrassment ever went unnoticed on Clare's fair skin.

"Yes! I'm going back to work! I start back this fall," she said excitedly.

Clare, in her former life —before Ethan had become sick and it had become too hard to take care of him and work at the same time —had been a high school history teacher.

"That's great! Is Logan excited?" I asked.

"Yes, it was his idea. He knew I was lonely in the house now that Maddie is in school. My mom will have to pick her up from school since the high school runs a bit later than her elementary school, but I will still be able to be here with her in the late afternoons. I honestly can't wait to get back into teaching."

"That's great. And hey, think of all the teenage boys who will have crushes on you! That will be a boost to the ego when you hit the big three-oh," I joked.

She threw a napkin at my face, and we continued to talk until Declan came over, announcing dinner.

"I cooked a mean steak, snickerdoodle. You have to try it."

"Nope."

"Nope to the steak or the pet name?"

"The pet name. It's awful. Call me that again, and I swear to God I will tell Clare right here in front of all our family and friends what your favorite movie is," I threatened.

His eyes widened.

"He told you?" Clare exclaimed, knowing all about my long, arduous ploy to get Declan to tell me his favorite movie.

It had taken months, but I'd finally gotten him to break down.

"Oh yeah, and it's good. Not something he'd want to share with his man buddies over there," I said, pointing to Logan and Colin.

Colin had his arm slung around his wife as he just laughed, and Logan gave me a goofy grin. They really, really wanted to know.

"What are you talking about?" Connor asked, coming from the playground with Maddie in tow.

"Declan's favorite movie," I answered, giving Declan a sly grin.

"Oh, you mean that movie, *The Notebook?*" Connor said.

Seconds after he'd said it, the backyard exploded. Logan and Colin doubled over in deep masculine laughter. Declan cursed, and all the women in the vicinity gave a collective sigh. I found it sexy that he loved that movie. It was seriously romantic...but for a dude, it wasn't a typical movie to love.

"Can't. Fucking. Breathe," Logan bellowed, clutching his side, before letting loose a string of jokes that addressed Declan's masculinity or the lack thereof that had the entire backyard in an uproar. *I had to admit, it was pretty damn funny.*

"I'm going to get you back for this, Matthews," Declan promised.

"Uh-huh, are you sure you can? I mean, don't you have a pedicure to go to or something? And besides, I really don't think I have anything that can top that, but I'd love to see you try."

"Oh, really?" Clare challenged. "I believe there's a frilly apron in there you love to use when cooking. Should I go get it and share?"

Logan went white, and it was Declan's turn to laugh.

"You use an apron, dude?" Declan chuckled.

"It keeps my clothes clean! And it's Clare's! I just use it because it's the only one we have." Logan pouted, making him look ridiculously handsome in a boyish way.

The entire time this was going on, Connor stood next to me, watching with a big grin on his face. Three months ago, if he'd said something like that and this had all happened, he would have run out of the room, worried that he'd ruined the party with his slip-up. But today, he was relaxed, and he understood we teased in good fun.

We all sat down at the picnic table after piling our plates full of food. Connor sat in between Declan and me.

Declan gave him a little nudge. "Last time I tell you anything, Little Man."

Connor giggled as Declan tried to pinch his side.

"I didn't know it was a secret!" Connor laughed again.

"Just remind me of this day when we meet your first girlfriend. I'll be sure to return the favor with something equally embarrassing," Declan said.


DECLAN

Dinner was finished, and I went wandering through the house in search of Connor. I hadn't seen him since we sat down to eat, and then he'd run off with Maddie to play again. I loved these visits I had with him —except for the end when I had to give him back. I hated that part. It reminded me of the fucked-up situation I was in —the fact that I still couldn't tell him who I was, the fact that my son was being raised by someone else, and the fact that he still thought of me as nothing more than a close family friend. I was basically the family equivalent to an uncle.

I understood Sarah and Devin's reluctance. I did. I was just impatient. Connor had made such strides in the last few months. Every obstacle he'd faced, he had overcome. It hadn't been easy.

There had been days he'd spent with us where he would still cry and ask, "Why? Why her?"

I couldn't answer that for him. I didn't know why his

mother had been taken so early in his life. Despite our falling-out, Heather had been a good person. I knew she'd made mistakes, and I hated that I couldn't get the first seven years of Connor's life back. *Did I wish things were different though? Hell yes.* If I could take his pain away, even at the cost of not knowing him, I would do it in an instant.

I found Maddie and Connor in the hallway downstairs, looking at old photos. There were photos of Clare and Logan, baby pictures of Maddie, and a few of Ethan, Clare's late husband. I thought it was cool of Logan to honor Ethan's memory. I wasn't so sure I'd be as accommodating as Logan was, but then again, I wasn't in his situation, so I guessed I'd never know. We all did what we had to do to love the person we were meant for, and Logan was doing just that. "That's my other Daddy. He's in heaven," I heard Maddie say to Connor.

I hung back, ducking into one of the spare bedrooms, curious to see their interaction.

"My mommy is in heaven, too," Connor said.

"Maybe they're friends!" Maddie suggested brightly, bringing a slight smile to Connor's face.

"Maybe. That would be cool. Was your Daddy nice?"

"He was really nice. He used to surf and take me to the beach when I was a baby."

"My mom liked the beach, too, so maybe they are surfing together in heaven."

"On pink waves!"

"Why would the waves be pink?" Connor asked.

"Because it's heaven. Duh," Maddie said.

I had to suppress a chuckle.

"Hey, look at this picture. That boy looks just like you!" Maddie said, pointing to a picture on the opposite wall.

I could just barely make it out. It was one I hadn't seen in a long time. It must have just been added to the wall. It was an old photograph of Logan and me from grade school. We had our arms around each other's shoulders in a boyish embrace, and we gave goofy smiles while looking at the camera.

"It does kinda. Who's the other boy?" Connor asked.

"I think that's my Daddy, Logan."

I heard Clare call for Maddie from the kitchen. Maddie had left a mess in the living room, and she was being told to clean it up. Maddie took off in a run, leaving Connor in the hallway. He stood frozen, staring at the photo of Logan and me.

"You know, we hated each other back then," I said, walking up next to him.

"That's you?"

"Yep. Logan and I go way back. We grew up together. Our fathers were close friends, and they figured their boys should be, too. Problem was, I hated Logan. He was annoying and pretentious."

"What does pretentious mean?"

"Stuck up."

"Oh, like Tyler at school. He says his dad is rich, and his room is filled with Iron Man toys."

"Yeah, exactly. Annoying, right?"

He nodded, slipping his hands into the pockets of his khakis shorts.

I continued, "So, we were forced to spend a lot of time

together. We'd play nice whenever our fathers were around, which is how we ended up with pictures like this." I pointed to the frame on the wall, "But when their backs were turned, we'd be on each other in a second. Fists would fly, and we'd go home bruised and battered, both lying that we fell down or got a bit rough while wrestling."

Connor stared quietly at the picture a few moments longer, and then he looked back at me. I could see his wheels turning. Maddie was right. The Declan in that picture was a spitting image of the boy standing next to me. It would be hard to miss, and my son wasn't stupid. He'd already begun to ask questions here and there. He'd asked one day after a walk in the park if I knew who his Dad was. Another time while we were out for ice cream, he asked about his mom's friends, trying to find the missing link. I couldn't lie to him, so I'd always changed the subject. I would not tell him any more lies.

"You know last month, when it was my birthday and Sarah and Leah got me that cake that looked like a stack of pancakes?"

"Mmhmm, that was awesome."

Sarah and Leah had gone to a fancy bakery in Williamsburg and had it custom made. It was a new twist on an old tradition. Heather had made him pancakes on his birthday. We had made him a pancake birthday cake. It was a perfect melding of the old and new. It had been Leah's idea, and when she'd told me, I had fallen in love with her all over again. She never ceased to amaze me.

"And remember how I blew out the candle and made a wish?" he asked.

"Yeah?"

"Do you know what I wished for?"

"For your mom to come back?"

"No," he answered, "I know that's not going to happen."

I was a little sad, but I was also proud of him for saying this. I was sad because he had to realize this at a young age, but I was so proud that he was finally able to come to terms with his mom's death.

"Well then, what did you wish for, Little Man?" I asked, looking down at his eyes that perfectly matched mine.

"I wished for my dad."

Words failed me. I forgot how to breathe.

He looked at that photo on the wall and then back at me. His eyes were so full of hope. "Declan, are you my dad?"

I just nodded and knelt down to catch him as he jumped into my arms. I held him tight, and tears stung my eyes as I finally was able to hold him as his father.

"I knew it. I knew you were my dad," he just kept saying over and over.

"I'm so sorry. I didn't know. I didn't know," I answered back.

We clung to each other in the empty hallway, crying until there were no tears left. We held each other for as long as we could as if making up for every hug we'd missed over the last eight years of his life —every milestone, birthday wish, and accomplishment I'd never get back because I hadn't been there.

But never again.

I never wanted him to wonder where his father was or

ask why his dad didn't care enough to there for him. Saying good-bye to him after our visits was becoming more and more difficult, and I wasn't sure how much longer I could stand being a visitor in his life. Now that he knew who I was, I didn't want to say good-bye. I shouldn't have to. He was mine to protect, and it was time I started doing that full-time.

I looked up then to see Leah standing in the hall. Her stunned tear-stained eyes were watching over us as she witnessed our emotional introduction. She stayed back, allowing us a moment as father and son. She gave me a loving smile and mouthed the words, *I love you.*

While holding my son finally, I realized I needed to step up and become the father he needed of me. It made me feel driven, but it also scared the living shit out of me. Clutching him as I gazed into the eyes of the woman I loved, I wondered if my decision would be the one thing that could tear us apart.

LEAH

"Now, tell me the reason we just watched that movie?" Declan asked as he rose from the couch to carry our empty mugs and soda cans into the kitchen.

He might have made fun of me for eating ice cream out of a coffee mug, but ever since he'd moved in, it was the only way he would eat it. I'd successfully converted him.

"Because it was an action movie. Guys like action movies, right?" I asked innocently.

"You know I like watching all sorts of movies, even romances. I'm not a typical guy when it comes to films. Everything else, yes," he said with a impish grin, "but films, no."

"I don't know. I just wanted something a bit different," I answered sweetly as I joined him in the kitchen, dumping the soda cans into the recycling bin.

"Wouldn't have anything to do with the fact that it starred Chris Hemsworth, would it?" he asked, leaning against the counter, which made his biceps flex against the fabric of his T-shirt.

"No. No, that had nothing to do with it," I answered, suddenly forgetting what we were talking about altogether as I stared at his rippling biceps.

He slowly made his way to me and captured me between his arms against the kitchen counter.

"Good, because if you ever, ever need a man to do something with a hammer, just let me know."

I couldn't help it. I snorted against his shoulder, laughter escaping me. "Oh God, that was awful. Worse than the last pet name you thought up."

"Precious?"

"Yes!"

"I liked that one. It was endearing. What's wrong with precious?" he asked.

"Nothing...if your name is Gollum!" I exclaimed.

Before I could let out another laugh, I was thrown over his shoulder, and we were in a dead run toward the bedroom.

"Declan, put me down!"

"Nope, you have officially hit your pain-in-the-ass quota for the day, and you must be punished!"

"I don't have a quota! And it was your cheeseball line, not mine!"

He threw me down onto the bed and pinned me beneath him, his chest heaving and his eyes bright with laughter and heat.

"You're crazy," I said.

"Maybe, but just about you."

He'd been like this all week —happy and full of boyish energy. He had his son finally, all of him, and I could see the weight being lifted off of Declan's shoulders minute by minute. But there were also times I'd seen him struggle, and I didn't know how to help. I'd see him staring at me from across the room with a pained look, but then he'd quickly look away and distract me with questions about work or the family before I could ask him what was wrong. Whatever he was trying to overcome, I only hoped he would share it soon because a female's mind was a powerful thing. Mine was already running wild with a million different reasons for his hot and cold mood swings and none of them were good. Life had just thrown us a new curve ball with Connor, and I could only hope we were strong enough to stabilize.

Our lovemaking started off playful and teasing. He nipped my shoulder, and I laughed. I pinned him beneath my thighs and gave him a show as I tore off my shirt and twirled it around in the air before letting it fly across the room. With Declan, there were a million different ways to make love, and I never seemed to get enough of any of it. He'd take me fast and hard, long and slow, or with a playful leisure that made me fall for him all over again.

When he entered me, hovering over me, with his fiery eyes locked on mine, I saw his playfulness melt away. He bent down and kissed my lips gently at first as if he were trying to savor the taste forever. Once locked into memory, he consumed me in a fevered kiss that hinged on the side of frantic.

Slipping one arm under me, he lifted me up against his

hard chest, making the angle ever so deep, bringing our bodies even closer. I looked into his eyes and saw desperation, like at any moment he was afraid I would slip through his fingers like sand.

"Please," he begged, "don't ever leave me."

"I won't leave you, Declan."

"Promise it," he said roughly as his body continued to master mine.

I felt the familiar flutter deep in my belly, and I knew I wouldn't be able to hold on much longer.

"I promise," I cried out as my body shook, sending waves of pleasure ricocheting through me.

Declan followed, letting out his own release, as mine continued to spasm around his shaft. He looked into my eyes, his own so full of love and adoration. I felt unworthy of such deep emotions.

"You're mine, Leah. Forever."

"Yes, and you're mine. Forever."

I fell asleep in his arms as I had every night. I couldn't help but wonder what had brought on his desperation, his need for promises.

*Where did he think I was going?*

DECLAN

The next morning, I awoke before the sun broke over the horizon. The room was still dark and gray. Leah was curled against my side, her breathing quiet and even, and her honey-colored hair was splayed wildly across my chest. I very rarely awoke before she did. As a nurse, she worked odd hours, and usually, she woke up before the sun did. Moments like this, I treasured. She looked softer and innocent when she slept, giving every ounce of trust to me as I held her through the night.

This week had been one of the best and worst of my life. I'd spent hours doing research on proving paternity and obtaining custody, and I had spoken with Sarah and Devin. They were in agreement with me, and they'd fully supported my decision. As much as they loved Connor, they wanted him to be happy, and they believed that I could provide that for him. Even though it wasn't what Heather wished, Sarah felt a child should be raised by a loving parent whenever possible. I was so incredibly touched by their willingness and dedication to Connor. At any point in this journey, they could have slammed the door in my face, and that would have made everything a giant mess.

I hadn't said a word to Leah. Through so many phone calls, research, and paperwork, I hadn't told the one person I cared about the most —the woman I lived with and loved with my entire being. *Why?* I was scared to death. *What would she say? Would she hate me for making such a huge decision without her? Was she ready to be a mother?* She could leave me. I couldn't live without her, but I couldn't ignore my duties as a father. I couldn't treat my son the way my father had treated me.

"Declan," Leah said, her voice soft and sleepy, "what are you doing awake?"

"Couldn't sleep," I simply stated.

"Are you okay?" she asked, lifting her head to meet my gaze.

"I want Connor."

"We get to see him this weekend," she encouraged, bending down to gently kiss my shoulder.

I should have said something. I should have talked to her before I contacted anyone. She should have been my first priority after Connor, but I'd panicked.

"I don't mean it like that. I mean, I want custody of him. I want all of him, all the time. I can't keep saying good-bye," I said without looking at her, afraid of her reaction.

*Did she expect this? Would she be angry? God, I'd never been so fucking scared in my life.*

"Say something," I whispered in the darkness.

"What do you want me to say?"

"That you won't leave me; that you'll stay."

"Is that what you're worried about?"

"Yes, this is a lot to ask of you. We aren't even married, and I'm asking you to be a mother to my child. How can I do that?"

"Declan, look at me."

I turned finally, and I saw none of the reactions I'd expected. Her eyes were not filled with anger or rejection. She wasn't turning to run or flee. She looked at me with nothing but love and compassion, reminding me of all the reasons I'd fallen for her. She was selfless in every way.

"How many times do I have to tell you? I'm not going anywhere. Am I scared that I won't be enough for him? Yes. I've worried about it every day since I saw that picture in your drawer. Since I was a child, I never planned on having children because I figured, after the upbringing I had, I could never be the type of mother any child deserved. What does a motherless child know about raising another?"

"You don't have anything to worry about. Don't you see it?" I asked, grasping her chin in my hand. "You're already there. You've been doing it ever since Connor came barreling down those stairs that first day...hell, ever since you sat with him in that hospital. Who do you think I've been learning from all these months? You might not be his mother, but that child adores you."

"I just...I don't know. I will always, always doubt myself," she whispered. "Why did she have to leave me, Declan? Why?"

It always came down to her mother. Every fear she had stemmed from the fact that she believed there was something innately wrong with her. Leah had come to the conclusion that this is the only reason her mother would have left.

I hadn't wanted to share this with her yet because I wasn't done with my investigation, but she needed it. She needed to know what I'd found since that day I sent her father packing.

"Get up," I commanded.

"What?"

"Get up, and put on your robe. We're going up to the attic."

"Why?" she scoffed.

"I have something I need to show you."

Five minutes later, she had her robe and signature fuzzy slippers on, and she was climbing the ladder to the attic.

"I hate this fucking ladder, Declan, so whatever is up

here better be good." I gave her a quick kiss and a slap on the ass pointing to the ladder. She groaned, but started climbing and I followed behind. *I won't lie —I checked out her ass the entire way up.*

As soon as we made it through the tiny entrance, we stood, or crouched rather, as Leah took an appraising gaze over the dimly lit space.

"Okay, you want to tell me what we're doing up here, Hotshot?"

"Before we sold your dad's house, I had him give me everything that belonged to your mother," I said, motioning to a small box near the Christmas decorations.

There hadn't been much, but what was there was enough to make a major impact on Leah's life.

"What? Why would you do that?" she asked, staring at the box as if it were going to jump up and attack.

"I wanted to know if there was anything else...anything we could find out about her to give you closure," I explained.

"But why are you just now telling me this?"

"I hired a private investigator who was going to go deeper and try to look up court documents. I wanted his work to be finished before I told you anything, but I think you need to know now."

"Need to know what?" she asked, taking a step toward the box and then a step back.

She was warring with herself, unable to decide if she wanted to open Pandora's box or leave well enough alone.

In less than ten seconds, she would have her answer.

"Your mother didn't abandon you."

My words hit her like a gust of wind. Her knees shook

before she quickly knelt, planting herself on the ground. I quickly joined her on the dusty wood floor and took her hand.

"What?"

"From what I can gather from the letters she sent your father, she tried to sneak the two of you out of the house one night, but your father caught her. She didn't love your father. She got caught in a bad situation and wanted out. She tried to save you both. When he found her, he kicked her out, saying he'd kill her if she ever came back. I think he kept you as a sick way of getting back at her. She left that night, but she never gave up on trying to get you back."

Leah couldn't speak.

After a few minutes, she said, "My whole life I thought she'd left because I'd done something or because I hadn't been good enough. But she'd left to protect me. I remember…I remember that night she left. She paused at my bedroom door on her way out. I always found it strange, but it suddenly makes so much sense. She loved me?"

"Yes, babe, she loved you. She spent the rest of her life trying to get you back until she died a few years later of pneumonia."

"But who put up the gravestone for her?" she asked.

"That's been a hard one. I was hoping there was a family member, someone you could reach out to, but the investigator says the plot was purchased by a woman who worked at the hospital your mother died in. She probably took pity on her and wanted her to have a nice burial plot."

"I can't believe you did this," she said, "I would have never known. My father never told me."

I kissed her forehead and then her cheek, kissing away the tears that stained her skin. "Now, you have no reason to doubt yourself. Your mother loved you. But even if she hadn't, you have enough love to overcome anything."

She threw her arms around me and cried tears of joy and relief. Years of thinking she was less than worthy of a mother's love evaporated in an instant because of a small cardboard box. Why her father had kept it, I would never know, but that small box saved a part of Leah, and to me, it was a miracle.

"Thank you, Hotshot," she said, pulling back to give me a weak smile.

Giving a quick grin, I replied, "Anytime, muffin."

# Chapter Twenty-Six



"Oh my God, Connor. My feet are going to fall off, and then you will have to carry me all the way home," I whined as we entered the fifth store of the day in search of the perfect bedding for his new room.

I thought girls were supposed to be picky. Apparently, boys could be equally so.

After visiting probably close to a gazillion houses, we'd finally found the perfect one to call home. Connor had thought house hunting was excellent.

He would always run inside every house we visited and yell, "My room!" when he'd found the one he wanted.

It didn't matter if the house had been a dump. He had always called dibs immediately. The idea of having a house he could call his own again excited him. Sarah and Devin had always treated him like a son, and he'd had his own room at their house, but for whatever reason, I didn't think he'd ever felt at home there. Maybe it was because his room had once been their guest room, and he had known that because he used to sleep there on visits with his mom. In any case, he couldn't wait to get a room of his own.

Declan and I had very different views when it came to houses. He was a man. I had thought he'd walk into a house and say, "Whatever you want, honey," like most men do. *As long as it had a garage and a place to put a big TV, what man cared? But no, not my man.* The granite had been too dark, or the cabinets had been too light. He hadn't liked the way the carpet felt under his toes. He had driven me insane. I'd scream in frustration and catch him smirking out of the corner of my eye, which had made me wonder if he had done all of this shit just to mess with me. But the instant we'd walked into the house on Maple Lane, I had known he was really that damn picky.

When we'd stepped inside, we'd both gasped. It was breathtaking. There were hardwood floors throughout, a kitchen any chef would die for, and a master bedroom fit for a king. The best part? The other four bedrooms were way down the hall. A bit of separation between Connor and our bedroom at night would be a good thing, especially when he got a little older. *Nothing worse than walking in on the parents. Yuck.*

We'd signed on the dotted line immediately, and our offer had been accepted. We'd officially moved in yesterday, and as Declan sat at home, unpacking, I'd taken Connor out to find bedding for his Iron Man–themed room. After four hours, I was starting to think Amazon would have been a better option.

"What if we got a solid red bedspread and painted the walls in an Iron Man theme?" I suggested brightly.

He gave me a look suggesting that was the lamest idea in history as he moved on toward the bedding section of store number five.

"What if we just bought a ton of Iron Man posters? Or glued a bunch of Iron Man action figures to the walls?"

"Le-ah!" he said, exasperated.

I laughed, messing up his hair, until he giggled.

"Okay, okay. I am at your service. Iron Man bedding or nothing! We will find it if we die trying!"

"That's the sprit!"

We walked through the bedding section, seeing every beloved childhood toy and action figure, except for the one we needed.

Connor sighed.

"Would you consider Bob the Builder?" I teased.

He gave me a goofy look and stuck out his tongue as we made our way out of the home section.

"Hey, Little Man, think I could interest you in an ice cream cone?"

"Is it vanilla?"

"Whatever floats your boat, dude."

We headed for the exit when a man came out of nowhere and collided with me. I immediately reached for Connor and righted my purse.

"I'm so sorry. I didn't see you," I began to apologize as I righted myself.

"You always were a bit of a klutz, weren't you, girl?"

Even though I hadn't heard it in almost a year, I'd recognize that ragged voice anywhere. My eyes lifted and fell in line with the hard, icy gaze of my father, the man I thought I'd never have to see again. He looked a bit cleaner, and his clothes were newer. But beyond the apparel, that same man I'd grown up hating was there. The blurred eyes and haggard demeanor told me he hadn't changed his lifestyle at all since leaving town.

"You have some balls coming back here," I said in a steady voice even though my heart rate had just kicked it into high gear. I felt like I was going to collapse.

Remembering I needed to stay calm for Connor, who was my number one priority, I took his hand and pulled him behind me, sheltering him with my body.

"I've been hanging low in Florida the last few months. I rented an apartment there, a nice one, thanks to your boyfriend. Figured I'd go someplace warm since I had spent my entire life living in a shithole because of you," he spat.

"Why did you come back? You weren't supposed to come back."

"Was at the store, getting some essentials," he said. *Essentials* was his key word for alcohol. "And imagine my surprise when I saw my baby girl on the front of a magazine, holding hands with the man who had run me out of town."

"No one ran you out of town," I corrected. "And I'm not your baby girl. Declan offered you money, and you took it."

"Yes, but I didn't realize he was a famous movie star and all. I'd say I was a bit shortchanged, don't you think?"

"What do you want?" I asked, grasping Connor's scared hand behind my back.

He hadn't said a word, but I knew he had to be frightened. I suddenly remembered the last store we'd visited. We'd seen a flowery pink sofa, and I'd taken a picture. I'd sent it to Declan and joked that I'd found a perfect addition to our living room. I'd slid my phone into my back pocket, waiting for his snarky reply, and it was still there.

Loosening my grip on Connor's hand, I pinched my phone between my fingers. Connor must have caught on because he grabbed it and took over.

"I want more money —a lot more."

"We're not giving you any more. You need to leave," I said.

"See, for a few days now, I've been watching you and that little boy you have behind you. Well, I'm guessing he's important to that boyfriend of yours. Wouldn't want anything to happen to him, would ya?"

"You wouldn't," I seethed.

"The gun tucked under my coat says otherwise," he sneered.

Any belief I'd had that there could be an ounce of good hiding somewhere deep down in my father was completely shattered in that instant. I knew he'd never cared or given two shits about me. I'd had enough run-ins and blowouts with him over the years to make that abundantly clear, but I had hoped that somewhere in that ice-cold, whiskey-soaked heart of his, there was some humanity left.

As I watched him look down on us with those familiar hazy eyes, now filled with hateful determination, I knew...he would always be the villain. Nothing could ever redeem him. When someone threatened the life of a child, there was no coming back from that. My father was a shell. He was nothing but a soulless alcoholic, intent on finding his next bottle, and nothing would ever get in his way.

"I think it's time the three of us took a little trip," he said, patting his hip, with a wicked smile.

With that gun in his possession, I was backed into a corner. Every molecule in my body was screaming to turn, run, and yell for help. But I looked at the man in front of me, and I didn't trust him. I didn't know what he would and wouldn't do. *Would he turn and run? Or would he shoot?* One thing my father had proven today was that he was unpredictable.

I should have known better after reading those letters he'd saved from my mother. I'd always cast him aside as a lifeless drunk, but behind those vacant eyes lay something much more sinister. Feeling Connor's small body behind me, knowing I was his sole protector in that moment, I knew I couldn't risk doing anything bold.

I gave a slight nod, squeezing Connor's hand, as he quickly shoved my phone back into my pocket.

"All right, Dad. You win. We'll go with you."

DECLAN

"One second, she was crying over a commercial she'd seen, and the next, she was shoving me down onto the couch, begging me to take her. It's weird, man," Logan said as we continued to unload boxes from the moving truck into the house.

This was our house —the house I owned with Leah,

the house we now shared with my son. Well, we would share it once all the court documents were filed. It was a surreal day.

"So, this is what I have to look forward to someday?" I asked with a grin.

"I think you have a few more steps to go through, dude, before you knock Leah up...unless you're planning on going the celebrity route and doing everything ass-backwards."

We set the boxes down in the formal living room, a room I didn't quite understand. *Why did a house need two living rooms?* It seemed redundant.

"No, I definitely plan on putting a ring on that woman before long. That way, she can't run," I said jokingly.

"Yeah? Good for you, man. Does Connor know?"

I nodded, remembering the conversation we'd had a week or so ago. Leah had been out, grabbing take-out, and I'd sat down with Connor to have a man-to-man chat. He had been excited as he'd asked how I was going to do it.

"You can't just ask her. You have to make it romantic, Dad."

I'd laughed and assured him I would do just that. It still tore me up every time he called me Dad.

"He's really happy," I said to Logan as we headed back outside to grab another box for the hundredth time. *How much damn shit did we have?* "But you can't tell Clare. Leah would know in five seconds flat. You know those two don't keep any secrets."

"What are you two talking about out here?" Clare asked, poking her head out the door.

"You weren't lifting anything, right? I told you to just put away small things, like kitchen things and clothes," Logan scolded, immediately taking residence next to his wife.

She was barely three months pregnant, but Logan was treating her like she was about to give birth any day. We'd all given him shit because he was so cautious and careful with her. As a doctor, he knew better, but apparently, that need to protect overrode all of his medical training. I knew it was a bit of a miracle that they'd conceived in the first place. They hadn't been planning on it, especially with Logan just recently going into remission. But here they were, expecting a child. I'd never seen my friend so frazzled and happy all at the same time. It was a look I hoped I'd have the pleasure of having someday.

"I was just saying how you and my lovely girlfriend can't keep secrets from each other," I said to Clare.

"Oh," she said with a giggle, "that's very true. Very true indeed."

"I don't even want to know what that smile means," I said.

She just laughed and headed back inside. I searched around the moving truck, grabbed another box, and took it inside, heading towards the kitchen. I found Clare sitting on the countertop with Logan standing between her legs. His arms were wrapped around her waist, and he was pulling her body closer as he kissed her.

"Dude! Could you at least let me be the one to deflower my kitchen?" I found a magnet on the counter and threw it at his head.

He ducked and laughed, chucking a kitchen towel in

my direction. Just as I was looking around the kitchen for something else I could launch at my horny friend, my phone vibrated in my back pocket.

Leah had been sending me funny texts all day, so I was curious to see what shenanigans she was up to this time. She had sent me pics of flowery bedspreads and another one of herself looking miserable as she and Connor entered yet another store. I'd also received a text saying that she was seriously considering painting his room pink as retribution. She'd thought she was getting off easy by taking Connor shopping for bedding and not having to unpack. Little had she known that it would turn out to be an all day affair. I felt bad for her, but then not so much while I stretched my aching back as I remembered when she'd told me we didn't need a mover.

With a goofy grin on my face, I pulled out my cell and saw that I did have a new message from Leah, but this one wasn't funny or snarky. This one stopped my blood cold and left me frozen in my tracks.

Dad, need U. At mall. Man with gun.

"Declan, you look like you just saw a ghost," Clare said.

Someone tugged at my arm, pulling the phone out of my hand, which snapped me back into reality.

*Leah and Connor needed me.* I didn't understand what was happening, but I needed to get to them —now.

I heard Logan and Clare's reaction to the text message a second later, and I didn't even need to voice my request as Logan grabbed his keys and headed to the door with me. He turned briefly and gave Clare a quick but passionate kiss that seemed to say everything all at once.

"Tell Maddie I'll be home soon," he said.

And we were gone.

I barely remember the car ride. Thank God Logan drove because I didn't know how the fuck I would have gotten there otherwise. Logically, I knew the mall was only five minutes away, but it felt like an eternity to get there.

"What do you think he meant?" I asked.

"I don't know," Logan stated.

"Do you think there's a shooter?"

"God, I hope not."

We arrived at the mall, and everything seemed normal. People were walking calmly to their cars, and others were walking in. I remembered which store Leah had said they were headed to in her last text, so I directed Logan there first. We leaped from the car and took off toward the entrance.

That was when I saw him —Clayton Morgan, Leah's father.

I'd never felt such instant rage before in my life. Leah and Connor were walking ahead of him in the parking lot, and they looked ashen and scared. Clayton kept close behind, no doubt covering the gun that was pointed into their backs.

*The motherfucker came back.* This was my fault. I'd assumed the money would be enough to keep him away. I'd thought he was so far gone into himself that once he got away, he wouldn't be able to find his way back. I'd seriously underestimated him, and now, Leah and Connor were paying the price.

He looked in our direction, and I dodged behind one of the cars. I didn't want to give up my position yet. If I knew the bastard at all, he had to have some alcohol running through that body, so he would be slow, and I'd use that to my advantage.

Crouched next to me, Logan asked, "Is that Leah's father?"

I just nodded.

"We need to take him out before he gets out of this parking lot." I said.

"Agreed."

Moving low, we managed to get behind Clayton. Taking quick steps, we caught up, and in one quick motion, Logan attacked Clayton from the right, and I slammed into Connor and Leah from the left, moving them out of the way.

My eyes briefly met Leah's before I quickly checked both of them for injuries.

"Run," I told them. "Use your phone and call the police. We'll detain him until then."

Leah nodded, looking vulnerable and scared but strong and determined as well. She grabbed Connor, who was clutching my shirt and crying, and then they took off toward the entrance of the mall. She already had her phone out and to her ear by the time she was to the doors.

I turned to see Logan straddling Clayton on the ground. The gun was tossed several feet away, and Leah's father was face down on the pavement with his hands behind his back.

"Sure you don't moonlight as a cop?" I asked Logan.

"I'm not just a pretty face, you know? I got skills."

I gave a ghost of a smile before focusing back on Clayton. My fists clenched, and I fought back the need to attack. I wanted vengeance so bad that I could taste it.

"Get him up," I said to Logan.

Logan lifted off of Clayton and roughly pulled him up from the ground. He wrapped his arm around Clayton's neck in a chokehold to make sure he wouldn't get away. Clayton's vision focused and unfocused for a minute, making his level of intoxication clear, and then his eyes finally settled on me.

"Well, well…if it isn't the movie star. Haven't gotten tired of my daughter yet, huh?"

My fist collided with his face so fast that I barely saw it. I only registered his head snapping back afterward.

"You shut the fuck up, do you understand? The police are going to be here in less than five minutes. Then, you will finally be arrested and punished for the multitude of sins you've committed over the years, including when you tried to kidnap my son today. You're going away for a long time, Mr. Morgan."

He just sneered at me, giving me that evil smile that said he didn't give a fuck about what I'd said.

"Do you remember what I told you about how much they love child abusers in prison?"

His eyes went wide just as I heard the sirens pulling into the parking lot. I gave a wave, and the police cars headed in our direction.

Turning my head back to Clayton, I gave a wicked grin and said, "You have fun in prison, you hear?"

His pleas for help and his cries declaring his innocence were the last things I heard as the cops shoved him in the police car before driving away.

# Chapter Twenty-Seven



I broke down the last box and took a final look around. We'd done it. Every box was unpacked, and everything was put away.

We had a new place to call home.

It had taken a solid week to unpack. Between my work schedule and driving back and forth to Williamsburg to visit Connor, we'd managed to cram the entire week full of activities, leaving little time for thinking.

I thought we were both avoiding the inevitable, but sooner or later, we'd have to talk about it.

Hands slid around my waist as Declan pulled me close.

"Looks good," he said, his mouth hovering over my shoulder.

"It does, doesn't it?"

"I wasn't talking about the room."

He dusted featherlight kisses on my skin that sent shivers down to my toes. He spun me around, and I immediately became lost in his dark gaze. Declan had the ability to say so much with even the slightest expression. Right now, I saw a million emotions churning under the surface of his intense stare.

"I love you, Leah," he said intently before bending down to touch my lips with his. "I love you so much," he murmured.

"I love you, too," I whispered.

He trailed kisses down my neck and shoulder. "The thought of losing you...I was sure I'd go mad from it," he admitted, bending down to bury his head in my shoulder.

I stroked his chestnut hair as he held my waist.

"I'm right here. Connor and I are fine. You saved us."

"I wanted to kill him. It took every ounce of control I had not to rip him apart right in the middle of that parking lot. If he had hurt you again, I don't know that I would have been able to control myself."

"Shhh...he's where he's supposed to be, Declan. He can't hurt any of us anymore."

"I was so stupid, Leah. So stupid. I should have let the police handle it in the beginning. I should have had him arrested the minute I saw the bruises on your face. None of this would have ever happened then."

"Declan," I said, pulling his face up to my eye level, "none of this is your fault. Do you hear me? None of it. You've done nothing but protect Connor and me. We could have never known what my father was capable of. Please don't let guilt take over."

He gave a brief nod, bending down to take my lips again, as if he needed proof that I was still there. I eagerly gave him all the reassurance he needed as I returned his kiss. I slightly moaned as he deepened it, sweeping his tongue against mine, like two bodies making love. He slowly led me across the room until I felt the back of the couch bump against my legs, and I fell backward. He laid me down and settled his weight on top of me, his eyes full of heat and need.

"I'm right here," I reminded him. I placed his hand on my heart, so he could feel it beating inside my chest.

"Show me," he said.

Declan's world had been rocked last week, and I could see in his eyes that he needed this. He needed me to show him we were still *us*. I was still Leah, and he was still Declan, and nothing could change that.

"Take off your clothes," I instructed.

He stood and shed his clothes, and then he watched as I did the same. I had him sit down and face me. If he needed to see, then I would show him.

I straddled him, placing one leg on each side of his massive thighs, and then I took him inside me. He hissed in pleasure, but his eyes never wavered from mine as I slowly slid myself down his length.

"Do you see me?" I asked.

"I see you," he answered.

I lifted, sliding up, and then I went back down again, slowly riding him. I grabbed the back of the couch for leverage as Declan wrapped his hands around my waist. He buried his head into my breasts, taking one nipple and then the other into his mouth.

"Do you feel me, Declan?"

"Yes...fuck yes."

I continued my torturous pace, over and over, moving

my hips back and forth. As I hit all the right places at once, I threw my head back and screamed my release just as Declan let out a guttural moan of his own.

"I'm yours, remember? I'm yours, and you are mine," I said breathlessly.

"Forever," he agreed.

DECLAN

The vision of Leah and Connor being pushed through that parking lot had startled me, and I awoke on the couch with the afternoon sun streaming through the curtains. I was alone, but I could hear Leah walking around upstairs, no doubt finishing up some odds and ends leftover from moving.

I wiped my brow and leaned back on the pillow, still trying to catch my breath. The image had been haunting me for days, so much so that I'd barely slept. Every morning since then, I'd woken up early to jog, unpack, or run errands. I'd done anything to keep my mind off of what had happened...what I'd almost lost.

Seeing that maniacal gleam in Clayton's eyes as he'd smiled at me before the police had come, I knew he would have done anything to get the money he'd so desperately believed he deserved. Leah and Connor had been nothing more than his ticket to an unlimited supply of booze, and that had been the one thing he needed above all else in life, the one thing he would do anything for.

That scared me beyond belief.

The police had tried to convince me that Clayton's threats were most likely those of a drunk man, and therefore, they were idle, but I had known better. Clayton had been desperate, having gone through half a million dollars in the blink of an eye. He'd needed more...and he hadn't planned on taking no for an answer.

We'd been assured that Clayton would be put away for a long time, but there was still a court hearing and a trial to go through —the very things I'd tried to avoid in the beginning with my ill-fated plan.

I'd thought I could fix everything with my money.

And it'd almost cost me everything.

Leah and Connor had recovered well, considering what they'd experienced. Leah had spent a lifetime with her father, and for her, seeing Clayton behind bars had been worth the fear. The only thing she'd had problems overcoming was that Connor was involved. After everything Connor had already been through in his short life, she hated that he'd had to go through something else horrific. But I'd assured her that he was fine. He'd told me shortly afterward that he'd known Leah would protect him and take care of him, no matter what. He saw her for more than she gave herself credit for.

I jumped to my feet, raking my hands through my hair. I looked around the house that was now void of the boxes that had invaded every square inch only days earlier. Now, it looked more like a home —our home.

I'd had a plan —buy the house, get settled, figure everything out with Connor. Once our lives had slowed down, I would propose, and then we could begin our lives together, finally.

But the only thoughts racing through my mind when I had seen her in that parking lot was the fact that I'd never asked her to marry me, I'd never told her that I wanted her to be my wife, that I wanted to love her for eternity.

In my old life, I'd lived from one day to another, never taking life too seriously. Since meeting Leah, I'd done nothing but plan —when I would first tell her I loved her, when I wanted to leave L.A. for her, and then when I wanted to marry her. I'd done nothing but plan.

It turned out the old Declan might have had the right idea.

Sometimes, you just had to fuck the plans and live. Otherwise, life would pass you by, and all you'd be left with was a bunch of useless, unexecuted plans.

*It was time I started living.*

"Hey, Leah...I have to run out for a bit. I'll be back."

I heard a mumbled, "Okay," as I hurried out the door.

If I wanted to get everything done, I needed to hurry.


LEAH

"So, do you think he got lost?" I asked Clare, holding the phone against my ear.

I sorted through the box of picture frames, trying to decide how to arrange them. I smiled, seeing a photo of Declan and me from Christmas. We were laughing, and Declan was looking at me with those eyes that made me melt. Those eyes could make me want to smile, cry with joy, and jump him all at the same time.

"How long has he been gone?" she asked.

"Um, about three hours, maybe four. He said he needed to run a few errands, but that was a while ago. I was going to order a pizza, but I wanted to wait for him."

"Ugh, don't mention food. Right now, food makes me want to hurl."

I laughed. "Morning sickness? Aren't you past three months? Shouldn't you be over that?"

"You'd think so, but apparently, Logan Matthew's child is an overachiever."

"It's Logan's child now?" I tried not to giggle.

"Yes. Until it does something redeeming, like flutter or kick, it's Logan's child."

"When was the last time you got laid, Clare?"

"What?"

"Seriously, you're about to explode. I'm going to hang up now, and you are going to go find that hot doctor of yours. Have him perform some sort of naughty exam on you, and you'll feel better soon, I promise."

"You're really bossy...and nosy. You know that, right?"

"Yes, and you love me anyway. Now, go have sexy time. I don't want my little goddaughter or godson coming out all frustrated and mean because of you."

She laughed, and we said our good-byes.

Just as I was setting the last photo on the mantle, I heard the door.

"Well, it's about time. I thought you got —"

I turned and saw Declan standing in the doorway, holding the biggest bouquet of red roses I'd ever seen. Next to him was Connor, holding a smaller version of the same bouquet.

"Connor! I thought we weren't going to see you until Saturday!"

"I needed him to help me with a small favor," Declan

said, closing the door and walking into the room with a slow swagger.

He had changed somewhere along the way during his errands. He was now dressed in dark jeans and a green button-up that brought out the green in his eyes.

"I should put these in water," I said, reaching out to grab the flowers.

He just set them down on the coffee table. "They can wait."

My heart kicked up a notch, and I looked from Declan to Connor, who had a huge smile on his face.

Declan bent down, and he kissed me slow and with purpose. "Do you remember asking me a long time ago about the tattoo on my chest?"

I nodded.

"And what did I tell you?"

I remembered that day in bed so long ago when I'd first run my fingers over the circular design on his chest. "You said people were essentially selfish, and when it came down to it, we would always choose ourselves because we loved ourselves first," I answered.

"God, hearing you say it makes me feel like even more of a moron," he said, shaking his head. "I got that tattoo when I was in a dark place. I thought I'd experienced love and loss, but I hadn't even scratched the surface. When I met you, I couldn't keep my eyes off you. I tried to tell myself it was because you were beautiful, attractive, and alluring. But it wasn't one particular thing that drew me in. It was you as a whole that I couldn't walk away from."

I was dumbstruck. I looked briefly down at Connor

and he was just staring up at his father beaming. My eyes met Declan's again and he continued.

"You are my other half, Leah, my soul mate, my missing piece. You showed me that there are still selfless people in this world who are worth all the risk that we go through to love another."

He reached up and wiped away my tears before turning to Connor.

He gave him a wink. "You ready?" he asked.

Connor gave an enthusiastic nod. Declan started undoing the buttons to his shirt, and Connor mimicked his father. When the two undid the last button and parted their shirts together, I gasped.

Where Declan's tattoo had been empty in the middle, it was now filled with an intricate *L*. I looked over at Connor, and he proudly displayed a smaller matching version of his father's tattoo.

"Oh my God, that better not be permanent!" I said quickly, pointing at Connor.

They both laughed.

"It's henna, Leah!" Connor said.

I blew out a short breath before turning my attention back to Declan.

"But mine is not," he said. "Like you, mine is permanent."

He dropped to one knee and pulled out a box. He slowly opened it, displaying an engagement ring that made my heart stop. On a platinum band, a diamond was flanked by two emeralds to match his eyes. It was perfect.

"I've been doing some thinking, and I think I've come up with the best pet name for you."

I meant to say something like, "Oh?" or "What is it?" But in the presence of Declan with his shirt open, displaying that new *L* on his chest, while he held out a ring, all I managed was a garbled mumble.

"Wife."

More tears slid down my face as I cried

"Marry me, Leah. Make me the happiest man alive. Take my name, be a mother for my children, and grow old with me."

I sobbed out a yes, and he jumped up. He twirled me around as Connor jumped up and down until we pulled him into a group hug.

Declan slipped the ring onto my finger, and we all gazed down at it, watching it sparkle and flash under the bright lights.

It was the beginning of a future —our future, completely unscripted, unwritten, and ready to be lived.

LEAH

"Have I mentioned how much I hate you for getting married less than a month after I gave birth?" Clare whined as she wiggled her perfectly fine-looking ass into her gown.

"Yes, you've mentioned it a time or two." I laughed. "But as I've said a hundred times, you look gorgeous, and seriously, take a gander at those tits. You need to show those off while you can. You should be the poster child for the many reasons women should breast-feed. Wowza!" I said, pointing to Clare's very enlarged breasts.

There was a knock on the bridal suite door, and Clare ran to open it. She poked her head out to make sure it wasn't Declan trying to get a peek before the ceremony.

Declan and I had chosen to have a small, intimate day with only family and a few friends in attendance. Even though Declan hadn't done an acting gig for a year, he was still in the tabloids. It had been only three months since his last movie premiere, and he still had one left, so it would be some time before our lives moved out of the limelight.

His life behind the camera had been going well. He was slowly making progress and working with the right people. He wasn't in a hurry, and he knew that it would take time. He wanted to do things right and earn his keep. It was paying off because last week, he'd received a call to work as an assistant director on a highly anticipated upcoming film. He would be gone during the week, and then he'd fly home on the weekends, but I was so happy to see him finally doing what he loved.

Putting the finishing touches on my makeup, I saw Connor appear in the reflection of the mirror. He looked around the room and made a sour face at the sight of all the girlie stuff.

"Hi, Connor," Maddie said as she twirled around in her flower girl dress in the corner.

"Hi, Maddie," he said before turning to me. "I was supposed to give you this. You look really pretty." He handed me a small box and then made his exit, fleeing the room as quickly as possible.

I gave a quick laugh, feeling bad that Declan had sent his poor son in here. There was makeup, curling irons, and dresses as far as the eye could see. It was a male's worst nightmare.

I looked down at the tiny box, running my hands along its edge, before cracking the lid. Inside was a small white gold necklace with three stones fitted together in a straight line.

Underneath, a note caught my attention. In Declan's handwriting, I read,

> *In the box I recovered from your parents' home, there was one item I didn't tell you about — a necklace. It was badly damaged, but I was able to recover a topaz stone. I've held on to it for months until this day when I could give you this necklace. These three stones together represent our family. Our birthstones —topaz for you, amethyst for me, and opal for Connor —are bonded together as we will be bonded together today. You are my forever, and today, you will become my wife. I love you. – Declan*

"Well, crap, there goes my makeup," I said out loud, looking down at the beautiful necklace.

Clare knelt down in front of me and wiped away my tears. "Let me put that on you, okay?"

I agreed and slid my hair to one side. After she closed the clasp, my hand immediately went to the stones, loving the feel of the necklace against my skin.

"Well, I hope you have something to top that," Clare said.

I smiled, looking at the envelope in front of me on the counter. "Oh, yes, I have something better.

"Christ, Declan. Calm down!" Logan said.

I was pacing the pathway for the twentieth time. "I'm not nervous," I said. "I just don't want to wait anymore."

He gave me a lopsided grin. "I get it, but at this rate, you're going to attack her the second she steps outside. So, do us all a favor, and calm the fuck down."

I looked at him and Connor. They were both grinning like damn fools, and I finally nodded, taking a deep breath, as I tried to stay in one place for more than five seconds.

I checked my watch. It was five minutes after six. *Why are we running late?*

Just as I was about to start pacing again, the minister told us to take our places. This was it. In just a few minutes, Leah would be my wife. Two months ago, I'd finally gotten full custody of Connor, and now, Leah and I were going to be married. My life was now complete.

The music started, and I watched as the bridesmaids made their way down the aisle. Colin and Logan both admired their wives, and Clare gave a little wave to their newborn son, Ethan, who was in the arms of her mother in the front row.

Someone tapped me on the shoulder, and I reluctantly pulled my eyes from the aisle. I was afraid I might miss Leah's grand entrance.

Logan was holding an envelope out to me. "Hey, man, Leah said I was supposed to give this to you right before she came out. It's your wedding gift."

"I'm supposed to open it now?" I asked.

He just shrugged and smiled.

I did as I'd been told. I lifted the lip of the envelope and pulled out the note.

> *Declan,*
> *I couldn't think of anything better to give to you for a wedding gift than the present that is now growing inside of me. Congratulations, Daddy.*
> *- Leah*

My eyes went wide as I pulled out the picture tucked inside the envelope. It was a close up shot of a small white pregnancy test. A test that had one word printed on its digital screen in bold letters —*pregnant.* I looked up just in time to see Leah turning onto the rose-covered path, and I lost the ability to breathe.

She looked absolutely stunning in a cream gown that hugged her curves and made her look like a goddess come to life.

She joined me at the end of the aisle, and I took her hand in mine.

"You're..." I started to say.

But she just smiled and answered with a simple, "Yes."

As we said our vows, binding our souls and lives together as one, I looked past her shoulder and saw my son. Then, I glanced down at the child growing in Leah's belly, and finally, I focused back on the face that had made it all possible. She was my world, my beginning and end, and she had shown me everything I never thought I wanted.

It was only supposed to be one night, but with Leah in my arms...only forever would do.

———

Don't miss the next chapter of the Ready series... Garrett and Mia's story continues in... *Ready for You*

# READY FOR YOU

## PROLOGUE



Eight Years Ago…

All I could see was blue and white. It stretched out beyond my field of vision, encompassing the grassy terrain completely, as if the entire football field had exploded into a sea of satin.

I was a high school graduate—finally.

Proud parents hugged their sons or daughters, congratulating their success with wishes for bright, happy futures. My fellow graduates had banded together, standing united on that vast green grass, feeling proud and utterly relieved. We had finally made it. Twelve years were behind us, and we had nothing but endless possibilities in our future. I smiled at the thought. There was only one person I wanted in my future, both imminently and permanently.

As my parents took what was probably the hundredth picture, I saw her. Chocolate-brown hair tumbled down her back, contrasting against the stark white robe she wore. When her gaze turned upward, our eyes locked briefly from across the field, and she smiled.

Mia Emerson. *My Mia.*

She'd been the first girl I noticed freshman year and the only girl I'd paid attention to since. She was my world, and I couldn't wait to spend the rest of my life with her. It wasn't exactly the life our parents had imagined for us, and I knew they would disagree with the plans we'd made, but everything would work out. With Mia by my side, everything would always work out.

Tomorrow was the beginning of us.

With slight hesitation, she shyly walked up to my large group of family members laughing and talking loudly. She was always a bit timid around my parents even though she had no reason to be. My mother and father adored her, and nothing would change that, not even the bomb we were about to drop tomorrow morning.

"Mia!" my mom said, greeting her enthusiastically, while pulling her into a tight hug. "Congratulations, my dear!"

"Thank you, Mrs. Finnegan."

"How many times do I have to tell you, sweetheart? There's no Mrs. Finnegan around here. You can call me Mom or Laura."

Mia gave her a sweet smile and nodded.

Mia hadn't known how to react to my family the first time she met them. Her family was vastly different. They loved her in their own way, but hugs and feelings were never easy to come by in the Emerson household. Mia came from wealth, and her family did things a certain way. My touchy-feely, middle-income family looked like *The Beverly Hillbillies* compared to hers, especially her mother.

"Garrett, put your arm around Mia. I need a quick picture!" Mom said, holding her digital camera up once again.

My father chuckled, giving my mom a squeeze, as she held the camera and waited for us to pose. My mouth curled into a grin, and I wrapped my arm around Mia's waist. I knew when my mom had said *picture*, she really meant we would be here for an eternity. Laura Finnegan was unable to take just one picture. I didn't mind. Mom clicked away as we smiled and laughed. I'd gladly hold Mia in my arms forever.

"Okay, okay, Mom! I think that's enough! He's going to break the camera!" my older sister, Clare, joked from behind us.

I turned around and gave her a stern look, and she laughed. Her giant basketball stomach bounced up and down as she turned her head to shield her laughter. If she got any bigger, I swore she was going to deliver an entire litter of babies and not just the one she'd kept telling me was in there. Her husband, Ethan, bent down to place a tender kiss on her round stomach. My big sister was going to be a mother. That freaked me out a little. I spent a moment too long staring at her stomach, wondering—

"Hey, I've got to meet my parents for dinner. Pick me up later?" Mia said suddenly, bringing me out of my wayward thoughts.

Her brilliant teal-blue eyes found mine, and I nodded, pulling her closer.

"I'll be there," I promised before bending down to kiss her softly.

Our kiss lingered a bit before she got embarrassed, giggling and pushing away. My parents already knew we were head over heels in love. *Did she really think I was going to keep my hands off just because my mom was around?*

Mia shot me a sly grin, promising retribution that I was sure to enjoy later, and then I watched her walk away, disappearing into the crowd of blue and white satin.

Had I known this would be the last time I saw her, I would have never let her go.

I would have fought for her. I would have done something, anything.

I would have done anything, except stand there and watch her disappear...forever.

# CHAPTER ONE

GARRETT

I gasped, desperately seeking air, as I tried clawing my way back to reality. Oxygen filled my airways too quickly and burned a fiery path to my overworked lungs. I felt myself gripping, holding on…trying not to let go.

*Don't let her go. Not again. Come back, Mia. Come back!*

My eyes flew open, and I found myself back in my cramped, lifeless bedroom, back in the present.

*Back to hell.*

I couldn't count the number of times I'd relived that day. I would relive what had started out as a perfect day in my past, and I'd wake back up to the hell that had become my life. It was like some sick, twisted curse I'd been given to remind me just how fucked-up fate could be.

The sheets felt cold against my sweat-slicked body, and my heart rate was still racing a marathon. A marathon I never won. Night after night, I'd awake from the same nightmare, my heart racing as I tried, over and over, to change history through my dreams.

*Good luck, buddy.*

I'd given up on that hope years ago. Sitting up, I ran my hands over my face and tried to calm my nerves. Out of the corner of my eye, I caught the glint of a mostly empty bottle of tequila sitting on my nightstand. Looking through my hands, which were still covering my face, I saw the bra first, then the dress, and finally the heels. They were all scattered among my own clothes on the floor.

My head began to pound like a drum as I slowly pieced together the night before, remembering the copious amounts of alcohol I'd consumed. I'd wandered into a bar after another long day at work, and there was a woman.

*Sarah or Sierra?* It didn't matter.

I'd told her she was beautiful and offered to buy her a drink. She'd laughed at my lame jokes, throwing her head back with enthusiasm, while resting her hand on my thigh. Her laugh had been all wrong—high-pitched and too bubbly. But nothing ever was right. I'd bought her another drink, and finally, I'd followed it up by asking if she would like to have a third one—back at my place.

*Shit.*

Running my hands through my disheveled dark hair, I slowly turned to my right, and there she was—the owner of the dress.

*Siena or Samantha?*

*Sadie?*

I had no clue.

I was not a player. I wasn't one of those guys who

would bring a different woman home every night and brag about it to his coworkers the next day. I didn't have notches on my bedpost, and I actually really hated the one-night stand routine. But I wasn't a saint, and sometimes, the solitude and quiet of being alone would get to be too much, overwhelming me to the point where I would become so weighed down by it that I thought I might drown. That was when I would end up here—with a nameless woman and a fucking mess to clean up.

She really was beautiful though.

*I'm a giant asshole.*

"Hey—" I started but stopped short, remembering I had no idea what to call her.

She stirred a bit, stretching like a cat, which made the sheet draped over her fall away to expose her naked body. I turned away.

"Oh." She giggled a bit. "Good morning, Adam," she nearly purred.

*Adam, huh?* I never gave my real name, but I hadn't ever used that one before.

She reached out, searching with her fingers, but I jumped off the bed before she could touch me. I was sober. There would be no touching now. I threw on my clothes and began running around to pick up hers. Once that was done, I risked turning around.

Sitting up now but using the sheet to cover herself, she had that look. It was the same look they would all give me when I did this one-eighty routine. Her eyes darted around the room, and the confidence from her good-morning purr was now replaced with insecurity and awkwardness.

"Am I missing something? I thought we had a good time last night," she said quietly.

I huffed out a breath. "We did," I said even though I didn't remember any of it. "But you need to go. I'm sorry."

She nodded silently, and I tried to ignore the sight of her lip quivering as I put her clothes on the bed before walking out.

My apartment was small, bordering on claustrophobic, and it took exactly five steps to reach my kitchen from my bedroom. If I were to give someone a tour, it would last about ten seconds. I had one solitary bedroom, and it was barely big enough to fit my bed, nightstand, and dresser. There was one bathroom, and the kitchen and living room bled into each other so much that they were really considered one entity. To complete the bachelor pad, I had a small kitchen table that most people would probably consider more of a card table.

My sister, Clare, hated this apartment. She would refuse to use the bathroom because it was too close to the couch, and she felt like people could hear her pee. She'd said the word *pee* in a hushed tone, like it was a bad word. I'd tried not to laugh, but she was kind of ridiculous. Also, she was right. We could hear her pee, but I wasn't about to tell her that. She would make me move.

After visiting for probably the tenth time and still refusing to use my bathroom, she had finally asked, *Why do you live in such a shithole, Garrett?*

It was a good question. I had a good job—one that would pay for a place that could eat my current apartment for breakfast. But why bother? It was just me. It would only ever be just me.

Just as I started to pour myself a cup of freshly brewed coffee, the smell beginning to do its job as my droopy eyes were prying themselves apart, my mystery date appeared in the kitchen. She looked awkward, tugging at her wrinkled black dress, as she stared at the floor. I got the feeling that she wasn't the type of girl who did this often.

"I'm going to take off," she said softly, her timid brown eyes peeking out from tousled blonde bangs.

"Okay," I answered, feeling like the worst kind of asshole on the planet.

She waited for a second, obviously stalling to see if I would follow up with anything. When I didn't, she reached for the door and took a step forward, but I stopped her.

"Hey, I'm sorry. I just…I'm…" I didn't know what to say. *I'm fucked-up? Permanently?*

She looked up at me with those sad brown eyes that were now rimmed with tears—tears that I'd put there.

"Just answer one question. Is your name even Adam?"

"No," I answered honestly. I didn't volunteer my real name. What was the point?

Her watery eyes peered up at me as if searching for something. "You're hurting…over a woman?" she asked, surprising me.

My silence was enough of an answer for her, and she seemed to recover a bit from her revelation. Seeing me as a victim suddenly made her feel better. Well, at least there was that.

"The tattoo on your arm…is it for her?"

*Inquisitive little thing, wasn't she?* I really needed to stop getting drunk.

Her eyes wandered down to the tattoo in question, stopping at the black tip of script peeking out of my T-shirt sleeve.

"No," I bit out. "That's for someone else."

Date night was definitely over.


MIA

It had been eight years since I was in my home state of Virginia. Eight years since I'd left the boy who stole my heart on a hot summer night under the stars. Eight years since I'd given him nothing more than a tear-stained note, destroying everything we'd planned. Eight years since I'd driven over that state line and never looked back, ruining my life from that moment on.

Now, fate had brought me home again. Why? I didn't know, but like a magnet, I'd felt drawn back here, and I only hoped it wouldn't be a mistake.

Virginia was beautiful and picturesque as I made my way down the tree-lined back roads dotted with small farms and forgotten towns. My roots were here, buried in the sweet Southern air and the historic countryside. Crossing the city limits into Richmond felt like coming home for the first time in almost a decade. No matter where I had gone, where I'd settled down, I never felt more at home than I did here. This is where I truly belonged and it was about time I came to accept that.

A few miles deeper into the city, I was pulling up to the curb of my longtime friend Olivia Prescott, or Liv, as I liked to call her. It had been years since we last spoke. That had been my fault, not hers. I'd cut ties with everyone from my former life when I quietly left town the night of our high school graduation. After what I'd done, I'd felt too ashamed to face anyone, even those I was closest to.

The house was drastically different than what I'd ever envisioned for Liv. Her family, like mine, came from money. Initially, it had been why we became friends. Our parents had attended the same country club, and we would end up attending many of the same functions together. We quickly realized that we had a lot in common, and we had become fast friends.

Liv had hated the country-club life almost as much as I had. It was so stuffy and stifling in there. I would feel like my lungs were tightening every time I'd walked inside those pretentious gilded walls. Our mutual hatred for the place had created a close bond, and we had always sought each other out when we were forced to attend parties or formal events. Our parents hadn't approved of our friendship. We had been expected to act a certain way, and neither Liv nor I had fit the mold of the perfect daughter. Being together had only exacerbated the situation in our parents' eyes.

I'd finally taken a stand against my parents, but by the time I had, it had been too late, and it had ended up costing me everything. I could only imagine what Liv had gone through alone. As I stepped out of my car, I took my first good look at Liv's house, and I knew she must have done the impossible. She'd done what I should have that night so long ago. She'd broken free.

Her house was small, too small for a trust-fund baby, which we both were—or at least, we used to be. Her trust fund was substantially larger than mine since she came from a family that had a name everyone knew. My family was well-off, more so than most, but my parents always strived to appear greater than they were. My father was a lawyer, a very successful one. I never understood why he'd felt the need to kiss ass with the rich elitists of the city. But maintaining their image had been everything to my parents—or rather my mother. My father loved me, but he had been my mother's puppet. She'd always come first. When I'd finally walked away, I'd told my mother to screw herself, and I'd left my inheritance behind. I hadn't heard from either of them since.

Liv lived in a part of town known for being eclectic. The neighborhood was full of artists and college students. Within walking distance, there was access to great restaurants, shops, and bars. The houses were small, historic, and full of Victorian charm. Most were divided into duplexes or townhouses to accommodate the amount of students attending the nearby university. But Liv's home looked to be all hers with only one address painted in hot pink stenciling on a wooden sign hanging by the side of the mossy green front door.

I pressed the buzzer and waited. I admired the bright colors she'd chosen for her trim and porch, and I hated the fact that she could keep her plants alive. I had the exact opposite of a green thumb. *What would that be? A black thumb?* Well, whatever it was, I had it. If they could, plants would scream and run away from my presence, knowing I would be their ultimate demise. I also couldn't cook worth a damn. I was the antithesis of Martha Stewart.

The door was suddenly thrown open, and I was engulfed in a sea of ebony hair as Liv dove forward and threw her arms around me.

"Mia!" Liv squealed, pulling back from her hug attack to give me her signature megawatt grin.

I always loved Liv's smile. It could light up an entire room. Her smile was genuine and encompassed her entire face. Her brown eyes twinkled and warmed, her right cheek dimpled, and her entire personality shined through. *God, I had missed her.*

"Amelia Emerson! You haven't changed a bit! You're just as skinny and gorgeous as ever. But wait, hold on," she said, stepping back to assess me for a moment. "Turn for me."

I rolled my eyes and did as she'd said, making a complete turn on her front stoop. I hoped her neighbors couldn't see this little spectacle. I would be staying here for a bit, and I didn't want them to think I was Liv's crazy relative coming to visit.

"Your boobs got bigger!" she practically announced to the entire block.

"Oh my God, they did not!" I said, folding my arms over my chest.

"They did so," she fired back, pulling my arms away to expose the area in question.

Suddenly, I felt underdressed next to my long-lost friend. She was very put together—in a strange way. It was much different than the Liv I remembered. She had on a gorgeous maxi dress that hugged her curves and highlighted her own rack nicely. Her jewelry all looked handmade, nothing like the pricey designer pieces our parents use to buy. The bold silver necklace and matching earrings she wore accentuated her long neck and shiny black hair. Her appearance was very eclectic and artsy but in a hip and sophisticated manner.

I looked like a bum standing next to her. Since I had been traveling all day, I wasn't wearing anything fancy. I had on a faded Old Navy tank top and a pair of jeans I'd probably owned since college. Besides the pendant around my neck that I never took off, I didn't have any other jewelry on. To complete my fashion train wreck, I was wearing flip-flops that didn't even match.

*Yay, me.*

"Well, whatever you say, but I still think they are bigger. Is that a thing? Are they supposed to get bigger in our twenties? Because mine sure haven't. I heard they sometimes grow with pregnancy, but that shit definitely isn't ever happening to me, so I'm stuck with my mediums. I've never had any complaints though. What do they say? A handful is all you need."

I just stared for a moment, thrown off guard by what she'd said, but I laughed it off. Shaking my head, I said, "You haven't changed a bit."

"Oh, but I have. Can't you tell?" She tossed her hands up as if to acknowledge her surroundings as validation of her epic change.

"Yes, you need to tell me all about this," I said, waving my pointer finger in a circle to incorporate her entire look.

"Oh, I plan to. Let's get you inside and make some tea."

*Of course she drank tea.*

As we made our way through her home, I took notice

of the hand-carved wood artwork on the walls and the unusual paintings scattered everywhere. I couldn't help but wonder how my privileged friend had gone from being a senator's daughter to wearing moonstones and making tea.

I settled into a chair at her worn kitchen table and drew my knees up to my chin.

"Still folding yourself into a ball, Mia?"

It was the second time I'd heard her say my former name. I'd given that name up when I left my old life behind. When I'd walked away from Virginia, I'd stopped being Mia, and I'd started using my proper name, Amelia.

Mia was the name *he* had given me, and I couldn't bear to hear it. I didn't deserve it anymore.

"I go by Amelia now," I simply said.

"Okay," she said, sending me a strange look. "Still folding yourself into a ball, *Amelia*?"

"Yes, I guess some things never change."

She gave me a long stare as she filled up the teakettle. "No, they don't."

We moved from awkward conversation to silence for a while as she moved about the kitchen, pulling out snacks and tea from some weird tin. She was so different, yet I could still see parts of my old friend there. Some of her mannerisms were the same, like how she bit her bottom lip as she became impatient while waiting for the water to boil and how she rocked her hips when she was standing. I used to call her a valley girl for that silly movement after seeing the girls on *Clueless* do it. She would just laugh it off and keep doing it.

Liv finished pouring our tea—some weird herbal

blend and set the mugs on a tray along with a plate of cookies. She brought everything over and set it on the table and joined me. I added a bit of cream to my tea and grabbed a spiced cookie to nibble on.

"So, are we going to talk about why you ran out of here like a demon on graduation night and then never came back? Or are we going to continue to ignore it?"

I knew she would ask, yet I still hadn't prepared an answer.

"I…had to leave. I just…I'm sorry, Liv. I'm not ready to talk about this yet."

I looked up, expecting to see hurt or anger, but she was radiating understanding.

"Okay, I can deal with that—as long as you'll be ready to talk someday."

"Okay," I agreed, not knowing if that day would ever come.

As we continued to eat our cookies and sip our teas, something was tugging at me, something I needed to know. It was more than what Liv had been doing since high school, more than whether that ice cream store was still down the street from my old house. I needed to know about him.

"Liv, I need to know. Does Garrett still live here?"

Saying his name out loud hurt. I didn't think I'd actually said those precious syllables in years. Hearing it spring free from my lips felt like I was cutting deep into my own flesh. It felt raw and ragged, like gravel against my vocal cords, and I was ashamed for even saying it.

She gave me a sympathetic gaze. "I don't know. After you…after that night, he hounded me for days that turned into weeks, trying to get a clue as to where you went. When I finally convinced him I was in the dark like he was, I didn't hear from him again. He went off to college, and that was it."

We were supposed to go to college together—the beginning to our *crazy life*, as he'd called it. We'd picked out all of our classes together. He was going to be my brainy architect, and I was going to be his sexy teacher. But I'd left, and he had gone alone.

Now, I was here. I wondered where life had taken him.

I only hoped he was happy.

BUY NOW

# ACKNOWLEDGMENTS

First and foremost, I have to thank my husband. Chris, you are my biggest supporter and I wouldn't be where I am without you. There hasn't been a single day since the beginning of this journey that you haven't supported me and my dream….pushing me when I needed it, letting me quit my job!! Simply put…you are amazing.

Secondly, I have to thank my kids who are the cutest little cheerleaders ever. Your enthusiasm is addictive.

I have an amazing family as a whole. Thank you so much to my parents, especially to my father for NOT reading my books.

To my beta readers - Evette Ashby, Michelle Kannan, Christy Towzen, Carey Heywood, Dixie Daniels and Whitney Baer. Thank you.

Blogs truly give books wings and I wouldn't be where I am today without some amazing bloggers. TotallyBooked - Jenny and Gitte, Tyhada Reads, Sassy Girls Books, Sinfully Sexy Book Review, Reader's Candy, All Romance Review, The Rockstars of Romance, Anna's Attic, Three Chicks and their Books, Jessica's Book Review and My Daily Romance.

A super, epic size thank you goes to my editors - Jovana Shirley and Ami Deason for both working so hard to help produce the best possible version of NBR. It really was a team effort.

Sarah Hansen made this gorgeous cover so many thanks to her.

I also have to thank my agent, Jill Marsal, for all the things.

Lastly, I have to thank my readers. Without you, I wouldn't be on this crazy and wild ride, living my dream every, single day. Keep believing in romance, and I'll keep writing it!

# ABOUT THE AUTHOR

J.L. Berg is the USA Today bestselling author of the Ready Series, the Lost & Found series, and many more. Originally from California, she now resides in central Virginia with her high school sweetheart, two children, and three dogs. When she's not writing, she enjoys spending time with her family or indulging in her love for Doctor Who. J.L. Berg is represented by Jill Marsal of Marsal Lyon Literary Agency, LLC. For the latest book updates, audio news, and more, be sure to visit her website.